GRANTA

DIRTY REALISM
NEW WRITING FROM AMERICA

8

Editor: Bill Buford
Assistant Editor: Diane Speakman
Administration: Tracy Shaw
Production: Claire Yerbury
Executive Editor: Pete de Bolla
Design: Chris Hyde
Editorial Assistants: Margaret Costa, Graham Coster,
Michael Hofmann
Editorial Board: Malcolm Bradbury, Elaine Feinstein,
Ian Hamilton, Leonard Michaels
US Editor: Jonathan Levi, 242 West 104th St., New York,
New York 10025

Editorial and Subscription Correspondence: Granta, 2–3 Hanover Yard,
Noel Road, Islington, London N1 8BE. Telephone: (071) 704 9776.
Fax: (071) 704 0474. Subscriptions: (071) 704 0470.
A one-year subscription (four issues) is £21.95 in Britain, £29.95 for the
rest of Europe and £36.95 for the rest of the world.

Set by Lindonprint Typesetters, Cambridge.

Granta is published by Granta Publications Ltd and distributed by
Penguin Books Ltd, Harmondsworth, Middlesex, England; Viking
Penguin, a division of Penguin Books USA Inc, 375 Hudson Street,
New York, NY 10014, USA; Penguin Books Australia Ltd, Ringwood,
Victoria, Australia; Penguin Books Canada Ltd, 2801 John Street,
Markham, Ontario, Canada L3R 1BR; Penguin Books (NZ) Ltd, 182–
190 Wairau Road, Auckland 10, New Zealand. This selection copyright
© 1983 by Granta Publications Ltd.

Cover by Chris Hyde.

Cover detail from Grant Wood, *American Gothic*, Art Institute of
Chicago. 'The Colonel' is from *The Country Between Us*, copyright
© 1983 by Carolyn Forché, reprinted with permission from
Jonathan Cape, Ltd.

ISSN 0017-3231
ISBN 014-00-6869-4

Published with the assistance
of the Eastern Arts Assocation

Granta 8, Autumn 1983. Fourth printing, May 1994.

CONTENTS

EDITORIAL

A new fiction seems to be emerging from America, and it is a fiction of a peculiar and haunting kind. It is not only unlike anything currently written in Britain,but it is also remarkably unlike what American fiction is usually understood to be. It is not heroic or grand: the epic ambitions of Norman Mailer or Saul Bellow seem, in contrast, inflated, strange, even false. It is not self-consciously experimental like so much of the writing—variously described as 'postmodern', 'postcontemporary' or 'decon-structionist'—that was published in the sixties and seventies. The work of John Barth, William Gaddis or Thomas Pynchon seem pretentious in comparison. It is not a fiction devoted to making the large historical statement.

It is instead a fiction of a different scope—devoted to the local details, the nuances, the little disturbances in language and gesture—and it is entirely appropriate that its primary form is the short story and that it is so conspicuously part of the American short story revival. But these are strange stories: unadorned, unfurnished, low-rent tragedies about people who watch day-time television, read cheap romances or listen to country and western music. They are waitresses in roadside cafés, cashiers in supermarkets, construction workers, secretaries and unemployed cowboys. They play bingo, eat cheeseburgers, hunt deer and stay in cheap hotels. They drink a lot and are often in trouble: for stealing a car, breaking a window, pickpocketing a wallet. They are from Kentucky or Alabama or Oregon, but, mainly, they could just about be from anywhere: drifters in a world cluttered with junk food and the oppressive details of modern consumerism.

This is a curious, dirty realism about the belly-side of contemporary life, but it is realism so stylized and particularized—so insistently informed by a discomforting and sometimes elusive irony—that it makes the more traditional realistic novels of, say, Updike or Styron seem ornate, even baroque in comparison. Many, like Richard Ford, Raymond Carver, or Frederick Barthelme, write

4

in a flat, 'unsurprised' language, pared down to the plainest of plain styles. The sentences are stripped of adornment, and maintain complete control on the simple objects and events that they ask us to witness: it is what's not being said—the silences, the elisions, the omissions—that seems to speak most. It is, as Frank Kermode has observed of Raymond Carver in particular, a 'fiction so spare in manner that it takes time before one realizes how completely a whole culture and a whole moral condition are being represented by even the most seemingly slight sketch.'

Jayne Anne Phillips describes the same work in a slightly different fashion—as being about 'how things fall apart and what is left when they do'—and her description could easily serve for her own work and for that of the other writers included here. These authors are, from one perspective, the youth of the sixties grown up, a generation that, having been raised on weed, whites and protest marches, is now suspicious of heroes, crusades and easy idealism. It is possible to see many of these stories as quietly political, at least in their details, but it is a politics considered from an arm's length: they are stories not of protest but of the occasion for it.

This issue of *Granta* selects seven authors—a more comprehensive collection might include Mary Robison, Ann Beattie, Richard Yates, Jean Thompson and Stephen Dixon—who share many of the same assumptions about language, character and narrative. It begins with Jayne Anne Phillips's memoir of the seventies as a kind of historical starting point and ends with Tobias Wolff's novella depicting the relationship between men and the military in the sixties—itself a work worthy of a cover.

The last issue of *Granta* was an extremely special issue devoted to new work from each of the twenty authors selected by the Book Marketing Council for its campaign to promote the 'Best of Young British Novelists'. It was, like this one, co-published with Penguin Books, but as this issue is our first proper issue under our new collaboration it is perhaps the most appropriate issue to give thanks to Penguin Books for being prepared to help in *Granta's* development and to undertake to get *Granta* to an audience much larger than what it has ever enjoyed before.

—Bill Buford

5

NOW IN SPHERE PAPERBACK

Fiction

THE THIRTEENTH VALLEY
JOHN DEL VECCHIO   £3.95
'One of the finest novels to come out of Vietnam...'
Publisher's Weekly

'There have been a number of excellent books about Vietnam...
but none has managed to communicate... the day-to-day pain,
discomfort, frustration and exhilaration... as well as this.'
New York Times Book Review
Short-listed for the American Book Award.

Humour

WARHEADS
ED. STEPHEN HELLER   £2.50
A sideways look at The Bomb by internationally well-known
cartoonists. Contributors include: Feiffer, Edward Koren, Gerald
Scarfe, Ronald Searle, Ralph Steadman, Garry Trudeau and Ken
Pyne. Royalties donated to CND.

Non Fiction

THE NUCLEAR BARONS
PETER PRINGLE AND JAMES SPIGELMAN   £3.50
'A comprehensive survey of the whole nuclear story.' **Spectator**

'Well written, thoroughly researched and comprehensive in its
detail... Best of all, it is objective.' **Sunday Telegraph**

S.I.O.P.
PETER PRINGLE AND WILLIAM ARKIN   £2.95
Nuclear war from the inside: the first popular account of the Single
Integrated Operational Plan – a four hundred billion dollar
hair-trigger for global devastation?

SPHERE

NOW IN ABACUS PAPERBACK

Fiction

SOUR SWEET

TIMOTHY MO £2.95

Short-listed for the 1982 Booker Prize.

'Brilliant... classic comic scenes... an excellent book.' *Sunday Times*

'In SOUR SWEET, Timothy Mo has brilliantly combined the comic with the frightening.' *Daily Telegraph*

Non Fiction

YELLOW RAIN

STERLING SEAGRAVE £3.25

Nominated for the Pulitzer Prize.

Sterling Seagrave's investigation into the development and use of chemical and biological weapons reveals widespread experimentation and huge stockpiling – a pattern with terrible implications for future warfare.

FROM BAUHAUS TO OUR HOUSE

TOM WOLFE £2.95

A devastating, timely attack on the monstrous follies created by modern architecture.

'Wolfe is to be congratulated for another blast of common sense and incisive writing.' *Punch*

THE DRAGON AND THE BEAR

Inside China and Russia Today

PHILIP SHORT £4.95

Published on 23rd June

By examining China in contrast to the Soviet Union, Philip Short highlights both the differences between the nations and the consequences of their political development for the West.

NEW FROM
PICADOR

MINOR CHARACTERS
Joyce Johnson

A memoir of a 1950s girlhood, a blind date with a man called Kerouac and the daring romance that followed. First British publication.
'A first-rate memoir, very beautiful, very sad' *E. L. Doctorow*

A BOY'S OWN STORY
Edmund White

A boy growing up gay in wholesome 1950s America comes to terms with his double life with devastating skill and deviousness. First British publication.
'An extraordinary novel . . . a clear and sinister pool in which goldfish and piranhas both swim' *New York Times Book Review*

A TRAVELLER'S LIFE
Eric Newby

A seasoned traveller and author shows how he made the great escape.
'A tonic and a pleasure' *Guardian*

LECTURES ON LITERATURE
LECTURES ON RUSSIAN LITERATURE
Vladimir Nabokov

The author of *Lolita* was also a stunning lecturer at American universities. The best of his lectures are collected in these two volumes.
'My own wife was so deeply under his spell that she attended one lecture with a fever high enough to send her to the infirmary' *John Updike*

FROM THE LAND OF SHADOWS
Clive James

The literary reviews from the *New Statesman, London Review of Books* and elsewhere are as entertaining as the famous TV column.
'Delightful writing' *Bernard Crick*

BURNING LEAVES
Don Bannister

When Paul Killick has a breakdown, he sets off on a Tom o'Bedlam journey amongst madmen and misfits, dossers and down-and-outs.
'An oddly powerful book' *Observer*

PICADOR
OUTSTANDING INTERNATIONAL WRITING

OBSERVATIONS

Claudia Cardinale is a Mexican Revolutionary

To the average viewer it's probably a film chiefly memorable for the fact that Claudia Cardinale gets tied up in it. What average viewer, you ask? Who knows. Male, Caucasian, as they say over the car radio in *Kojak* (or, as I prefer to call it, *Kapok*). Like the man said, someone who just wants to watch that TV advert all night with the girl's wet T-shirt clinging to her tits in all that surf.

Claudia Cardinale is a Mexican revolutionary. Not that you know that straight away. She's married to a rich American rancher (Ralph Bellamy). But she's been kidnapped and taken over the border by this bandit, Raza, played by (who else?) Jack Palance. Except, she hasn't really been kidnapped. She's escaped. But you don't know that either yet. Nor do Lee Marvin and Burt Lancaster, who the rich American rancher hires to bring her back.

Lee Marvin is an armaments expert and Burt Lancaster a dynamiter. They're old buddies. These days, though, they're both drifters, desperados, mercenaries awash from their last professional war. But they're the best there is on armaments and dynamite. Lee Marvin's in charge of things. He has a persisting air of military authority, and wears a hat like a scoutmaster's, only tipped forward more. They must have worn them in the Texas Rangers or the Cavalry. Burt Lancaster is unshaven, a rough diamond and something of a womanizer. He seems always to be in grimy longjohns and pulling a whisky-cork out with his teeth. Sounds corny when you try to write it down, and perhaps it is. But I've always liked Lancaster's style. He's good at things like that.

Anyway, Ralph Bellamy, the rich American rancher, tells them that Jack Palance is holding his wife for $100,000 ransom. And he offers them ten grand apiece for her return.

At first they're not too sure. They know Raza. He's a dangerous hombre. And, down there in Mexico, he'll be on his home ground. But in the end they go along with the deal. It's work. The only kind that men like them can do.

So the rancher shows them a photograph of his wife. Marvin looks at it and passes it to Lancaster. You don't see it. And they don't comment. But you know it must be Claudia Cardinale. You can tell Ralph Bellamy, the rich American rancher, is a weak and desperate man from the way he begged them to accept the job. You sense that he's besotted by this new young wife.

'You get some women,' says Lee Marvin later, 'who can turn a boy into a man. And others who can change a man into a boy.'

Lancaster bares his tombstone teeth into a grin at this remark. 'That,' he says, 'is the only kinda woman worth a hundred grand.'

(Except you know there's never been a woman capable of doing that to Lancaster...)

Anyway, they recruit two other drifters. One turns out to be no less a man than Robert Ryan; and the other is Woody Strode, who seems to be a kind of bounty hunter. And that's their outfit: just the four of them against Raza and his hordes. But all good actors.

Of course, even getting to Palance's hideout they have to cross an allegory of desert, salt flats, rock terrain. That bit I always like. The scenery. A landscape of mesas, canyons, gulches. Horses plunging down sandbluffs. Duststorms. A single canteen of water shaken, listened to, reslung unopened. Hard faces creased against the sun. Wiping their brows with sleeved forearms, squinting upwards at its pitilessness.

'What a country,' Robert Ryan complains, standing in the saddle and surveying it with that unique grimness he has.

Lee Marvin looks at him. 'The kind of country only scorpions and men tempered like steel survive in.'

Ryan gives his dry, humourless laugh. 'Men like us.'

Marvin squints beyond the heat wobble, to the mountains of rock they have to get past. 'Men like Raza.'

They push on, eyes wrinkled slits beneath the hatbrims, that impossible patch of sweat between the shoulderblades. A progress in framed images, like a picturestrip. Like that one of riders coming at last upon water. But a crude wooden sign in its shallows warns: alkaline. And, drawn large in the foreground, at eye-level, a horned skull on the ground: a maverick steer's. Picked clean by vultures, scoured by wind, with dark eyesockets, like the human skull in a Renaissance painting: an iconography of the badlands from childhood cowboy comics.

11

Anyway, after the customary hardships, escapes and escapades, they get to Raza's. It is after dark. As they peer down at the camp it is a typical Tuesday night in those little Mexican towns south of the border. A permanent low party. Guitars. Trumpets. Tequila. Laughing dancing girls throwing their hair, black as a horse's mane, over one shoulder. Bandidos stubbled, greasy with sweat, bandoleers crossed on their chests, clutching a bottle by the neck. They're always laughing too. But their laughter is dangerous. A Mexican: part grinning imbecile, part joyful murderer. They have gaps in their teeth. They give out whoops and let off random shots.

But for Lee Marvin and Burt Lancaster the next real problem is not Raza's drunken soldiery but Claudia Cardinale. Disguised in ponchos, faces hidden underneath sombreros, they have penetrated the camp under cover of the general festivity, edging along each wall to the apexed shadow at its corner. (It is a brilliant Hollywood night, noonbright, blue-filtered cirrus skies.) And now they have entered Claudia Cardinale's room by stealth, two vaulting shadows, and are hidden, like voyeurs, in an alcove of it, behind a screen of beads.

Claudia Cardinale lies abandoned in repose upon the bed. They are about to reveal themselves when suddenly the door of the room opens and Jack Palance enters.

They freeze.

Jack Palance looks at Claudia Cardinale domineeringly, and bolts the door behind him. He unbuckles his heavy gunbelt and hangs it on the bedpost. Then he slowly loosens the laces of his shirt, looking at her steadily throughout.

She sits and looks at him, skirts high, thighs open, on the bed. Pouting that mouth, and tumblehaired as if from sleep. His coming is at this point still equivocal, perhaps suggestive of a routine nightly rape.

Then, as we watch, she slips the dress aside, in readiness, from those superb gold shoulders.

Marvin and Lancaster, highlighted silhouettes in profile, exchange a glance significantly. They are beginning to understand that this is not quite as the rich American rancher led them to believe. (Her readiness too, though, is at this point still equivocal. Has Cardinale's passion been unbridled by habituation to Palance's ruthless lust? I am ever alert to such moments, rife with tacit implications.)

It is only later that you learn that she and Raza are in fact true lovers, have been since she was a girl. Jack Palance is the one man in her life, and always will be. Ralph Bellamy, the rich American rancher, had only bought her for his wife, after her father died. But now she has escaped from Bellamy. And she and Raza had planned the whole thing; the ransom money was to help the Revolution. Yet the Revolution is almost finished, has degenerated into random skirmishes and banditry. Raza is a tired man. But Claudia Cardinale still believes in their cause, still loves only him.

Anyway, you don't know any of this till later. There's a struggle and the two stars finally knock Jack Palance out.

Now the real kidnap takes place. But, of course, Claudia Cardinale doesn't want to go. She resists strenuously. So this is where, as I promised you, Lancaster ties her up.

Pinioning her wrists behind her back with one hand, he lashes her together tightly with the other. And, as he does this, she turns slightly for the camera, to a profile, showing her magnificent *embonpoint*. The shot does not dwell on her, of course, on that accentuated, out-thrust bosom nor the helpless, fluttering hands. But the director has evidently instructed her, as it were, to totemize the moment by holding her arms rigidly behind her as if they were bound not at the wrist but at the elbow. Her splendid head is thrown back, so that you may sense the musculature of her throat. And for those seconds—feet of screentime—her sexuality, proud but powerless, is delineated as graphically as in a semi-pornographic drawing.

Your expectation, now aroused, is, naturally, agonizingly prolonged: for even after their immediate escape from the camp has been accomplished, on their flight back through the badlands, they still keep her bound. But, erect in the saddle, with her head flung back, she is now no more than one of the riders in the longshots of those fleeting frames. The director, having baited you, will now, as always, withhold the long, slow closeup you are chafing for. I am an expert on the coy sadism the cinema practises upon its audience.

And, in the next time-cut, morning in the broiling desert sun, and after all those hours (screenminutes) of her bondage, she is freed: simply riding between Marvin and Lancaster, her hands in front of

13

her upon the reins. No mention of the circulation cramps. No closeshot of the herringbone imprinted by the rope upon the flesh. It is as if those thoughts were your responsibility.

There is only, as a consolation, in the frankly open throat of her brown dress, the space between her glistening breasts. Her breasts are round, pneumatic. And she holds herself proudly upright upon the horse and, almost insistently, thrusts them forward as she rides: almost like a ship's figurehead, or as if she were at all times bound. But that is all....

You ought to know that I don't go for that in any case, that rounded fullness. I see it. I know what she's doing with it. And I describe it for your delectation. But I don't go for it myself. I can see why she's in films, but you could say Claudia Cardinale's not my type.

Me, I go for breasts in earlier films. Films made in the 40s, early 50s. A triumph of circular stitching, wire, and elastic. They're slung brazenly high, and are almost conical in shape. They look hard, as if they'd feel like pointed baskets if you grabbed them. It's all that support they give. The miracle of uplift. Uplift? Thrustout. From some décolleté ballgown or one of those tight sweaters they all wore (white or near white, to show that pointed shadow underneath). Rita Hayworth. Rhonda Fleming. Dorothy Malone. Janet Leigh. Those are the ones I go for. Even bit-part actresses, walk-on cigarette-girls whose names nobody ever knew, nor what became of them. The kind of breasts Howard Hughes finally invented the cantilever bra for. I could hardly have been born when it came out.

Anyway, my interest in these things stops at that period of Hollywood. You could say it's a regressive taste. Like some men go for shy Victorian nudes on the original brownish postcards, collectors' items. Me, I'm a man for breasts in 50s movies.

And not just the breasts. I go for the ensemble, the whole damn style. The look itself, the hairstyles, skirts, the high-heeled shoes. Or those gorgeous glistening gowns (half of those films seem to have been shot in a nightclub or a cocktail bar so they could wear those gowns). Or those long, three-quarter-length black gloves Hayworth peeled off in *Gilda*. I've seen the odd strip in my time: I'm a kibitzer of the underside of cities. But I've never seen anything to equal

14

Hayworth just taking off a pair of gloves in that dance. Black, they were, up past the elbow. Shiny black. Colour? Who needed it? I prefer the satin blacks and halftone greys before Eastmancolor (or whatever it was) came in. The composition and play of light and sheen and shadow, that vicious studio elegance.

People think it's just the films that are all different. But it's also the film. The thing itself. Mere celluloid stock. I'm a connoisseur of chiaroscuro, tone. I like everything in black and livid white and grey. Stark or shimmery. A closeup of Jennifer Jones shot through gauze, wetmouthed, enraptured for the camera's kiss, with starpoints in her eyes and on her teeth tips. Or Expressionism: that murderous, dull glint you get in life only on a city street at night after the rain. I'm a romantic, if you like. A cinéaste. A filmbuff, anyway. Girls in the buff don't interest me at all. Even on film. The bared *bronzage,* the fuzzy triangle, the beavershot. I go for clarities and contrasts, the bare white shoulders and the ballgown's cups. The world's in colour. I dream in black and white. *Odds Against Tomorrow* (one of Ryan's best) or Fritz Lang's *While the City Sleeps.* Anything by Robert Siodmak. Stuff like that. The filmnoir atmosphere, that old RKO B-movie look. Even earlier stuff, with those corny credits: the titles coming up on scrolled vellum or on turned pages of a morocco tome.

I don't go much for realism, unless it's outdoor shots of New York at night or something, streets and skyline: or the Arizona desert (that impossible geology). And for interiors, I prefer the set. Its depthlessness. Its studied lifelikeness. Those shaded reading-lamps that throw a whole room into savagery. The obvious backdrop view outside a window.

Sometimes I feel as if I grew up, spent my whole childhood and adolescence, in a studio where all of Brooklyn lived on one lot: those deteriorating brownstone houses, railing steps up to the doors, the urchins playing in the street. The soda parlour, like in Hopper's *Nighthawks,* and the little store run by a kindly old Pole. Or that junction, more familiar and nostalgic than your own street corner, with a line of shop-fronts, fine quoined buildings built by studio carpenters, where extras pass each other endlessly on pavements never littered, and a real car comes around the corner (one with a runningboard) and pulls up at the City Bank, the inevitable fire hydrant at the kerb.

I'm not much into sex on film either, let alone the porn stuff now. Sylvia Kristel, Marilyn Chambers, they're not my scene. Simulated or otherwise, who needs that kind of thing? Me, I'm happier in the days when they had to keep one foot on the floor. Bo Derek, Maria Schneider, their breasts feed everyone these days. Not me. These days, that's all they want. Softcore. With now and then a quick glimpse of the heavy trade. Claudia Cardinale with her hands tied. Charlotte Rampling with her hair shaved, in a Nazi uniform. I know what these things mean. But in the old days films were more subtle. If you wanted sadism you had to buy detective magazines. That kind of thing was only available in line drawings, terrified kidnap victims, gagged, their skirts up round their arse, their coneshaped breasts thrust out at their assailant. All drawn in loving, intent detail by the artist. Some hack, but with a gift for that. Nothing he drew he hadn't pulled off himself: that was your guarantee. I've got some of those mags. I save Americana from that period. So I know.

But now the sadism's less undercover, and it's lost that tacky feel. It's loose in the system. It's been given style. And it's not the helpless victim it's directed at, but you. In the fleeting glimpse, in the suggestion. In the framing, editing. In the whole, unconsummated ocular pricktease. Like that TV ad for bathsoap, where the girl doesn't quite turn round enough for you to see the nipple. That's not delicacy, taste, despite the dreamy look. It's a sadistic practice. That hardcore stuff I've seen is child's play in comparison. I know exactly what they're doing when I see these things. I've got their number. But it doesn't work on me. Not me.

In the old days Hollywood knew what eroticism was. It was smooth and white, but had a shadow cast upon it (stark or subtle). It was a skiamachy, to use a term from Greek: a struggle between white and dark, a dark encroaching from the edges in a room lit by one source. And beauty was more abstract then, more masklike. No flaws or freckles. No wrinkles under the eyes, like Jane Fonda's getting. Even with Joan Crawford. They just used the gauze. No marks of the bra-strap across the back when they unhook it. I shrivel when I see something like that. People are like that. Pored. Pockmarked. Wrinkled. Hirsute. Who wants to see that kind of thing on film?

So, Claudia Cardinale's not my type. Oh, she's smooth enough, handsome enough, statuesque enough. And it's still film. But, I don't know, somehow you can guess her naked, even though she never is. She was making films at the wrong time, it's as simple as that: when Technicolor meant you had to get even your tits tanned. She's not blank and white enough. Let's face it, she's not Dietrich in black stockings. Sitting on that chair turned back to front in *The Blue Angel*, icy in all the smoke and lights. But then, I'm not the average viewer.

So: it was a film. Helped kill the first part of a Tuesday night. And on the TV films are free.

Most of my money goes on films. I work to watch. There's usually a good old one on somewhere. At the Electric or the Scala or the Ritzy. Or they'll have a season at the NFT. Sometimes I think the afternoon show's best. I take a couple of cans of Long Life and a quarterbottle of Scotch in. I like to lurch out of the darkness at the end into the dislocated, dazzled roar of day. Or I'll go down to the BFI and spend an hour just going through their lists. It's almost more fun choosing one than seeing it. You get a private booth, an individual screening, like they have for couples in some of the porno joints. At home I've got the rented VCR and a whole shelf of films taped from TV. But tapes are dear. If I could afford it, I'd live like Howard Hughes right at the end. Just watching old films in his bedroom all day long. Except, the only one he ever watched by then was *Ice Station Zebra*, with Rock Hudson. Over and over again. By then he'd lost his marbles.

One of these days, I've often thought, I'll go to Hollywood. Just to see if the old studios are standing, wander round the lots. See the famous palmprints in cement outside that Chinese restaurant. The usual rubbernecking tourist trip, its falsity and crassness savoured through the sad joy of a real nostalgia. I could even get a Greyhound out of Arizona or Sonora. See the mesas from Red River, all that giant cactus.

But there's a sense in which I'd be afraid to set real foot upon the landscape of my soul. I like the slow pan and the framed view and the music: theme tunes out of Dvorak, or a lone guitar. And sight itself's too all-inclusive, cluttered. I'd rather see it simplified to legend through a good director or a cameraman like James Wong Howe.

My real dream'd be to fly to New York City, book into a precipice hotel room, put the chain up on the door. And sit there with the *TV Guide* beside me and the curtains drawn all day so that the sun can't dull the screen. Switching through all twenty-eight damn channels or whatever, watching the old movies from eight in the morning till the early hours, bleak black and white, the men in gangster trilbies and the girls in lowfront cocktail gowns. And hear the prowlcars wail that terrible, attenuating, eerie wail far down there in the street, another rape or murder crackling in over their radios, the city a long, long scream in me, me prince of it.

Duncan Bush

The State of The State of Things

I don't give a fuck how things worked out, I gave you your first job, all right? I had my choice of twenty-five directors just sitting around the Chateau Marmont. Twenty-five directors from Europe, just looking for their first American film....

Gordon

'A few words to cross the waters,' as the director puts it, preparing to address his cast and crew, all of them drunk, stranded together under contract on location in Portugal, in mid-schedule, with the last of the film and the Los Angeles money run out and no relief in sight. Their project, referred to as 'The Survivors' (but called *The State of Things* on the clapboard, as if to give it its real name) is an unbearably gloomy science-fiction story—if story is the appropriate word—about survival in the post-apocalypse, four adults and two children trekking painfully over a blasted landscape looking for the payoff, the sea; mercy-killing their children as they go, straggling out of an environment so poisoned that they can't touch anything for fear of melting, all of it filmed entirely in black and white. Or, as the finished film called *The State of Things* insists in every shot, in glorious black and white, profound, poetic, *true* black and white. Even though the people call the director Friedrich, or Fred, or Fried Rice, his name in the film is Fritz, a great movie name, and everything he touches turns to remembered images.

A few beautiful frames to cross the waters, a few obsessive images, signs as stable, abiding and recurring as the seasons, an arc of film to cross the dangerous waters to generic Hollywood. So much accumulated pan-Atlantic yearning, so much *hommage* and genre-refreshment: Italian Westerns, German private-eyes, French Hollywood musicals, Godard inventing the open-ended reference dictionary to all the great American moments that most Americans missed because we thought we were just going to the movies. As though American light and shadow were the best; no highway, city street, nightclub or open country filmed like ours, no gun showed up like an American gun filmed by Fuller or Lewis or Ray, in illuminating, haunting black and white. The big European romantic hearts fell for it completely, those gorgeous businesslike shapes growing and focusing into symbols, objects of reverence.

The Germans in particular were never more epic in European ciné-mind than when they worked in Hollywood, against the odds and obstacles of studios that were putting out fifty-two features a year, with all the trimmings: cartoons, newsreels, shorts, trailers, advertising, publicity, distribution, the investments, the insurance, 'the whole equation of pictures' that Fitzgerald said only a few men—geniuses—could keep all together at once in their heads.

'You writers and artists get all mixed up,' the Last Tycoon says, 'and somebody has to come in and straighten you out.' There weren't a lot of producer-directors in those days.

Lots of films are mentioned and suggested in *The State of Things*, but never the one that's closest to the nerve, and probably inspired it. Like his spiritual film fathers, Wim Wenders once wanted to make an American film, and like them, he got the chance; the project and everything else.

Looking at *Hammett*, you can see the marks of all the strong hands that held it, and all the different directions it was pulled in, until it became a torn film, whose pieces were edited but never really joined: a producer's film, an art director's film, certainly a director's

19

film, but a thwarted director; several mutually exclusive films in one, or in none, a beautiful and even unforgettable 'failure' that gives you more to look at and take out with you than any of the current successes, a bit of a mess, but unique. If for some reason someone wanted to make another film like *Hammett*, they could never find the formula.

They say the reason that movie people give each other such expensive presents after a film is finished is that they've behaved so terribly during the shooting. Before shooting on *Hammett* had even begun, the talk had started. Rumour, the fourth horseman of the movie business, was out of the gate on his promiscuous talking horse Gossip, honking all over the international back lot. They'd made up the T-shirts before they even had the story down; there was big trouble, bad relations, script problems, Differences. Shooting was interrupted twice, once for over a year. They couldn't work out the story, the money was variable, the working was turning into something that nobody had wanted. The producer was behaving like a director—which shouldn't have surprised anyone, since he was Francis Coppola—and had, anyway, disappeared into fresh enthusiasms, wider plans, new chaos. Wenders was in, he was out, his credit was removed, restored, hanging by a thread. He was on non-speaking terms with Coppola, through in Hollywood, through *with* Hollywood, and had gone out to make his own movie about the movies, a 'revenge' film called *The State of Things*. Some revenge.

Having been around at the beginning of *Hammett,* I can verify the one about the T-shirts. There was great optimism at the start, and warmth, but I don't doubt that as things went on there were a lot of hard feelings. As for Wenders and Coppola not speaking, Coppola is a very difficult man not to speak to, or even to maintain irreconcilable differences with for very long, whether out in the open at meetings, or in your heart. And as for Wenders's revenge, it seems to have been carried out with much more love than cunning. Perhaps revenge is really a dish best eaten long after you've lost your appetite for it.

To be obvious on purpose for a moment: all good books are finally books about writing, and the best paintings have painting as their ultimate subject/object, but even the worst movies are about movie-making. Great movies, then, are twice about movie-making, and great films with film as their actual subject are many times about film, *all* about film, but there aren't many of them.

So many directors pass through *The State of Things* that it's like *Forty Guns,* with movie directors instead of guns. In fact, a lot of the directors invoked and remembered functioned something like hired guns who, through cleverness and passion, remained their own men while still riding for the brand. Forced against their wishes to shoot in colour, they made beautiful colour film, and when the orders changed, they shot in black and white, with even more triumph. Required, ordered, to incorporate elements and expressions alien to their own, they subverted the project while they served it, and left their personalities everywhere. If an absurd story was imposed on them, they imposed their style on the absurd story; most people who love movies don't care that much about stories anyway. Those were always the hired director's conditions. They were Wenders's on *Hammett,* they're Fritz's on 'The Survivors'. But *Hammett* at least had a strong commercial hook to lift it up off the table and on to a set. The very idea that any American producer today would go anywhere near a story as depressing and down as 'The Survivors' would almost have to be some kind of joke. A German movie-director's joke, for instance.

> *I told you that day-for-night is for the birds if you want to see anything.*
>
> Joe Corby

Nobody ever confused the megalomaniac amoralist director-protagonist of *The Bad and the Beautiful* with Vincent Minnelli, or imagined that the lost-and-found adolescent dreamer of *8½* was anybody but Fellini. Fritz, in *The State of Things,* has both those links with the real director. He's not Wim Wenders, but he's having a few of Wenders's experiences, and they're all coming out on exposed film.

In the long middle section, the eponymous state of things is more or less like this: the tight common energy of a working company breaks and runs back into its solitary individual containers, where it goes nervous and ragged. They're like a commando unit moved suddenly to a rest area, not knowing whether it's for a day, weeks, forever, wanting to decompress but afraid of losing their edge in case the order comes through, and they have to go back into the line. In spite of a few mild eruptions, their tenderness and respect for each other holds them together to a degree, but without the regulator of the schedule, they're losing their precision, and for the moment, time is not money.

'I can't stop speeding,' one of the actresses says, but she's very high-strung anyway. 'The Survivors' was going to be her ticket to Hollywood influence. She's slept with the producer, maybe even with the writer, like the heroine of the starlet joke, except that she's not dumb, far from it, just a bit crazy. She prowls around the hotel, around her room, around inside her skin, practising the violin, sawing into poor Mendelssohn as though he were the composer of her misfortune, and generally acts out the fears and frustrations of her colleagues.

Another actress, Anna, goes the other way, trying to keep herself still, half glad that the shooting has been interrupted so that they can all do some serious work on themselves. Her lover and co-star, Mark, compulsively rehearses a drowning scene in his bath over and over like Narcissus, a role he could well be up for one day. Another actor, Robert, recalls his less-than-golden childhood in southern California: buckteeth, braces, cross-eyed, stuttering, double-pimples, overweight, racked by genital-fear and allergies and one other problem—what was it?—oh yes, he had cancer too, and not that many friends. The writer drinks from the bottle and worries endlessly, seemingly about his credit. He taunts the director, insults the cast and plays the classic rôle of writers on movie-sets: sour conscience of the company and all-round monumental pain in the ass. The director tries to keep everyone, including his wife and daughters and himself, from sliding into despair, shooting film in his head until relief comes. The money is the most obvious and mysterious element in the problem, a problem in which the things that are missing are also most present. Gordon, the vanished producer, is very much in everyone's thoughts. He's the phantom of the location.

Everybody thinks that they're waiting for a signal, when actually they're waiting for a signal that they can bear to receive. There's no shortage of signals, a profusion of totally distinct unacceptable signals coming in every minute, but the only one there who can see clearly enough to read and decode them is Joe Corby, the cameraman. His translations are explicit, to say the least, but nobody wants to know. He doesn't particularly want to know either, but that doesn't stop him from knowing, and saying, and everything he says is simultaneously practical, poetic and 'true'. Played by Sam Fuller, Corby seems to be holding both films together, a legend playing a legend, filling something more than an actor's space on the screen, a strange extra dimension. His heart is the secret engine that makes film, both the hard boring work that goes on a day at a time, 'from shot to shot', and the long unbroken romantic rhapsody-history of movies that Fritz, and Wenders, are so madly in love with. In the grimy, all-too-human terms of a movie-set, Joe Corby is a lion, the one true seer in a film about vision.

'A lot of things are happening simultaneously,' Fritz says. 'If we had more than one camera....' Of course, that's a sentence best left unfinished, or at least open, and not only because, for the moment, he doesn't have even one camera.

Boom-time is running out fast, maybe even time itself: in the toxic melting world of the interrupted 'foldero' movie called 'The Survivors'; in Sintra and the vast unfinished hotel there, like a giant shell left on the beach by some abomination that crawled into the ocean to die; in Hollywood itself, the fallen Capitol of the ancient dream. The shadow of Incompletion moves over everything, the old references have lost their currency, the old forms are turning to dust, film is a basket case. Fritz stares in revulsion and fascination at the computer screen, 'a piece of Gordon's mind' left behind when he disappeared, and sees the new movie that's oozing out of the decay of the old, the whole equation of what had been his film—the budget, the schedule, his own vital statistics and credits, 'his' movie, broken down scene by scene and shot by shot into alien unwatchable images, bathed in a cold monstrous light, a bad dream of a film. You can almost hear the thought in his head, What if I made a movie, and it looked like *that*?

The world of *The State of Things* is composed mostly of edges, and they aren't the clean edges of the beloved inevitable arbitrary rectangle, either. The movie-makers are on the edge of themselves and all their expectations, on the beach in every way in beautiful Sintra-by-the-sea on the edge of Europe, holding tight and trying not

Michael Herr

to stare too long or hard at 'the hole where the land runs out and the sea comes in', because you'd need Joe Corby's eye, and his courage, ever to look really at that. When Fritz goes looking for Gordon and the action moves to Los Angeles, it reaches the sharpest, farthest edge of all, and then, as if things weren't extreme enough, story comes into it.

It's a hell of a shot. One of the best in the whole picture, if you can get it.

Joe Corby

People talk about story all through the movie, and they're seldom talking about the same thing. Fritz seems to regard it as a rather rude and vulgar thing, a polluter of film. Whether story is the walls of the house of movies, as Gordon thinks, or exists only in the space between characters, as Fritz believes, they both agree that there are only two stories that can be filmed, the love story and the death story, and Wenders has filmed them both. In terms of its plot, *The State of Things* is almost a home movie, but in the space between characters, it's richer and warmer than all but a few recent films. Wenders's ensemble isn't uniformly wonderful, there are some rough strange moments, but they *are* resonant and real, and the three main performances—Patrick Bauchau as Fritz, Sam Fuller as Fuller-Corby and Allen Goorwitz as the demonically brilliant Gordon—are so complex and wonderful that they make a story out of themselves. It's a cast, and a story, that Renoir could have assembled.

The State of Things is like a movie version of 'Dover Beach', about a darkening entropic planet floating lost in a universe of love. For all the talk about what a cold and unreadable 'deaf mute German' Fritz is, the clearest thing about him is that he's a lover, and that his love is practically unconditional, going out even to Gordon, who seems to have betrayed him, and to his 'enemy', Dennis the Menace the writer. When Fritz accuses him of knowing nothing about love, Dennis makes one of the most touching speeches in the movie.

'I think I know something about it,' he says. 'I mean, I wish I did. I mean, I hope I do. I would like to hope I do.'

He needn't worry. Love and death are subjects that everyone

24

knows much more about than is usually imagined. As far as those stories go, if you're breathing, you're an expert. What Fritz probably means is that Dennis knows nothing about pictures.

Gordon's a lover too, a very passionate one, and his passions have got him into serious trouble. He may be just another self-destructive flash Los Angeles genius, he may be a man of great courage and creative vision, but either way, he's gone far over the border of what people in Hollywood usually mean when they speak of risk-taking. The Killers are looking for him, and they don't just want the money back anymore. He's gone into a fabulous kind of Hollywood hiding, in a mobile home driven by a psychotic movie-mad goon who's as dangerous as the people trying to find him. He cruises Los Angeles non-stop, making like Hamlet, making like Wagner, making like Che Guevara, hit, run and hide (one description of movie-making), while Fritz the Searcher tracks him down, maybe like the hero of his last completed film, which was called *An American Hunter*. When he steps on Fritz Lang's star in the pavement of Hollywood Boulevard he presses the button that lets in the rest of the movie, and then heads out into *Big Heat* country.

It's appropriate to a film that is so much about film to pay tribute to the mythical incubator of the medium. Except maybe with my own eyes, I've never seen Los Angeles in such combinations of clinical and supernatural views. It's as though the place had perpetrated so many unwholesome fantasies and played so ruthlessly and carelessly with the lights and darks of its home industry that its living spirit bailed out, and the town that was founded on sunshine was no longer fit to be seen in daylight. It's not filmed for obvious surreality, which would be so easy, and so disrespectful. The tribute is genuine, the images are at least as beautiful as they are repellent. Los Angeles, in *The State of Things,* is a city laid out for an autopsy.

Hollywood, what a great idea, but maybe the place itself isn't so great. Together again, Fritz and Gordon drive by night all night long, talking over the state of things in love and reconciliation, and together they draw their bottom line, and not a moment too soon.

Fritz talks story, and Gordon sings *The Hollywood Song,* 'Hollywood, Hollywood, Never been a place people had it so good,' a love song, a death chant, a cry for whatever there is for you when you're beyond help, a hell song about the place where your soul leaves your body and goes to hell while you're still alive and trying to use it.

'In the beginning it was easy,' Fritz remembers, thinking back over his ten films. 'I just went from shot to shot... but now, I'm scared... now I know how to tell stories, and relentlessly...as the story comes in, life sneaks out....'

It's a rare and moving sight in Hollywood, a producer and his director going to the wall for each other: Gordon's notes are all called in and Fritz, his camera up like Dirty Harry's Magnum, films the big one, the death scene. But it's only a camera. In some situations there are serious limitations to a medium that shoots footage instead of bullets.

All the elements intersect and become one element; the movie, the movies, the movie-makers and the money. All stories and genres rush into one another and pour back into the camera through the lens, just another hole where the land runs out and the sea comes in. The state of things has gone right to the edge of the frame and beyond, out of it completely, no more film, and then it's time for all good survivors to say goodbye.

Michael Herr

Fragments of a Lament for Thelonious Monk

Here I am sitting in front of my computer monitor looking at dates and times in luminous green letters on the screen. I've typed a memo of travel and engagements into the computer. From my tape recorder comes music with that bright okay sound that you hear from the curtained screen in the cinema before the lights are dimmed. It is, yes, it is also that music you hear in the echoing and vasty spaces of airports. It makes me feel good, makes me feel neither here nor there but comfortably in between. Airports have many monitors with arrival and departure times on their screens, flights designated by letters and numbers in luminous characters that don't move but are full of subliminal motion, full of dancingness and quivering.

Here at my desk I've put together that airport feeling, that wonderful airport state of mind, everything for the present suspended, the traveller out of reach of the usual daily bother, out of reach of all those daily systems by which the extraordinary is reduced to a grey and manageable tedium.

Not everything is suspended; no, only the grey and manageable tedium is suspended; the extraordinary is once more available to the soul that is hungry and thirsty for it. Yes, yes, anything at all may happen now. The hitherto unrecognized may suddenly be recognized. The ungraspable mountain may suddenly present itself to one's vision. Transcendence!

Listening now to an effigy of Thelonious Monk, a dome of the dummy world, that midnight dome, those caves of nice. Always the slant rhyme with Thelonious, that was his Thelonious assault on the grey and civil devils of the ordinary. Walk tall and slanty, Thelonious; you live.

There was a little bit of spring sunshine, and already the girls were on their summer legs, the ravishing Persephones of the Fulham Road on their beckoning and procreative summer legs, trundling their goodies in the thin, in the vernal, in the London sunshine and I went into what looked like a record shop. I shaped words with my lips in the noise to the smiling and undoubtedly deaf young man, I don't remember what words were on his T-shirt at first. WE HAVE NO THELONIOUS MONK maybe, I don't know.

I shaped the words, 'Have you got any Thelonious Monk?'

Shake of his head, smiling, uncaring, deaf.

'Call yourself a record shop and you haven't got any Thelonious Monk?'

THERE IS NO SUCH THING AS THELONIOUS MONK, said his T-shirt.

Thelonious Monk! Ah! Thelonious! How you are gone, how I lament your death now! You are of the fabric of my perception, yes that is not too much to say. In The Five Spot in Cooper Square I sat long ago in the blue smoke and the buzz of night-murmurers and saw you under your magical hat at the helm, your keyboard was the wheel by which you steered precariously our frail vessel on the edgelines of the actual. Peerless navigator, ardent darer that you were, dark albatross of the farther frequencies.

Russell Hoban

The letters on the screen of my computer are made up of a continual
dancing; letter by letter I see my thoughts appear on the screen. My
thoughts and the mind that thinks them are equally composed of the
dancing; the dancing is there before anything else. You are in that
dancing, Thelonious Monk, in that green dancing in which letter by
letter my thoughts appear this midnight, round about this midnight
mindnight. On the margin of the moment where you made notations,
Thelonious, at The Five Spot in Cooper Square in the rain and in the
fog when I was young.

Russell Hoban

On the Bus

Bus No. 122 was going down Belvederska Street. The
passengers sat in silence. Of late, people tend to sit in
silence on buses. None of the arguments, none of the
jokes you used to get. The bus halted sharply at a crossing but even
that failed to provoke a comment. A ribbon of army transporters and
lorries stretched out in front of us while the bus waited. Guns
wobbled under tarpaulins. A Gazik brought up the rear. As soon as
the convoy had passed, the bus moved forward cautiously over the icy
asphalt. It passed the 'colony', a row of buildings of differing heights
surrounded by a wall, housing Russian diplomats and advisers.

'Walled themselves in, the Russkis!' said a nondescript young
man in a fur hat which had seen better days. 'Must be afraid of an
attack.' His voice was surprisingly loud and penetrating. He ended
with a crazy sort of giggle.

A few passengers looked at the walled quarters. Nobody spoke.

'What was that you said?' Another voice, from the front of the
bus. A fat squat man. Good fur hat, shiny face, clean shaven. He
elbowed his way towards the young man, who was standing by the
middle door.

The young man looked anxious. He glanced instinctively at the
door.

The driver was watching the incident in his mirror. He jammed on
his brakes suddenly, then accelerated just as abruptly. The standing
passengers were precipitated to the front, taking the fat man in the fur

hat with them. He resisted, but was swept along by the crush of bodies and pinned to the glass partition dividing the driver's cab from the passengers.

The driver smiled, but then the smile vanished at once. He drove on, concentrating on the icy surface. He looked tired and unshaven.

The fat man in the fur hat struggled to get free but to no avail. He gripped the back of a seat with both hands and tried to pull himself up. He managed to move a bit but couldn't pass one of the seats reserved for the disabled. The cripple sitting there held his stiff leg fully extended across the aisle.

A request stop. The impetus of all those bodies once again immobilized the fat man in the fur hat. The driver pressed a button. The automatic doors opened with a hiss. The middle door first. The nondescript young man, who was standing right by the steps, jumped out nimbly.

The fat man in the fur hat laboriously fought his way towards the door at the front. He was at some disadvantage. A raging, red-faced bulldog. The driver watched him coolly, waiting politely. The fat man made it in the end. Once outside he peered helplessly in every direction. The young man was nowhere to be seen. He took down the number of the departing bus.

The Steel-Clawed Glove

They had had a good journey. Only four of them in the compartment. The country looked fresh, alive with the first green of the spring. Not just peaceful: serene. It passed gently across the carriage windows.

A stocky priest looked into the breviary opened on his knees, then raised his eyes and turned his face closer to the window. Ploughing and sowing had started. The slow unalterable rhythm of peasant life. A man following a plough bent to the effort. Crows flew behind him and settled on to the upturned soil.

A white horse was grazing in a meadow with a wood in the background.

'A good horse,' said the old man in the blue uniform, gazing through the window.

Merek Nowakowski

The two other passengers in the compartment showed no interest
in the view. The man wearing glasses seemed absorbed in the thick
volume he was reading. His eyesight must have been very poor: he
held the book close despite his glasses. A soldier, corporal's stripes on
his shoulder, sat near the door. He had undone his belt, placed his cap
on the seat beside him. He sat with his head bent down. But he wasn't
asleep. His short fingers drummed nervously on his seat. The middle
finger carried a thick gold wedding ring.

The old man in the blue uniform yawned. He looked round the
compartment. His eyes rested on the priest for a moment. The priest's
lips were moving. In prayer, no doubt.

'Yes,' said the old man. 'Prayer is our only hope. Holy scripture
alone carries the truth. But not everything has been revealed yet.' He
frowned and turned to watch the moving country outside. Cottages.
A stork. Green trees. A tractor on a field track. Children waving
handkerchiefs at the train.

The familiar scenes floated by. Life renewing itself, the same from
year to year.

'How long will it go on?' The old man had difficulty putting his
words together. 'What can we do about it all? Only don't tell me,
Father, that we need compassion and patience and humility!' His
pale blue eyes clouded over.

The priest sighed and spread his hands helplessly.

The man in glasses, until then absorbed in a thick volume with an
exotic god on the dust jacket spouting liquid fire from his funnelled
mouth, broke off his reading. With the gesture of a practised reader,
he pushed a finger between the pages and closed the book.

'I'm reading about the Aztecs, about Montezuma, about priests
tearing children's hearts out to sacrifice them to their gods. The
Spaniards were only a handful, yet they crushed the mighty empire of
the sun! And without much difficulty.' He banged his hand on the
closed book. His face was thin, birdlike, and behind the thick glasses
the eyes blinked incessantly with a nervous tick.

'That empire was built on slavery, injustice, it was rotten. Cortez
had the will to win and nothing to lose!'

'Like the proletariat,' said the old man. 'It had nothing to lose but
its chains.'

The corporal raised his head. But not to look at his fellow-

30

passengers. He concentrated on the opposite wall which was embellished with an advertisement for Orbis restaurant cars. He looked tense. His lips were tight, his legs were drawn up uncomfortably.

The old man gave the soldier a careful, appraising glance.

'Don't worry so much, soldier,' he said gently. He took his briefcase down from the rack. Opened it. Took out a bottle filled with an opaque yellow liquid. Pushed it towards the soldier. 'Cheer up, corporal. I made it myself. With sugar.'

The corporal accepted the bottle and took a hefty swig of moonshine. Didn't even pull a face. Wiped his mouth with the back of his hand: 'The buggers! They've postponed our discharge for a year.' His eyes, apathetic earlier, now lit up with rage. 'It's a year since I saw my child. I've got a pass now because the child's ill. I don't know what things are like at home.' The tension made him clench his teeth, the veins stood out on his hands.

'My own boy,' said the old man in his quiet voice, 'worked down the mine. They've put him in clink. Three years he got.'

The corporal shyed, and looked anxiously at the old man. 'I had nothing to do with all that. Not me. The riot squads, the militia took the mines. We were only in reserve, I swear it.' In desperation, he turned to the others. They kept silent and looked away.

'It's all right, lad.' The old man placed his large heavy hand over the corporal's. 'I bear no grudges. Are *they* to blame?' The question was directed to the priest.

The priest closed his breviary.

'Even the militia . . . ,' the old man said thoughtfully, 'they're only a blind tool.'

The man in glasses cleared his throat and said in a near whisper: 'Here we are. Spring's coming. The journey is comfortable. No crowds. We trust one another. And what good is it all?' He looked out of the window. 'It's terrible! It's all so terrible!'

The old man pushed the bottle towards the soldier again. But he wouldn't have any more.

'No, thank you. Makes you feel better for a bit but then it's worse than ever.'

The old man pushed the cork back and returned the bottle to his battered briefcase. He fastened the straps. Carefully replaced it on the rack.

31

'You are quite right,' the priest spoke for the first time, 'they are only a blind tool.'

'When they went in to storm the mine,' said the old man, 'they looked like devils. The gloves they had on'—his hand stretched out, the fingers wide apart—'they had claws, of steel. If they got you in those claws, you'd had it. You'd never break loose from them.'

The man in glasses stared at the cruel, clutching fingers. 'Claws of steel,' he repeated in a whisper.

They sat in silence. The country outside darkened. The paw with steel claws hovered over them. They could feel them, claws that raked body and soul.

The old man shut his eyes. The corporal curled up in his corner. The train sped over the green plain. It was spring.

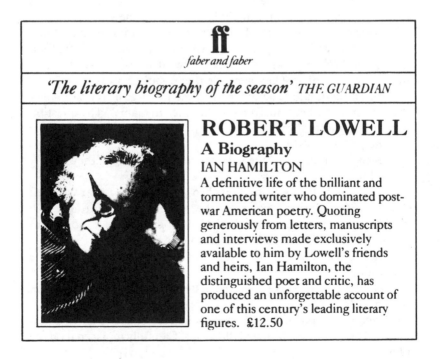

JAYNE ANNE
PHILLIPS
RAYME—A MEMOIR
OF THE SEVENTIES

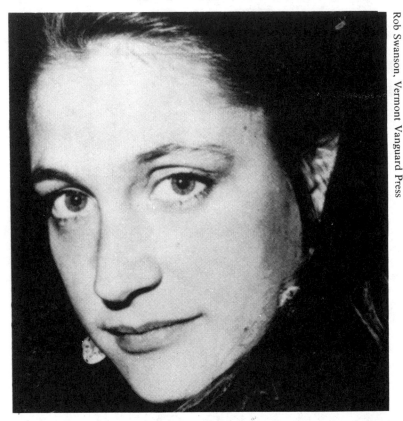

Rob Swanson, Vermont Vanguard Press

Jayne Anne Phillips was born in Buckhannon, West Virginia, in 1952. She grew up in the Appalachians, and has worked in amusement parks and restaurants, and travelled door-to-door in mining camps selling home improvements and bathroom appliances. Her short fiction has appeared in the *Atlantic* and a number of literary magazines, and has been included in the *Pushcart Prize Anthology*, the *Best American Short Stories*, and the *O'Henry Prize* collection. She has won a number of prizes, including the Academy of Arts and Letters Sue Kaufman Award for first fiction, and the National Endowment of the Arts Award for fiction. She has published one collection of short stories, *Black Tickets*, available in Britain in King Penguin, and is currently working on a novel.

In West Virginia in 1974 we were all in need of fortune-tellers. No one was sure what was happening in the outside world and no one thought about it much. We had no televisions and we bought few newspapers. Communal life in Morgantown seemed a continual dance in which everyone changed partners, a patient attempt at domesticity by children taking turns being parents. We were adrift but we were together. A group of us floated between several large ramshackle houses, houses arranged above and below each other on steep streets: a gritty version of terraced dwellings in some exotic Asia. The houses were old and comfortable, furnished with an accumulation of overstuffed chairs and velveteen sofas gleaned from rummage sales. There were no curtains at the large windows, whose rectangular sooty light was interrupted only by tangles of viney plants. The plants were fed haphazardly and thrived, like anything green in that town, enveloping sills and frames still fitted with the original wavy glass of seventy years before. The old glass was pocked with flaws and minute bubbles, distorting further the vision of a town already oddly displaced and dreamed in jagged pieces. Houses of the student ghetto were the landscape of the dream—a landscape often already condemned.

I lived in a house on Price Street with three male housemates: a Lebanese photographer from Rochester, New York, a Jewish instructor of transcendental meditation from Michigan, and a carpenter-musician, a West Virginian, who'd worked in the doomed McCarthy campaign and dropped out of Harvard Law to come home and learn house-building.

This story could be about any one of those people, but it is about Rayme and comes to no conclusions.

Perhaps the story is about Rayme because she lived in all the communal houses at one time or another. Intermittently, she lived with her father and stepmother and brother. Or she lived with one of her two older sisters, who had stayed in town and were part of our group of friends. Or she lived in her own small rooms, a bedroom, kitchen and bath in a house chopped into three or four such apartments. She lived alone in several of those single-person places, and in all of them she kept the provided mattress and box springs tilted upright against the wall. She slept on a small rug which she unrolled at night, or she slept on the bare floor with the rug precisely folded as a pillow. She shoved most of the other furniture into a corner or put it outside on the porch. Skirts and coats on hangers, swatches of fabric, adorned the walls. Rayme brought in large branches, a brick, a rock. Usually there were no utilities but running water; her father paid the rent and that is all that was paid. She wore sweaters and leggings and burned candles for light. She used the refrigerator as a closet for shoes and beads, and seemed to eat almost nothing. She kept loose tea and seeds in jars and emptied coffee cans which she filled with nutshells and marbles.

A long time ago her mother had committed suicide in Argentina. No one ever talked about the death, but one of Rayme's sisters told me the suicide was slow rather than overtly violent. 'She stopped eating, she'd been sick, she wouldn't go to the hospital or see a doctor,' the sister said. 'It took her several months to do it.' Rayme seldom mentioned her mother and didn't seem certain of any particular chain of events concerning the past. The facts she referred to at different times seemed arbitrary, they were scrambled, they may have been false or transformed. It is true that her parents married each other twice and divorced twice; the father was a professor, the mother had musical talent and four children. Rayme told me her father wouldn't let his wife play the piano; he locked the baby grand because she became too 'detached' when she played.

The first time her parents divorced, Rayme was six years old, the only child to go with her mother. They lived alone together in Kansas. Rayme didn't remember much about it. She said sometimes she came home from school and the door was locked and she would sit outside past dark and listen to the owls in the trees. Once there was a tornado in Kansas; Rayme's mother opened all the windows 'so the wind can blow *through* the house instead of breaking it.' Then they sat on the sofa wrapped in their winter coats, rather than hiding in the basement, so they could watch the rattling funnel cloud twist and hop across the flat fields behind the town.

In Kansas, Rayme said her mother kept things, like bracelets and rings, costume jewellery, under the pillows of the bed. They used to play games with those things before they went to sleep at night, and tell stories. Rayme slept by the wall because her mother sleepwalked, and needed a clear path to the open.

At the time of the second divorce, Rayme was twelve. She said her father stood in the middle of the living-room and called out the names of the children. He pointed to one side of the room or the other. 'When we were lined up right, he said *those* kids would stay with him and *those* kids would go with her.' Rayme went to Argentina with her mother and oldest sister. A family friend there paid airplane fares and found housing; Rayme's father paid child support. Rayme learned some Spanish songs. Her sister went out on chaperoned dates; there was a terrace; it was sunny. Their mother died down there after a few months, and the two children came back on a boat, unchaperoned.

Rayme's sister told me Rayme didn't react when their mother died. 'Everyone else cried, but Rayme didn't. She just sat there on the bed. She was our mother's favourite.' The funeral was in Argentina, and the service was Catholic. 'I was standing by the door while the priest was in the bedroom,' Rayme's sister said. 'Rayme looked up at me wearing our mother's expression, on purpose, to say *I'd* lost my mother but *she* hadn't.'

Once Rayme sent her oldest sister a group of wallet-sized photographs in the mail. They were all pictures of Rayme taken in various years by public school photographers, and they were all dotted with tiny pinholes so that the faces were gone. Another time she came to her sister's Christmas party with one eyebrow shaved off. Her sister demanded that she shave the other one off as well so at least they'd match, and Rayme did.

Sometime late that winter, Rayme went to stay in the country at the cabin of a friend. She was living there alone with her cat; she said she could marry the snow. The cat wandered into the woods and Rayme wandered down the middle of the dirt road six miles to the highway. There was rain and a heavy frost, sleet flowers on the pavement. Rayme wore a summer shift and a kitchen knife strapped to her arm with leather thongs. She had hacked her waist-length hair to the shape of a bowl on her head and coiled her thick dark braids tightly into the pockets of her dress.

She had nothing to say to the farm couple who found her sitting on the double line of the highway in a meditative pose, but she did nod and get into the car as though expecting them. They took her to the university hospital and she committed herself for three weeks. I visited her there; she sat stiffly by a window reinforced with chicken wire between double panes, her back very straight, her hands clasped. She said it was important to practise good posture, and she moved her head, slowly, deliberately, when she looked to the right or left. Her skin was pale and clear like white porcelain. Before I left, we repeated some rituals evolved earlier in half-serious fun: children's songs with hand motions ('here is the church and here is the steeple...I'm a little teapot, short and stout...along came the rain and washed the spider out'), the Repulse Tiger movement from T'ai Chi, a series of Chinese bows in slow motion. She said the hospital was like a big clock and she was in the floor of the clock; every day she went to Group, and played dominoes in the common room. She ate her lunch in a chair by the nurses' desk; she liked their white clothes and the sighing of the elevators.

By the time she was released, the TM instructor living at Price Street had moved to Cleveland. Rayme moved in with me, with the Harvard carpenter, with the Lebanese photographer. She wasn't paying rent but we had the extra room anyway and sometimes she cooked meals.

Once she cooked soup. For an hour, she stood by the stove, stirring the soup in a large dented kettle. I looked into the pot and saw a jagged object floating among the vegetables. I pulled it out, holding the hot thin edge: it was a large fragment of blackened linoleum from the buckling kitchen floor.

I asked Rayme how a piece of the floor got into the soup.

'I put it there,' Rayme said.

I didn't answer.

'It's clean,' Rayme said, 'I washed it first,' and then, angrily, 'If you're not going to eat my food, don't look at it.'

That was her worst summer. She told me she didn't want to take the Thorazine because it made her into someone else. Men were the sky and women were the earth; she liked books about Indians. She said cats were good and dogs were bad; she hated the lower half of her body. She didn't have lovers but quietly adored men from her past—relatives, boyfriends, men she saw in magazines or on the street. Her high-school boyfriend was Krishna, a later one Jesus, her father 'Buddha with a black heart'. She built an altar in her room out of planks and cement blocks, burned candles and incense, arranged pine needles and pebbles in patterns. She changed costumes often and moved the furniture in her room several times a day, usually shifting it just a few inches. She taped pictures on her wall: blue Krishna riding his white pony, Shiva dancing with all her gold arms adorned, Lyndon Johnson in glossy colour from *Newsweek,* cutouts of kittens from a toilet-paper advertisement. Her brother, three years younger than she and just graduated from high school, came to see her several times a week. He brought her a blue bottle full of crushed mint, and played his guitar. He seemed quiet, witty, focused; he looked like Rayme, the same dark hair and slender frame and chiselled bones. She said he was the angel who flew from the window with sleep-dust on his shoes; he used to tell his sisters, when they were all children, that he was the one who'd sealed their eyes shut in the night, that they would never catch him because boys could be ghosts in the dark.

On an afternoon when we'd taken mescaline, Rayme sat weeping on the couch at Price Street. The couch was brown and nubby, and people had to sit towards its edge or the cushions fell through to the floor. The cushions had fallen through, and Rayme sat in the hole of the frame comfortably, her legs splayed up over the board front. She sat looking at the ceiling, her head thrown back like a woman trying to keep her mascara from running. She remained still, as though enthroned, waiting, her face wet, attentive. I watched her from across the room. 'Yes,' she said after a long while, as though apprehending some truth, 'tears wash the eyes and lubricate the skin of the temples.'

All of us were consulting a series of maps bearing no relation to any physical geography, and Rayme was like a telephone to another world. Her messages were syllables from an investigative dream, and her every movement was precise, like a driver unerringly steering an automobile by watching the road through the rear-view mirror.

I'd met her when we were both working at Bonanza Steak House as servers. She liked the cowboy hats and the plaid shirts with the braid trim, and she insisted on completing the outfit by wearing her brother's high-heeled boots and a string tie from Carlsbad Caverns emblazoned with a tiny six-gun. She got away with these embellishments of restaurant policy because her compulsions seemed harmless. She would stand erect behind plates of crackling steaks bound for numbered trays, looking intently into the vacuous faces of customers shuffling by in the line. She did tap-dance steps in place, wielding her spatula and tipping her hat, addressing everyone as Sir or Madam. She liked the ritual of the totally useless weekly employee meetings, in which skirt lengths and hairnets and customer quota were discussed. She admired the manager and called him Mr Fenstermaker, when everyone else referred to him derisively as Chester, after the gimp on *Gunsmoke.* He was a fat doughy boy about thirty years old who walked around what he called 'the store' with a clipboard of names and work hours. During meetings, Rayme sat at his elbow and took down his directives in careful, cursive script, posting them later on the door to the employees' bathroom. She also posted the covers of several *True Romance* comic books. She got in trouble once for mixing the mashed potatoes with nutmeg and banana slices, and again when she arranged the plastic steak tags across the raw meat in a mandala bordered by white stones. In the centre of the mandala was the small, perfect egg of a bird. The egg was purely blue; on it Rayme had painted a Chinese word in miniature gold characters. Later she told me she'd looked the word up especially in a language textbook; the word meant *banquet.*

R ayme was protected at Price Street. She stopped losing jobs because she stopped having them; instead, she worked in the tumbledown garden, tying tomato plants to poles with strips of heavy satin and brocade—draperies she'd found in a junk pile. Meticulously, she cut the fabric into measured lengths and hemmed the pieces. She kept the house full of wild flowers and blossoming weeds, and hung herbs to dry in the hallways. The summer was easy. No one expected her to talk on days when she didn't speak. She was calm. She pretended we were mythical people and brought us presents she'd made: a doll of sticks and corn silk, with a shard of glass for a face, or the skeleton of a lizard laid out perfectly in a velvet-lined harmonica box.

In late August we were told that Price Street and the abandoned houses near it would be demolished by the city, 'to make the city hospital a more attractive property.' The rest of us complained resignedly but Rayme made no comment; quietly, she began staying awake all night in the downstairs of the house. Day after day, we awoke to find the furniture turned over and piled in a heap, the rugs rolled up, pictures turned upside-down on the walls. She took personal possessions from the bedrooms, wrapped them in her shirts and jeans, and tied the carefully-folded parcels with twine. We called a house meeting to discuss her behaviour, and Rayme refused to attend. She went upstairs and began throwing plates from the windows.

We asked her brother to come to Price Street and talk to her. They sat in her room for a couple of hours, then they came downstairs. Rayme said she didn't have any money, maybe she'd live with her sister for a while. She unwrapped the stolen possessions with great ceremony and gave them back to us as gifts while her brother watched, smiling. At midnight, we made wheat pancakes and ate them with molasses, Indian-style, on the dark porch.

Several years later, when all the houses we'd lived in together had been torn down, Rayme's brother would shoot himself with a pistol. He would do it beside a lean-to he'd built as a squatter at an isolated camp site, five miles up a steep mountain trail. He would leave no notes; his body would not be discovered for some time. When they did find him (they meaning people in uniforms), they would have trouble getting a stretcher down the path and over the rocks.

But this was before that. It was September of 1974, most of us would leave town in a few weeks, and I had been recently pregnant. Some of us were going to Belize to survive an earthquake. Some of us were going to California to live on 164th Street in Oakland. A few were staying in West Virginia to continue the same story in even more fragmented fashion. My lover, the carpenter, was going to Nicaragua on a house-building deal that would never materialize. We'd had passport photos taken together; he would use his passport in the company of someone else and I would lose mine somewhere in Arizona. But on this day in September I had never seen Arizona, and we all went to a deserted lake to swim despite the fact the weather had turned.

I remember going into the lake first, how the water was warmer than the air. On the bank the others were taking off their clothes—

Jayne Anne Phillips

denim skirts and jeans, soft, worn clothes, endlessly utilitarian. Their bodies were pale and slow against the dark border of the woods. They walked into the lake separately, aimlessly, but Rayme swam straight towards me. It was almost evening and the air smelled of rain. Noise was muffled by the wind in the leaves of the trees, and when Rayme was suddenly close the splash of her movement was a shock like waking up. Her hands brushed my legs—her touch underwater as soft as the touch of a plant—and she passed me, swimming deeper, swimming farther out.

I wanted to stand on something firm and swam to the dock, a stationary thickness for mooring motor boats. It stretched out into the water a long distance. Who had built it in this deserted place? It was old, the weathered black of railroad ties. I pulled myself on to the splintery wood and began to walk along its length, touching the pylons, hearing the *swak* of stirred water as the storm blew up, hearing my own footsteps. Where were we all really going, and when would we ever arrive? Our destinations appeared to be interchangeable pauses in some long, lyric transit. This time that was nearly over, these years, seemed as close to family as most of us would ever get.

Now the rain was coming from far off, sweeping across the water in a silver sheet. The waiting surface began to dapple, studded with slivers of rain. Rayme was a white face and shoulders, afloat two hundred yards out.

'Janet,' she called across the distance, 'when you had your abortion, did you think about killing yourself?'

'No,' I yelled back. 'Come out of the water.'

42

RICHARD FORD
ROCK SPRINGS

Richard Ford was born in 1944 in Jackson, Mississippi. He has taught creative writing at Princeton University, Michigan University, and William and Mary College. He is the author of two novels, *A Piece of My Heart* and *The Ultimate Good Luck*. He is currently living in Missoula, Montana, and is working on his third book.

E dna and I had started down from Kalispell heading for Tampa-St Pete, where I still had some friends from the old glory days who wouldn't turn me in to the police. I had managed to scrape with the law in Kalispell over several bad cheques—which is a prison crime in Montana. And I knew Edna was already looking at her cards and thinking about a move, since it wasn't the first time I'd been in law scrapes in my life. She herself had already had her own troubles, losing her kids and keeping her ex-husband, Danny, from breaking in her house and stealing her things while she was at work, which was really why I had moved in in the first place, that and needing to give my little daughter, Cheryl, a better shake in things.

I don't know what was between Edna and me, just beached by the same tides when you got down to it. Though love has been built on frailer ground than that, as I well know. And when I came in the house that afternoon, I just asked her if she wanted to go to Florida with me, leave things where they sat, and she said, 'Why not? My datebook's not that full.'

Edna and I had been a pair eight months, more or less man and wife, some of which time I had been out of work, and some when I'd worked at the dog track as a lead-out and could help with the rent and talk sense to Danny when he came around. Danny was afraid of me because Edna had told him I'd been in prison in Florida for killing a man once, though that wasn't true. I had once been in jail in Tallahassee for stealing tyres and had got into a fight on the county farm where a man had lost his eye. But I hadn't done the hurting, and Edna just wanted the story worse than it was so Danny wouldn't act crazy and make her have to take her kids back, since she had made a good adjustment to not having them, and I already had Cheryl with me. I'm not a violent person and would never put a man's eye out, much less kill someone. My former wife, Helen, would come all the way from Waikiki Beach to testify to that. We never had violence, and I believe in crossing the street to stay out of trouble's way. Though Danny didn't know that.

But we were half down through Wyoming, going toward Interstate 80 and feeling good about things, when the oil light flashed on in the car I'd stolen, a sign I knew to be a bad one.

I'd got us a good car, a cranberry Mercedes I'd stolen out of an ophthalmologist's lot in Whitefish, Montana. I stole it because I thought it would be comfortable over a long haul, because I thought it got good mileage, which it didn't, and because I'd never had a good car in my life, just old Chevy junkers and used trucks back from when I was a kid swamping citrus with Cubans.

The car made us all high that day. I ran the windows up and down, and Edna told us some jokes and made faces. She could be lively. Her features would light up like a beacon and you could see her beauty, which wasn't ordinary. It all made me giddy, and I drove clear down to Bozeman, then straight on through the park to Jackson Hole. I rented us the bridal suite in the Quality Court in Jackson and left Cheryl and her little dog, Duke, sleeping while Edna and I drove to a rib barn and drank beer and laughed till after midnight.

It felt like a whole new beginning for us, bad memories left behind and a new horizon to build on. I got so worked up, I had a tattoo done on my arm that said FAMOUS TIMES, and Edna bought a Bailey hat with an Indian feather band and a little turquoise-and-silver bracelet for Cheryl, and we made love on the seat of the car in the Quality Court parking lot just as the sun was burning up on the Snake River, and everything seemed then like the end of the rainbow.

It was that very enthusiasm, in fact, that made me keep the car one day longer instead of driving it into the river and stealing another one, like I should have done and *had* done before.

Where the car went bad there wasn't a town in sight or even a house, just some low mountains maybe fifty miles away or maybe a hundred, a barbed-wire fence in both directions, hardpan prairie, and some hawks sailing through the evening air seizing insects.

I got out to look at the motor, and Edna got out with Cheryl and the dog to let them have a pee by the car. I checked the water and checked the oil stick, and both of them said perfect.

'What's that light mean, Earl?' Edna said. She had come and stood by the car with her hat on. She was just sizing things up for herself.

'We shouldn't run it,' I said. 'Something's not right in the oil.'

She looked around at Cheryl and Little Duke, who were peeing on the hardtop side by side like two little dolls, then out at the mountains, which were becoming black and lost in the distance. 'What're we doing?' she said. She wasn't worried yet, but she wanted to know what I was thinking about.

'Let me try it again,' I said.

'That's a good idea,' she said, and we all got back in the car.

When I turned the motor over, it started right away and the red light stayed off and there weren't any noises to make you think something was wrong. I let it idle a minute, then pushed the accelerator down and watched the red bulb. But there wasn't any light on, and I started wondering if maybe I hadn't dreamed I saw it, or that it had been the sun catching an angle off the window chrome, or maybe I was scared of something and didn't know it.

'What's the matter with it, Daddy?' Cheryl said from the back seat. I looked back at her, and she had on her turquoise bracelet and Edna's hat set back on the back of her head and that little black-and-white Heinz dog on her lap. She looked like a little cowgirl in the movies.

'Nothing, honey, everything's fine now,' I said.

'Little Duke tinkled where I tinkled,' Cheryl said, and laughed.

'You're two of a kind,' Edna said, not looking back. Edna was usually good with Cheryl, but I knew she was tired now. We hadn't had much sleep, and she had a tendency to get cranky when she didn't sleep. 'We oughta ditch this damn car first chance we get,' she said.

'What's the first chance we got?' I said, because I knew she'd been at the map.

'Rock Springs, Wyoming,' Edna said with conviction. 'Thirty miles down this road.'

She pointed out ahead. I had wanted all along to drive the car into Florida like a big success story. But I knew Edna was right about it, that we shouldn't take crazy chances. I had kept thinking of it as my car and not the ophthalmologist's, and that was how you got caught in these things.

'Then my belief is we ought to go to Rock Springs and negotiate ourselves a new car,' I said. I wanted to stay upbeat, like everything was panning out right.

'That's a great idea,' Edna said, and she leaned over and kissed me hard on the mouth.

'That's a great idea,' Cheryl said. 'Let's pull on out of here right now.'

Richard Ford

T he sunset that day I remember as being the prettiest I'd ever
seen. Just as it touched the rim of the horizon, it all at once
fired the air into jewels and red sequins the precise likes of
which I had never seen before and haven't seen since. The West has it
all over everywhere for sunsets, even Florida, where it's supposedly
flat but where half the time trees block your view.

'It's cocktail hour,' Edna said after we'd driven a while. 'We ought
to have a drink and celebrate something.' She felt better thinking we
were going to get rid of the car. It certainly had dark troubles and was
something you'd want to put behind you.

Edna had out a whiskey bottle and some plastic cups and was
measuring levels on the glove-box lid. She liked drinking, and she
liked drinking in the car, which was something you got used to in
Montana, where it wasn't against the law, where, though, strangely
enough, a bad cheque would land you in Deer Lodge Prison for a
year.

'Did I ever tell you I once had a monkey?' Edna said, setting my
drink on the dashboard where I could reach it when L was ready. Her
spirits were already picked up. She was like that, up one minute and
down the next.

'I don't think you ever did tell me that,' I said. 'Where were you
then?'

'Missoula,' she said. She put her bare feet on the dash and rested
the cup on her breasts. 'I was waitressing at the Amvets. It was before
I met you. Some guy came in one day with a monkey. A spider
monkey. And I said, just to be joking, "I'll roll you for that monkey."
And the guy said, "Just one roll?" And I said, "Sure." He put the
monkey down on the bar, picked up the cup, and rolled out boxcars. I
picked it up and rolled out three fives. And I just stood there looking
at the guy. He was just some guy passing through, I guess a vet. He got
a strange look on his face—I'm sure not as strange as the one I
had—but he looked kind of sad and surprised and satisfied all at
once. I said, "We can roll again." But he said, "No, I never roll twice
for anything." And he sat and drank a beer and talked about one
thing and another for a while, about nuclear war and building a
stronghold somewhere up in the Bitterroot, whatever it was, while I
just watched the monkey, wondering what I was going to do with it
when the guy left. And pretty soon he got up and said, "Well,

48

goodbye, Chipper," that was this monkey's name, of course. And then he left before I could say anything. And the monkey just sat on the bar all that night. I don't know what made me think of that, Earl. Just something weird. I'm letting my mind wander.'

'That's perfectly fine,' I said. I took a drink of my drink. 'I'd never own a monkey,' I said after a minute. 'They're too nasty. I'm sure Cheryl would like a monkey, though, wouldn't you, honey?' Cheryl was down on the seat playing with Little Duke. She used to talk about monkeys all the time then. 'What'd you ever do with that monkey?' I said, watching the speedometer. We were having to go slower now because the red light kept fluttering on. And all I could do to keep it off was go slower. We were going maybe thirty-five and it was an hour before dark, and I was hoping Rock Springs wasn't far away.

'You really want to know?' Edna said. She gave me a quick, sharp glance, then looked back at the empty desert as if she was brooding over it.

'Sure,' I said. I was still upbeat. I figured *I* could worry about breaking down and let other people be happy for a change.

'I kept it a week,' she said. She seemed gloomy all of a sudden, as if she saw some aspect of the story she had never seen before. 'I took it home and back and forth to the Amvets on my shifts. And it didn't cause any trouble. I fixed a chair up for it to sit on, back of the bar, and people liked it. It made a nice little clicking noise. We changed its name to Mary because the bartender figured out it was a girl. Though I was never really comfortable with it at home. I felt like it watched me too much. Then one day a guy came in, some guy who'd been in Vietnam, still wore a fatigue coat. And he said to me, "Don't you know that a monkey'll kill you? It's got more strength in its fingers than you got in your whole body." He said people had been killed in Vietnam by monkeys, bunches of them marauding while you were asleep, killing you and covering you with leaves. I didn't believe a word of it, except that when I got home and got undressed I started looking over across the room at Mary on her chair in the dark watching me. And I got the creeps. And after a while I got up and went out to the car, got a length of clothesline wire, and came back in and wired her to the doorknob through her little silver collar, and went back and tried to sleep. And I guess I must've slept the sleep of the dead—though I don't remember it—because when I got up I

found Mary had tupped off her chair back and hanged herself on the
wire line. I'd made it too short.'

Edna seemed badly affected by that story and slid low in the seat
so she couldn't see out over the dash. 'Isn't that a shameful story,
Earl, what happened to that poor little monkey?'

'I see a town! I see a town!' Cheryl started yelling from the back
seat, and right up Little Duke started yapping and the whole car fell
into a racket. And sure enough she had seen something I hadn't,
which was Rock Springs, Wyoming, at the bottom of a long hill, a
little glowing jewel in the desert with Interstate 80 running on the
north side and the black desert spread out behind.

'That's it, honey,' I said. 'That's where we're going. You saw it
first.'

'We're hungry,' Cheryl said. 'Little Duke wants some fish, and I
want spaghetti.' She put her arms around my neck and hugged me.

'Then you'll just get it,' I said. 'You can have anything you want.
And so can Edna and so can Little Duke.' I looked over at Edna,
smiling, but she was staring at me with eyes that were fierce with
anger. 'What's wrong?' I said.

'Don't you care anything about that awful thing that happened to
me?' she said. Her mouth was drawn tight, and her eyes kept cutting
back at Cheryl and Little Duke, as if they had been tormenting her.

'Of course, I do,' I said. 'I thought that was an awful thing.' I
didn't want her to be unhappy. We were almost there, and pretty soon
we could sit down and have a real meal without thinking somebody
might be hunting us.

'You want to know what I did with that monkey?' Edna said.

'Sure I do,' I said.

She said, 'I put her in a green garbage bag, put it in the trunk of my
car, drove to the dump, and threw her in the trash.' She was staring at
me darkly, as if the story meant something to her that was real
important but that only she could see and that the rest of the world
was a fool for.

'Well, that's horrible,' I said. 'But I don't see what else you could
do. You didn't mean to kill it. You'd have done it differently if you
had. And then you had to get rid of it, and I don't know what else you
could have done. Throwing it away might seem unsympathetic to
somebody, probably, but not to me. Sometimes that's all you can do,

and you can't worry about what somebody else thinks.' I tried to smile at her, but the red light was staying on if I pushed the accelerator at all, and I was trying to gauge if we could coast to Rock Springs before the car gave out completely. I looked at Edna again. 'What else can I say?' I said.

'Nothing,' she said, and stared back at the dark highway. 'I should've known that's what you'd think. You've got a character that leaves something out, Earl. I've known that a long time.'

'And yet here you are,' I said. 'And you're not doing so bad. Things could be a lot worse. At least we're all together here.'

'Things could always be worse,' Edna said. 'You could go to the electric chair tomorrow.'

'That's right,' I said. 'And somewhere somebody probably will. Only it won't be you.'

'I'm hungry,' said Cheryl. 'When're we gonna eat? Let's find a motel. I'm tired of this. Little Duke's tired of it too.'

Where the car stopped rolling was some distance from the town, though you could see the clear outline of the Interstate in the dark with Rock Springs lighting up the sky behind. You could hear the big tractors hitting the spacers in the overpass, revving up for the climb to the mountains.

I shut off the lights.

'What're we going to do now?' Edna said irritably, giving me a bitter look.

'I'm figuring it,' I said. 'It won't be hard, whatever it is. You won't have to do anything.'

'I'd hope not,' she said, and looked the other way.

Across the road and across a dry wash a hundred yards was what looked like a huge mobile-home town, with a factory or a refinery of some kind lit up behind it and in full swing. There were lights on in a lot of the mobile homes, and there were cars moving along an access road that ended near the freeway overpass a mile the other way. The lights in the mobile homes seemed friendly to me, and I knew right then what I should do.

'Get out,' I said, and opened my door.

'Are we walking?' Edna said.

'We're pushing,' I said.

'I'm not pushing,' Edna said, and reached up and locked her door. 'All right,' I said. 'Then you just steer.'

'You pushing us to Rock Springs, are you, Earl? It doesn't look like it's more than about three miles,' Edna said.

'I'll push,' Cheryl said from the back.

'No, hon. Daddy'll push. You just get out with Little Duke and move out of the way.'

Edna gave me a threatening look, just as if I'd tried to hit her. But when I got out she slid into my seat and took the wheel, staring angrily ahead straight into the cottonwood scrub.

'Edna can't drive that car,' Cheryl said from out in the dark. 'She'll run it in the ditch.'

'Yes, she can, hon. Edna can drive it as good as I can. Probably better.'

'No, she can't,' Cheryl said. 'No, she can't either.' And I thought she was about to cry, but she didn't.

I told Edna to keep the ignition on so it wouldn't lock up and to steer into the cottonwoods with the parking lights on so she could see. And when I started, she steered it straight off into the trees, and I kept pushing until we were twenty yards into the cover and the tyres sank in the soft sand and nothing at all could be seen from the road.

'Now where are we?' she said, sitting at the wheel. Her voice was tired and hard, and I knew she could have put a good meal to use. She had a sweet nature, and I recognized that this wasn't her fault but mine. Only I wished she could be more hopeful.

'You stay right here, and I'll go over to that trailer park and call us a cab,' I said.

'What cab?' Edna said, her mouth wrinkled as if she'd never heard anything like that in her life.

'There'll be cabs,' I said, and tried to smile at her. 'There's cabs everywhere.'

'What're you going to tell him when he gets here? Our stolen car broke down and we need a ride to where we can steal another one? That'll be a big hit, Earl.'

'I'll talk,' I said. 'You just listen to the radio for ten minutes and then walk on out to the shoulder like nothing was suspicious. And you and Cheryl act nice. She doesn't need to know about this car.'

'Like we're not suspicious enough already, right?' Edna looked up at me out of the lighted car. 'You don't think right, did you know that, Earl? You think the world's stupid and you're smart. But that's not how it is. I feel sorry for you. You might've *been* something, but things just went crazy someplace.'

I had a thought about poor Danny. He was a vet and crazy as a shit-house mouse, and I was glad he wasn't in for all this. 'Just get the baby in the car,' I said, trying to be patient. 'I'm hungry like you are.'

'I'm tired of this,' Edna said. 'I wish I'd stayed in Montana.'

'Then you can go back in the morning,' I said. 'I'll buy the ticket and put you on the bus. But not till then.'

'Just get on with it, Earl,' she said, slumping down in the seat, turning off the parking lights with one foot and the radio on with the other.

The mobile-home community was as big as any I'd ever seen. It was attached in some way to the plant that was lighted up behind it, because I could see a car once in a while leave one of the trailer streets, turn in the direction of the plant, then go slowly into it. Everything in the plant was white, and you could see that all the trailers were painted white and looked exactly alike. A deep hum came out of the plant, and I thought as I got closer that it wouldn't be a location I'd ever want to work in.

I went right to the first trailer where there was a light and knocked on the metal door. Kids' toys were lying in the gravel around the little wood steps, and I could hear talking on TV that suddenly went off. I heard a woman's voice talking, and then the door opened wide.

A large Negro woman with a wide, friendly face stood in the doorway. She smiled at me and moved forward as if she was going to come out, but she stopped at the top step. There was a little Negro boy behind her peeping out from behind her legs, watching me with his eyes half closed. The trailer had that feeling that no one else was inside, which was a feeling I knew something about.

'I'm sorry to intrude,' I said. 'But I've run up on a little bad luck tonight. My name's Earl Middleton.'

The woman looked at me, then out into the night toward the freeway as if what I had said was something she was going to be able to see. 'What kind of bad luck?' she said, looking down at me again.

'My car broke down out on the highway,' I said. 'I can't fix it myself, and I wondered if I could use your phone to call for help.'

The woman smiled down at me knowingly. 'We can't live without cars, can we?'

'That's the honest truth,' I said.

'They're like our hearts,' she said firmly, her face shining in the little bulb light that burned beside the door. 'Where's your car situated?'

I turned and looked over into the dark, but I couldn't see anything because of where we'd put it. 'It's over there,' I said. 'You can't see it in the dark.'

'Who all's with you now?' the woman said. 'Have you got your wife with you?'

'She's with my little girl and our dog in the car,' I said. 'My daughter's asleep or I would have brought them.'

'They shouldn't be left in that dark by themselves,' the woman said, and frowned. 'There's too much unsavouriness out there.'

'The best I can do is hurry back,' I said. I tried to look sincere, since everything except Cheryl being asleep and Edna being my wife was the truth. The truth is meant to serve you if you'll let it, and I wanted it to serve me. 'I'll pay for the phone call,' I said. 'If you'll bring the phone to the door I'll call from right here.'

The woman looked at me again as if she was searching for a truth of her own, then back out into the night. She was maybe in her sixties but I couldn't say for sure. 'You're not going to rob me, are you, Mr Middleton?' she said, and smiled like it was a joke between us.

'Not tonight,' I said, and smiled a genuine smile. 'I'm not up to it tonight. Maybe another time.'

'Then I guess Terrel and I can let you use our phone with Daddy not here, can't we, Terrel? This is my grandson, Terrel Junior, Mr Middleton.' She put her hand on the boy's head and looked down at him. 'Terrel won't talk. Though if he did he'd tell you to use our phone. He's a sweet boy.' She opened the screen for me to come in.

The trailer was a big one with a new rug and a new couch and a living room that expanded to give the space of a real house. Something good and sweet was cooking in the kitchen, and the trailer felt like it was somebody's comfortable new home instead of just temporary. I've lived in trailers, but they were just snail backs with one room and no toilet, and they always felt cramped and unhappy—

though I've thought maybe it might've been me that was unhappy in them.

There was a big Sony TV and a lot of kids' toys scattered on the floor. I recognized a Greyhound bus I'd got for Cheryl. The phone was beside a new leather recliner, and the Negro woman pointed for me to sit down and call and gave me the phone book. Terrel began fingering his toys, and the woman sat on the couch while I called, watching me and smiling.

There were three listings for cab companies, all with one number different. I called the numbers in order and didn't get an answer until the last one, which answered with the name of the second company. I said I was on the highway beyond the Interstate and that my wife and family needed to be taken to town and I would arrange for a tow later. While I was giving the location, I looked up the name of a tow service to tell the driver in case he asked.

When I hung up, the Negro woman was sitting looking at me with the same look she had been staring with into the dark, a look that seemed to want truth. She was smiling, though. Something pleased her and I reminded her of it.

'This is a very nice home,' I said, resting in the recliner, which felt like the driver's seat of the Mercedes and where I'd have been happy to stay.

'This isn't *our* house, Mr Middleton,' the Negro woman said. 'The company owns these. They give them to us for nothing. We have our own home in Rockford, Illinois.'

'That's wonderful,' I said.

'It's never wonderful when you have to be away from home, Mr Middleton, though we're only here three months, and it'll be easier when Terrel Junior begins his special school. You see, our son was killed in the war, and his wife ran off without Terrel Junior. Though you shouldn't worry. He can't understand us. His little feelings can't be hurt.' The woman folded her hands in her lap and smiled in a satisfied way. She was an attractive woman and had on a blue-and-pink floral dress that made her seem bigger than she could've been, just the right woman to sit on the couch she was sitting on. She was good nature's picture, and I was glad she could be, with her little brain-damaged boy, living in a place where no one in his right mind would want to live a minute. 'Where do *you* live, Mr Middleton?' she said politely, smiling in the same sympathetic way.

'My family and I are in transit,' I said. 'I'm an ophthalmologist, and we're moving back to Florida, where I'm from. I'm setting up practice in some little town where it's warm year-round. I haven't decided where.'

'Florida's a wonderful place,' the woman said. 'I think Terrel would like it there.'

'Could I ask you something?' I said.

'You certainly may,' the woman said. Terrel had begun pushing his Greyhound across the front of the TV screen, making a scratch that no one watching the set could miss. 'Stop that, Terrel Junior,' the woman said quietly. But Terrel kept pushing his bus on the glass, and she smiled at me again as if we both understood something sad. Except I knew Cheryl would never damage a television set. She had respect for nice things, and I was sorry for the lady that Terrel didn't. 'What did you want to ask?' the woman said.

'What goes on in that plant or whatever it is back there beyond these trailers, where all the lights are on?'

'Gold,' the woman said, and smiled.

'It's what?' I said.

'Gold,' the Negro woman said, smiling as she had for almost all the time I'd been there. 'It's a gold mine.'

'They're mining gold back there?' I said, pointing.

'Every night and every day,' she said, smiling in a pleased way.

'Does your husband work there?' I said.

'He's the assayer,' she said. 'He controls the quality. He works three months a year, and we live the rest of the time at home in Rockford. We've waited a long time for this. We've been happy to have our grandson, but I won't say I'll be sorry to have him go. We're ready to start our lives over.' She smiled broadly at me and then at Terrel, who was giving her a spiteful look from the floor. 'You said you had a daughter,' the Negro woman said. 'And what's her name?'

'Irma Cheryl,' I said. 'She's named for my mother.'

'That's nice,' she said. 'And she's healthy, too. I can see it in your face.' She looked at Terrel Junior with pity.

'I guess I'm lucky,' I said.

'So far you are,' she said. 'But children bring you grief, the same way they bring you joy. We were unhappy for a long time before my husband got his job in the gold mine. Now, when Terrel starts to school, we'll be kids again.' She stood up. 'You might miss your cab, Mr Middleton,' she said, walking toward the door, though not to be forcing me out. She was too polite. 'If *we* can't see your car, the cab surely won't be able to.'

'That's true,' I said, and got up off the recliner where I'd been so comfortable.

'None of us have eaten yet, and your food makes me know how hungry we probably all are.'

'There are fine restaurants in town, and you'll find them,' the Negro woman said. 'I'm sorry you didn't meet my husband. He's a wonderful man. He's everything to me.'

'Tell him I appreciate the phone,' I said. 'You saved me.'

'You weren't hard to save,' the woman said. 'Saving people is what we were all put on earth to do. I just passed you on to whatever's coming to you.'

'Let's hope it's good,' I said, stepping back into the dark.

'I'll be hoping, Mr Middleton. Terrel and I will both be hoping.'

I waved to her as I walked out into the darkness toward the car where it was hidden in the night.

The cab had already arrived when I got there. I could see its little red and green roof lights all the way across the dry wash, and it made me worry that Edna was already saying something to get us in trouble, something about the car or where we'd come from, something that would cast suspicion on us. I thought, then, how I never planned things well enough. There was always a gap between my plan and what happened, and I only responded to things as they came along and hoped I wouldn't get into trouble. I was an offender in the law's eyes. But I always *thought* differently, as if I weren't an offender and had no intention of being one, which was the truth. But as I read on a napkin once, between the idea and the act a whole kingdom lies. And I had a hard time with my acts, which were oftentimes offender's acts, and my ideas, which were as good as the gold they mined there where the bright lights were blazing.

'We're waiting for you, Daddy,' Cheryl said when I crossed the road. 'The taxi-cab's already here.'

'I see, hon,' I said, and gave Cheryl a big hug. The cabdriver was sitting in the driver's seat having a smoke with the lights on inside. Edna was leaning against the back of the cab between the tail-lights, wearing her Bailey hat. 'What'd you tell him?' I said when I got close.

'Nothin',' she said. 'What's there to tell?'

'Did he see the car?'

She glanced over in the direction of the trees where we had hid the Mercedes. Nothing was visible in the darkness, though I could hear Little Duke combing around in the underbrush tracking something, his little collar tinkling. 'Where're we going?' she said. 'I'm so hungry I could pass out.'

'Edna's in a terrible mood,' Cheryl said. 'She already snapped at me.'

'We're tired, honey,' I said. 'So try to be nicer.'

'She's never nice,' Cheryl said.

'Run go get Little Duke,' I said. 'And hurry back.'

'I guess *my* questions come last here, right?' Edna said.

I put my arm around her. 'That's not true,' I said.

'Did you find somebody over there in the trailers you'd rather stay with? You were gone long enough.'

'That's not a thing to say,' I said. 'I was just trying to make things look right, so we don't get put in jail.'

'So *you* don't, you mean,' Edna said and laughed a little laugh I didn't like hearing.

'That's right. So I don't,' I said. 'I'd be the one in Dutch.' I stared out at the big, lighted assemblage of white buildings and white lights beyond the trailer community, plumes of white smoke escaping up into the heartless Wyoming sky, the whole company of buildings looking like some unbelievable castle, humming away in a distorted dream. 'You know what all those buildings are there?' I said to Edna, who hadn't moved and who didn't really seem to care if she ever moved anymore ever.

'No. But I can't say it matters, 'cause it isn't a motel and it isn't a restaurant,' she said.

'It's a gold mine,' I said, staring at the gold mine, which, I knew now from walking to the trailer, was a greater distance from us than it seemed, though it seemed huge and near, up against the cold sky. I thought there should've been a wall around it with guards instead of just the lights and no fence. It seemed as if anyone could go in and take what they wanted, just the way I had gone up to that woman's trailer and used the telephone, though that obviously wasn't true.

Edna began to laugh then. Not the mean laugh I didn't like, but a laugh that had something caring behind it, a full laugh that enjoyed a joke, a laugh she was laughing the first time I laid eyes on her, in Missoula in the Eastgate bar in 1979, a laugh we used to laugh together when Cheryl was still with her mother and I was working steady at the track and not stealing cars or passing bogus cheques to merchants. A better time all around. And for some reason it made me laugh just hearing her, and we both stood there behind the cab in the dark, laughing at the gold mine in the desert, me with my arm around her and Cheryl out rustling up Little Duke and the cabdriver smoking in the cab and our stolen Mercedes-Benz, which I'd had such hopes for in Florida, stuck up to its axle in sand, where I'd never get to see it again.

'I always wondered what a gold mine would look like when I saw it,' Edna said, still laughing, wiping a tear from her eye.

'Me too,' I said. 'I was always curious about it.'

'We're a couple of fools, ain't we, Earl?' she said, unable to quit laughing completely. 'We're two of a kind.'

'It might be a good sign, though,' I said.

'How could it be?' she said. 'It's not our gold mine. There aren't any drive-up windows.' She was still laughing.

'We've seen it,' I said, pointing. 'That's it right there. It may mean we're getting closer. Some people never see it at all.'

'In a pig's eye, Earl,' she said. 'You and me see it in a pig's eye.'

And she turned and got into the cab to go.

The cabdriver didn't ask anything about our car or where it was, to mean he'd noticed something queer. All of which made me feel like we had made a clean break from the car and couldn't be connected with it until it was too late, if ever. The driver told us a lot about Rock Springs while he drove, that because of the gold mine a lot of people had moved there in just six months, people from all over, including New York, and that most of them lived out in the trailers. Prostitutes from New York City, who he called 'B-girls', had come into town, he said, on the prosperity tide, and Cadillacs with New York plates cruised the little streets every night, full of Negroes with big hats who ran the women. He told us that everybody who got in his cab now wanted to know where the women were, and when he got our call he almost didn't come because some of the trailers were brothels operated by the mine for engineers and computer people away from home. He said he got tired of running back and forth out there just for vile business. He said that *60 Minutes* had even done a programme about Rock Springs and that a blowup had resulted in Cheyenne, though nothing could be done unless the prosperity left town. 'It's prosperity's fruit,' the driver said. 'I'd rather be poor, which is lucky for me.'

He said all the motels were sky-high, but since we were a family he could show us a nice one that was affordable. But I told him we wanted a first-rate place where they took animals, and the money didn't matter because we had had a hard day and wanted to finish on a high note. I also knew that it was in the little nowhere places that the police look for you and find you. People I'd known were always being arrested in cheap hotels and tourist courts with names you'd never heard of before. Never in Holiday Inns or Travelodges.

I asked him to drive us to the middle of town and back out again so Cheryl could see the train station, and while we were there I saw a pink Cadillac with New York plates and a TV aerial being driven slowly by a Negro in a big hat down a narrow street where there were just bars and a Chinese restaurant. It was an odd sight, nothing you could ever expect.

'There's your pure criminal element,' the cabdriver said, and seemed sad. 'I'm sorry for people like you to see a thing like that. We've got a nice town here, but there're some that want to ruin it for everybody. There used to be a way to deal with trash and criminals, but those days are gone forever.'

'You said it,' Edna said.

'You shouldn't let it get *you* down,' I said to the cabdriver. 'There's more of you than them. And there always will be. You're the best advertisement this town has. I know Cheryl will remember you and not *that* man, won't you, honey?' But Cheryl was asleep by then, holding Little Duke in her arms on the taxi seat.

The driver took us to the Ramada Inn on the Interstate, not far from where we'd broken down. I had a small pain of regret as we drove under the Ramada awning that we hadn't driven up in a cranberry-coloured Mercedes but instead in a beat-up old Chrysler taxi driven by an old man full of complaints. Though I knew it was for the best. We were better off without that car, better, really, in any other car but that one, where the signs had turned bad.

I registered under another name and paid for the room in cash so there wouldn't be any questions. On the line where it said 'Representing', I wrote 'ophthalmologist' and put 'MD' after the name. It had a nice look to it, even though it wasn't my name.

When we got to the room, which was in the back where I'd asked for it, I put Cheryl on one of the beds and Little Duke beside her so they'd sleep. She'd missed dinner, but it only meant she'd be hungry in the morning, when she could have anything she wanted. A few missed meals don't make a kid bad. I'd missed a lot of them myself and haven't turned out completely bad.

'Let's have some fried chicken,' I said to Edna when she came out of the bathroom. 'They have good fried chicken at the Ramadas, and I noticed the buffet was still up. Cheryl can stay right here, where it's safe, till we're back.'

'I guess I'm not hungry anymore,' Edna said. She stood at the window staring out into the dark. I could see out the window past her some yellowish foggy glow in the sky. For a moment I thought it was the gold mine out in the distance lighting the night, though it was only the Interstate.

'We could order up,' I said. 'Whatever you want. There's a menu on the phone book. You could just have a salad.'

'You go ahead,' she said. 'I've lost my hungry spirit.' She sat on the bed beside Cheryl and Little Duke and looked at them in a sweet way and put her hand on Cheryl's cheek just as if she'd had a fever. 'Sweet little girl,' she said. 'Everybody loves you.'

'What do you want to do?' I said. 'I'd like to eat. Maybe I'll order up some chicken.'

'Why don't you do that?' she said. 'It's your favourite.' And she smiled at me from the bed.

I sat on the other bed and dialled room service. I asked for chicken, garden salad, potato, and a roll, plus a piece of hot apple pie and ice tea. I realized I hadn't eaten all day. When I put down the phone I saw that Edna was watching me, not in a hateful way or a loving way, just in a way that seemed to say she didn't understand something and was going to ask me about it.

'When did watching me get so entertaining?' I said, and smiled at her. I was trying to be friendly. I knew how tired she must be. It was after nine o'clock.

'I was just thinking how much I hated being in a motel without a car that was mine to drive. Isn't that funny? I started feeling like that last night when that purple car wasn't mine. That purple car just gave me the willies, I guess, Earl.'

'One of those cars *outside* is yours,' I said. 'Just stand right there and pick it out.'

'I know,' she said. 'But that's different, isn't it?' She reached and got her blue Bailey hat, put it on her head, and set it way back like Dale Evans. She looked sweet. 'I used to like to go to motels, you know,' she said. 'There's something secret about them and free—I was never paying, of course. But you felt safe from everything and free to do what you wanted because you'd made the decision to be there and paid that price, and all the rest was the good part. Fucking and everything, you know.' She smiled at me in a good-natured way.

'Isn't that the way this is?' I said. I was sitting on the bed, watching her, not knowing what to expect her to say next.

'I don't guess it is, Earl,' she said, and stared out the window. 'I'm thirty-two and I'm going to have to give up on motels. I can't keep that fantasy going anymore.'

'Don't you like this place?' I said, and looked around at the room. I appreciated the modern paintings and the lowboy bureau and the big TV. It seemed like a plenty nice enough place to me, considering where we'd been already.

'No, I don't,' Edna said with real conviction. 'There's no use in my getting mad at you about it. It isn't your fault. You do the best you can for everybody. But every trip teaches you something. And I've learned I need to give up on motels before some bad thing happens to me. I'm sorry.'

'What does that mean?' I said, because I really didn't know what she had in mind to do, though I should've guessed.

'I guess I'll take that ticket you mentioned,' she said, and got up and faced the window. 'Tomorrow's soon enough. We haven't got a car to take me anyhow.'

'Well, that's a fine thing,' I said, sitting on the bed, feeling like I was in a shock. I wanted to say something to her, to argue with her, but I couldn't think what to say that seemed right. I didn't want to be mad at her, but it made me mad.

'You've got a right to be mad at me, Earl,' she said, 'but I don't think you can really blame me.' She turned around and faced me and sat on the windowsill, her hands on her knees. Someone knocked on the door. I just yelled for them to set the tray down and put it on the bill.

'I guess I *do* blame you,' I said. I was angry. I thought about how I could have disappeared into that trailer community and hadn't, had come back to keep things going, had tried to take control of things for everybody when they looked bad.

'Don't. I wish you wouldn't,' Edna said, and smiled at me like she wanted me to hug her. 'Anybody ought to have their choice in things if they can. Don't you believe that, Earl? Here I am out here in the desert where I don't know anything, in a stolen car, in a motel room under an assumed name, with no money of my own, a kid that's not mine, and the law after me. And I have a choice to get out of all of it by getting on a bus. What would you do? I know exactly what you'd do.'

'You think you do,' I said. But I didn't want to get into an argument about it and tell her all I could've done and didn't do. Because it wouldn't have done any good. When you get to the point of arguing, you're past the point of changing anybody's mind, even though it's supposed to be the other way, and maybe for some classes of people it is, just never mine.

Edna smiled at me and came across the room and put her arms around me where I was sitting on the bed. Cheryl rolled over and looked at us and smiled, then closed her eyes, and the room was quiet. I was beginning to think of Rock Springs in a way I knew I would always think of it, a low-down city full of crimes and whores and disappointments, a place where a woman left me, instead of a place where I got things on the straight track once and for all, a place I saw a gold mine.

'Eat your chicken, Earl,' Edna said, 'Then we can go to bed. I'm tired, but I'd like to make love to you anyway. None of this is a matter of not loving you, you know that.'

S ometime late in the night, after Edna was asleep, I got up and walked outside into the parking lot. It could've been any time because there was still the light from the Interstate frosting the low sky and the big red Ramada sign humming motionlessly in the night and no light at all in the east to indicate it might be morning. The lot was full of cars all nosed in, most of them with suitcases strapped to their roofs and their trunks weighed down with belongings the people were taking someplace, to a new home or a vacation resort in the mountains. I had laid in bed a long time after Edna was asleep, watching the Atlanta Braves on cable television, trying to get my mind off how I'd feel when I saw that bus pull away the next day, and how I'd feel when I turned around and there stood Cheryl and Little Duke and no one to see about them but me alone, and that the first thing I had to do was get hold of some automobile and get the plates switched, then get them some breakfast and get us all on the road to Florida, all in the space of probably two hours, since that Mercedes would certainly look less hid in the daytime than the night, and word travels fast. I've always taken care of Cheryl myself as long as I've had her with me. None of the women ever did; most of them didn't even seem to like her, though they took care of me in a way so that I could take care of her. And I knew that once Edna left, all that was going to get harder. Though what I wanted most to do was not think about it just for a little while, try to let my mind go limp so it could be strong for the rest of what there was. I thought that the difference between a successful life and an unsuccessful one, between me at that moment and all the people who owned the cars that were nosed in to their proper places in the lot, maybe between me and that woman out in the trailers by the gold mine, was how well you were able to put things like this out of your mind and not be bothered by them, and maybe, too, by how many troubles like this one you had to face in a lifetime. Through luck or design they had all faced fewer troubles, and by their own characters, they forgot them faster. And that's what I wanted for me. Fewer troubles, fewer memories of trouble.

I walked over to a car, a Pontiac with Ohio tags, one of the ones with bundles and suitcases strapped to the top and a lot more in the trunk, by the way it was riding. I looked inside the driver's window. There were maps and paperback books and sunglasses and the little plastic holders for cans that hang on the window wells. And in the back there were kids' toys and some pillows and a cat box with a cat sitting in it staring up at me like I was the face of the moon. It all looked familiar to me, the very same things I would have in my car if I had a car. Nothing seemed surprising, nothing different. Though I had a funny sensation at that moment and turned and looked up at the windows along the back of the Ramada Inn. All were dark except two. Mine and another one. And I wondered, because it seemed funny, what would you think a man was doing if you saw him in the middle of the night looking in the windows of cars in the parking lot of the Ramada Inn? Would you think he was trying to get his head cleared? Would you think he was trying to get ready for a day when trouble would come down on him? Would you think his girlfriend was leaving him? Would you think he had a daughter? Would you think he was anybody like you?

'Dazzling' *
Martyn Goff
'Extraordinary'
Anthony Thwaite
'True originality'
Victoria Glendenning
'Wholly believable'
Paul Theroux
'Attempts the impossible and achieves it'
Bernard Levin
RUSSELL HOBAN
follows his 'masterpiece' (Observer)
RIDDLEY WALKER*
with a novel of genius, set at the time of the First Crusade of AD1096
PILGERMANN
JONATHAN CAPE

RAYMOND CARVER
THE COMPARTMENT

Raymond Carver

Raymond Carver was born in Clatskanie, Oregon, in 1939. He is the author of seven books, including four books of poetry, and three collections of short stories. His most recent collection, *What We Talk About When We Talk About Love*, was published in Britain last year. Raymond Carver is one of the most prolific and the most popular short story writers in the United States, and his fiction has appeared in the *New Yorker*, the *Atlantic, Esquire, Antaeus, Triquarterly*, and a number of literary magazines. His previous contribution to *Granta* appeared in issue number four. He has won the National Endowment of the Arts award for both poetry and fiction, and the Academy of Arts and Letters has recently awarded him a 'Living' of $35,000 a year for the next five years—and, if renewed, for the rest of his life—to enable him to write full time.

The Compartment

Myers was travelling through France in a first-class rail car on his way to visit his son in Strasbourg, who was a student at the university there. He hadn't seen the boy in eight years. There had been no phone calls between them during this time, not even a postcard since Myers and the boy's mother had gone their separate ways—the boy staying with her. The final breakup was hastened along, Myers always believed, by the boy's malign interference in their personal affairs.

The last time Myers had seen his son, the boy had lunged for him during a violent quarrel. Myers' wife had been standing by the sideboard, dropping one china plate after the other on to the dining-room floor. Then she'd gone on to the cups. 'That's enough,' Myers had said, and at that instant the boy charged him. Myers sidestepped and got him in a headlock while the boy wept and pummelled Myers on the back and kidneys. Myers had him, and while he had him he made the most of it. He slammed him into the wall and threatened to kill him. He meant it. 'I gave you life,' Myers remembered himself shouting, 'and I can take it back!'

Thinking about that horrible scene now, Myers shook his head as if it had happened to someone else. And it had. He was simply not that same person. These days he lived alone and had little to do with anybody outside his work. At night he listened to classical music and read books on waterfowl decoys.

He lit a cigarette and continued to gaze out the train window, ignoring the man who sat in the seat next to the door and who slept with a hat pulled over his eyes. It was early in the morning and mist hung over the green fields that passed by outside. Now and then Myers saw a farmhouse and its outbuildings, everything surrounded by a wall. He thought this might be a good way to live—in an old house surrounded by a wall.

It was just past six o'clock. Myers hadn't slept since he'd boarded the train in Milan at eleven the night before. When the train had left Milan, he'd considered himself lucky to have the compartment to himself. He kept the light on and looked at guide books. He read things he wished he'd read before he'd been to the place they were about. He discovered much that he should have seen and done. In a way, he was sorry to be finding out certain things about the country now, just as he was leaving Italy behind after his first and, no doubt, last visit. He put the guide books away in his suitcase, put the suitcase on the overhead rack, and took off his coat to drape over himself. He switched off the light and sat there in the darkened compartment with his eyes closed, hoping sleep would come.

After what seemed a long time, and just when he thought he was going to drop off, the train began to slow. It came to a stop at a little station outside Basel. There, a middle-aged man in a dark suit, and wearing a hat, entered the compartment. The man said something to Myers in a language Myers didn't understand, and then the man put his leather bag up on to the rack. He sat down on the other side of the compartment and straightened his shoulders. Then he pulled his hat over his eyes. By the time the train was moving again, the man was asleep and snoring quietly. Myers envied him. In a few minutes, a Swiss official opened the door of the compartment and turned on the light. In English, and in some other language—German, Myers assumed—the official asked to see their passports. The man in the compartment with Myers pushed the hat back on his head, blinked his eyes, and reached into his coat pocket. The official studied the passport, looked at the man closely, and gave him back the document. Myers handed over his own passport. The official read the data, examined the photograph, and then looked at Myers before nodding and giving it back. He turned off the light as he went out. The man across from Myers pulled the hat over his eyes and put out his legs. Myers supposed he'd go right back to sleep, and once again he felt envy.

He stayed awake after that and began to think of the meeting with his son, which was now only a few hours away. How would he act when he saw the boy at the station? Should he embrace him? He felt uncomfortable with that prospect. Or should he merely offer his hand, smile as if these eight years had never occurred, and then pat the boy on the shoulder? Maybe the boy would say a few words—'*I'm glad to see you. How was your trip?*' And Myers would say—something. He really didn't know what he was going to say.

The French *contrôleur* walked by the compartment. He looked in on Myers and at the man sleeping across from Myers. This same *contrôleur* had already punched their tickets, so Myers turned his head and went back to looking out the window. More houses began to appear. But now there were no walls, and the houses were smaller and set closer together. Soon, Myers was sure, he'd see a French village. The haze was lifting. The train blew its whistle and sped past a crossing over which a barrier had been lowered. He saw a young woman with her hair pinned up and wearing a sweater, standing with her bicycle as she watched the cars whip past.

'How's your mother?' he might say to the boy, after they had walked a little way from the station. 'What do you hear from your mother?' For a wild instant, it occurred to Myers she could be dead. But then he understood that it couldn't be so, he'd have heard something—one way or the other, he'd have heard. He knew if he let himself go on thinking about these things, his heart could break. He closed the top button of his shirt and fixed his tie. He laid his coat across the seat next to him. He laced his shoes, got up, and stepped over the legs of the sleeping man. He let himself out of the compartment.

Myers had to put his hand against the windows along the corridor to steady himself as he moved towards the end of the car. He closed the door to the little toilet and locked it. Then he ran water and splashed his face. The train moved into a curve, still at the same high speed, and Myers had to hold on to the basin to keep his balance.

The boy's letter had come to him a couple of months ago. The letter had been brief. He wrote that he'd been living in France and studying for the past year at the university in Strasbourg. There was no other information about what had possessed him to go to France, or what he'd been doing with himself during those years before France. Appropriately enough, Myers thought, no mention was made in the letter of the boy's mother—not a clue to her condition or whereabouts. But, inexplicably, the boy had closed the letter with the word 'Love', and Myers had pondered this for a long while. Finally, he'd answered the letter. After some deliberation, Myers wrote to say he had been thinking for some time of making a little trip to Europe. Would the boy like to meet him at the station in Strasbourg? He signed his letter, 'Love, Dad'. He heard back from the boy and then he'd made his arrangements. It struck him there was really no one, besides his secretary and a few business associates, that he felt it was necessary to tell he was going away. He had accumulated six weeks of vacation at the engineering firm where he worked, and he decided he would take all of the time coming to him for this trip. He was glad he'd done this, even though he now had no intention of spending all that time in Europe.

He'd gone first to Rome. But after the first few hours walking around by himself on the streets, he was sorry he hadn't arranged to be with a group. He was lonely. He went to Venice, a city he and his wife had always talked of visiting. But Venice was a disappointment. He saw a man with one arm eating fried squid, and there were grimy, water-stained buildings everywhere he looked. He took a train to Milan, where he checked into a four-star hotel and spent the night watching a soccer match on a Sony colour TV until the station went off the air. He got up the next morning and wandered around the city until it was time to go to the station. He'd planned the stopover in Strasbourg as the culmination to his trip. After a day or two, or three days—he'd see how it went—he would travel to Paris and fly home. He was tired of trying to make himself understood to strangers and would be glad to get back.

Someone tried the door to the toilet. Myers finished tucking in his shirt. He fastened his belt. Then he unlocked the door and, swaying with the movement of the train, walked back to his compartment. As he opened the door, he saw at once that his coat had been moved. It lay across a different seat than the one where he'd left it. He felt he had entered into a ludicrous but potentially serious situation. His heart began to race as he picked up the coat. He put his hand into the inside pocket and took out his passport. He carried his wallet in his hip pocket. So he still had his wallet and the passport. He went through the other coat pockets. What was missing was the gift he'd bought for the boy—an expensive Japanese wristwatch purchased at a shop in Rome. He had carried the watch in his inside coat pocket for safekeeping. Now it was gone.

'*Pardon,*' he said to the man who slumped in the seat, legs out, the hat over his eyes. '*Pardon.*' The man pushed the hat back and opened his eyes. He pulled himself up and looked at Myers. His eyes were large. He might have been dreaming. But he might not.

Myers said, 'Did you see somebody come in here?'

But it was clear the man didn't know what Myers was saying. He continued to stare at him with what Myers took to be a look of total incomprehension. But maybe it was something else, Myers thought. Maybe the look masked slyness and deceit. Myers shook his coat to focus the man's attention. Then he put his hand into the pocket and rummaged. He pulled the sleeve back and showed the man his own wristwatch. The man looked at Myers and then at Myers' watch. He seemed mystified. Myers tapped the face of his watch. He put his other hand back into his coat pocket and made a gesture as if he were fishing for something. Myers pointed at the watch once more and waggled his fingers, hoping to signify the wristwatch taking flight through the door.

The man shrugged and shook his head.

'God dammit,' Myers said, in frustration. He put his coat on and went out into the corridor. He couldn't stay in the compartment another minute. He was afraid he might strike the man. He looked up and down the corridor, as if hoping he could see and recognize the thief. But there was no one around. Maybe the man who shared his compartment hadn't taken the watch. Maybe someone else, the person who tried the door to the toilet, had walked past the compartment, spotted the coat and the sleeping man, and had simply opened the door, gone through the pockets, closed the door, and gone away again.

Myers walked slowly to the end of the corridor, peering into the other compartments. It was not crowded in this first-class car, but there were one or two people in each compartment. Most of them were asleep, or seemed to be. Their eyes were closed, and their heads were thrown back against the seats. In one compartment a man about his own age sat by the window looking out at the countryside. When Myers stopped at the glass and looked in at him, the man turned and regarded him fiercely.

Myers crossed into the second-class car. The compartments in this car were crowded—sometimes five or six passengers in each, and the people, he could tell at a glance, were more desperate. Many of them were awake—it was too uncomfortable to sleep—and they turned their eyes on him as he passed. Foreigners, he thought. It was clear to him that if the man in his compartment hadn't taken the watch, then the thief was from one of these compartments. But what could he do? It was hopeless. The watch was gone. It was in someone else's pocket

Raymond Carver

now. He couldn't hope to make the *contrôleur* understand what had happened. And even if he could, then what? He made his way back to his own compartment. He looked in and saw that the man had stretched out again with his hat over his eyes.

Myers stepped over the man's legs and sat down in his seat by the window. He felt dazed with anger. They were on the outskirts of the city now. Farms and grazing land had given way to industrial plants with unpronounceable names on the fronts of the buildings. The train began slowing. Myers could see automobiles on city streets, and others waiting in line at the crossings for the train to pass. He got up and took his suitcase down. He held it on his lap while he looked out the window at this hateful place.

It came to him that he didn't want to see the boy, after all. He was shocked by this realization and for a moment felt diminished by the meanness of it. He shook his head. In a lifetime of foolish actions, this trip was possibly the most foolish thing he'd ever done. But the fact was, he really had no desire to see this boy whose behaviour had long ago isolated him from Myers' affections. He suddenly, and with great clarity, recalled the boy's face when he had lunged that time, and a wave of bitterness passed over Myers. This boy had devoured Myers' youth, had turned the young girl he had courted and wed into a nervous, alcoholic woman whom the boy alternately pitied and bullied. Why on earth, Myers asked himself, would he come all this way to see someone he disliked? He didn't want to shake the boy's hand, the hand of his enemy, nor have to clap him on the shoulder and make small-talk. He didn't want to have to ask him about his mother.

He sat forward in the seat as the train pulled into the station. An announcement was called out in French over the train's intercom. The man across from Myers began to stir. He adjusted his hat and sat up in the seat as something else in French came over the speaker. Myers didn't understand anything that was said. He grew more agitated as the train slowed and then came to a stop. He decided he wasn't going to leave the compartment. He was going to sit where he was until the train pulled away. When it did, he'd be on it, going on with the train to Paris, and that would be that. He looked out the window cautiously, afraid he'd see the boy's face at the glass. He

74

didn't know what he'd do if that happened. He was afraid he might shake his fist. He saw a few people on the platform wearing coats and scarves who stood next to their suitcases, waiting to board the train. A few other people waited, without luggage, hands in their pockets, obviously expecting to meet someone. His son was not one of those waiting, but of course that didn't mean he wasn't out there somewhere. Myers moved the suitcase off his lap on to the floor and inched down in his seat.

The man across from him was yawning and looking out the window. Now he turned his gaze on Myers. He took off his hat and ran his hand through his hair. Then he put the hat back on, got to his feet, and pulled his bag down from the rack. He opened the compartment door. But before he went out, he turned around and gestured in the direction of the station.

'Strasbourg,' the man said.

Myers turned away.

The man waited an instant longer, and then went out into the corridor with his bag and, Myers felt certain, with the wristwatch. But that was the least of his concerns now. He looked out the train window once again. He saw a man in an apron standing in the door of the station, smoking a cigarette. The man was watching two trainmen explaining something to a woman in a long skirt who held a baby in her arms. The woman listened and then nodded and listened some more. She moved the baby from one arm to the other. The men kept talking. She listened. One of the men chucked the baby under its chin. The woman looked down and smiled. She moved the baby again and listened some more. Myers saw a young couple embracing on the platform a little distance from his car. Then the young man let go of the young woman. He said something, picked up his valise, and moved to board the train. The woman watched him go. She brought a hand up to her face, touched one eye and then the other with the heel of her hand. In a minute, Myers saw her moving down the platform, her eyes fixed on his car, as if following someone. He glanced away from the woman and looked at the big clock over the station's waiting room. He looked up and down the platform. The boy was nowhere in sight. It was possible he had overslept or it might be that he, too, had changed his mind. In any case, Myers felt relieved. He looked at the clock again, then at the young woman who was hurrying up to the window where he sat. Myers drew back as if she were going to strike the glass.

The door to the compartment opened. The young man he'd seen outside closed the door behind him and said, *'Bonjour.'* Without waiting for a reply, he threw his valise on to the overhead rack and stepped over to the window. *'Pardon.'* He pulled the window down. 'Marie,' he said. The young woman began to smile and cry at the same time. The young man brought her hands up and began kissing her fingers.

Myers looked away and clamped his teeth. He heard the final shouts of the trainmen. Someone blew a whistle. Presently, the train began to move away from the platform. The young man had let go of the woman's hands, but he continued to wave at her as the train rolled forward.

But the train went only a short distance, into the open air of the rail yard, and then Myers felt it come to an abrupt stop. The young man closed the window and moved over to the seat by the door. He took a newspaper from his coat and began to read. Myers got up and opened the door. He went to the end of the corridor where the cars were coupled together. He didn't know why they had stopped. Maybe something was wrong. He moved to the window. But all he could see was an intricate system of tracks where trains were being made up, cars taken off or switched from one train to another. He stepped back from the window. The sign on the door to the next car read, *Poussez.* Myers struck the sign with his fist, and the door slipped open. He was in the second-class car again. He passed along a row of compartments filled with people settling down, as if making ready for a long trip. He needed to find out from someone where this train was going. He had understood, at the time he purchased his ticket, that the train to Strasbourg went on to Paris. But he felt it would be humiliating to put his head into one of the compartments and say, *'Paree?'* or however they said it—as if asking if they'd arrived at a destination. He heard a loud clanking, and the train backed up a little. He could see the station again, and once more he thought of his son. Maybe he was standing back there, breathless from having rushed to get to the station, wondering what had happened to his father. Myers shook his head.

The car he was in creaked and groaned under him, then something caught and fell heavily into place. Myers looked out at the maze of tracks and realized that the train had begun to move again. He turned and hurried back to the end of the car and crossed back into the car he'd been travelling in. He walked down the corridor to his compartment. But the young man with the newspaper was gone. And Myers' suitcase was gone. It was not his compartment, after all. He realized with a start they must have uncoupled his car while the train was in the yard and attached another second-class car to the train. The compartment he stood in front of was nearly filled with small, dark-skinned men who spoke rapidly in a language Myers had never heard before. One of the men signalled him to come inside. Myers moved into the compartment, and the men made room for him. There seemed to be a jovial air in the compartment. The man who'd signalled him laughed and patted the space next to him. Myers sat down with his back to the front of the train. The countryside out the window began to pass faster and faster. For a moment, Myers had the impression of the landscape shooting away from him. He was going somewhere, he knew that. And if it was the wrong direction, sooner or later he'd find it out.

He leaned against the seat and closed his eyes. The men went on talking and laughing. Their voices came to him as if from a distance. Soon the voices became part of the train's movements—and gradually Myers felt himself being carried, then pulled back, into sleep.

ARENA

The new paperback imprint created specifically for readers interested in exciting, intelligent and original fiction and non-fiction.

Lord of the Dance

ROBIN LLOYD-JONES. The stunning winner of the BBC Bookshelf/Arrow First Novel Competition. A brilliantly imagined, picaresque novel, LORD OF THE DANCE is set in 16th century India and tells of the travels and misadventures of two Englishmen as they journey to Agra, the centre of the Mogul court and the great libraries of knowledge amassed there.

£2.50

Published simultaneously in hardback by Gollancz at £8.95

Ten years in an open necked shirt

JOHN COOPER CLARKE. Rock poet, storyteller, comic, John Cooper Clarke is a prime moving force in the revival of contemporary poetry. This is the authorised collection of his engaging and extraordinary off-beat verse. Brilliantly illustrated by Steve Maguire.

£2.50

ELIZABETH TALLENT
WHY I LOVE
COUNTRY MUSIC

Elizabeth Tallent was born in Washington DC in 1954, and now lives with her husband in Colorado. Her stories have appeared in the *New Yorker*, and have been included in the *Pushcart Prize Anthology* and the *Best American Short Stories*. 'Why I Love Country Music' will be included in her first collection of short stories, *In Constant Flight*, to be published by Chatto and Windus in August.

Nod is a miner. He has long dark hair and owns probably a hundred different pairs of overalls; he likes to go dancing in cowboy bars. Because he weighs about two hundred pounds and is no taller than I am—about 5' 4" in my bare feet—the sight of Nod, dancing, has been known to arouse the kind of indignation in the hearts of cowboys that, in New Mexico, can be dangerous to the arouser. Cowboys in slanting hats—not only their Stetsons, in fact, but often their eyes are slanting, and the dark cigarettes stuck in one corner of their mouths, the ash lighting only with the brief, formal intake of each breath—watch Nod dancing with the slight contemptuous smiles with which they slice off a bull calf's genitals on hot afternoons in July. The genitals themselves are like plums buried in soft pouches made of cat's fur; if you are not quick with the small curved knife the scrotum slides between your fingers, contracting against the calf's ermine-slick black belly, the whites of its eyes almost phosphorescent with fear. The cowboys, with what seems to me an unnecessary lack of tact, often feed the remains to the chickens. Sometimes, living in the desert, you understand the need for an elaborate code of ritual laws; without them, the desert makes you an accomplice in all kinds of graceless crimes. They are not even crimes of passion—they are crimes of expediency, small reckonings made on the spur of the moment before the white chickens boil around the rim of the bloody, dented bucket.

Want to go dancing?' Nod says. It is still early and he has just called. I stare at the picture on the wall by the phone: my ex-husband, standing up to his knees in a stream, holding a trout. In the picture my husband is wearing a dark T-shirt and the water in the stream is the colour of iodine. Only the trout is silver. 'That job came through,' Nod says. 'The one in Texas, you remember? It put me in a bad mood. I want to go sweat out my anguish in a dim-lit bar. And it's Saturday night and you're a lonely woman with love on her mind. Come with me. You've got nothing else to do.'

I pause. It is true, I'm not doing anything else: on the television in the other room a long-haired Muppet with a quizzical expression is banging on a black toy piano with a toy hammer. My ex-husband is in Oregon. The trout, when he had opened it, was full of beautiful parallel bones. I was amazed by the transparency of the bones, and the fact that they had been laid down so perfectly inside the fish, lining the silvery gash of its intestines. My husband was pleased that I was taking such an interest in the trout; 'This is an art,' he said. He showed me the tiny minnow he had found, perfectly whole, inside the belly cavity. The minnow had tiny, astonished eyes. I wanted to put it in water. He refused. He wrapped it in a scrap of newspaper and threw it away. 'It was *dead*,' he told me. When he finally called me from Oregon, I could hear a woman singing in the background. My husband pretended it was the radio.

Nod waits a moment longer. 'Come on,' he says, 'I already told you I'm in a bad mood. I don't want to wait around on the phone all night.'

'Why are you in a bad mood?' I counter. 'Most people would be in a good mood if their job had just come through.'

'Coal mining always puts me in a bad mood,' Nod says. 'Now get dressed and let's go to the Line Camp. I'll be at your house in twenty minutes.'

I hang up the phone and go into the other room to get dressed, pulling on my Calvin Klein jeans while the long-haired Muppet sings *The Circle Song*.

T he cowboys, leaning against the left-hand wall as you go in, look you over with the barest movement of the eye, the eyelid not even contracting, the pupil dark through the haze of cigarette smoke, the mouth downcurved, the silent shifting of the pelvis against the wall by which one signals a distant quickening of erotic possibility. The band is playing *Whisky River*. My white buckskin cowboy boots—I painted the roses myself, tracing the petals from a library book—earn me a measure of serious consideration, the row of Levi-shaded pelvises against the wall swivelling slightly (they can swagger standing still, for these are the highest of their art, O men) as I go by, the line of cigarettes flicking like the ears of horses left standing in the rain, movement for the sake of movement only. The cowboys stand, smoking, staring out at the dance floor. Everyone who comes in has to pass by them. My hair has been brushed until it gleams, my lips are dark with costly gels. I pay my five dollars. Nod follows me. He pays his five dollars. The man at the card table, collecting the money, has curly sideburns that nearly meet under his chin. He whistles under his breath, so softly I can't tell whether it is *Whisky River* or something else. He keeps the money in a fishing-tackle box, quarters and dimes in the metal compartments which should have held coiled line, tiny amber flies. The cowboys shift uneasily against the wall. Nod graces them with a funereal sideways miner's glance, the front of his overalls decorated with an iron-on sticker of Mickey Mouse, giving the peace sign. There is one like it on the dashboard of his jeep. Nod is nostalgic for Mickey Mouse cartoons, which I do not remember. Fingers in their jeans, the cowboys watch us like the apostles confronted with the bloody, slender wrists: horror, the shyest crease of admiration, hope.

In Nod's arms I feel, finally, safe: a twig carried by lava, a moth clinging to the horn of a bull buffalo. Nod, you see, thinks I am beautiful—a beautiful woman—and that in itself is an uplifting experience. Nod is, for the most part, oddly successful with women; he has been married twice, both times to women you would think, if not beautiful, at least strikingly good-looking. Nod faltered through his second divorce, eking out his unemployment with food stamps, too depressed to look for work. He listened to Emmylou Harris records day and night in his bare apartment; his second wife had taken everything, even the *Aloe vera*. In the end, Nod says, it was *Defying Gravity* that saved him. He had the sudden revelation that there were always other women, deeper mines; he got dressed for the first time in months and sent a résumé to Peabody Coal. Peabody Coal, Nod claims, knows how to appreciate a man who has a way with plastic explosives. Don't they use dynamite anymore? I asked him. Nod grinned. Dynamite, he said, is the missionary position of industrial explosives; some men won't try anything else. He described the way explosives are placed against a rock face; in the end it often comes down to a matter of intuition, he said. You just *know* where it should go. Now, in the half-dark of the Line Camp dance floor, Nod is not unattractive. I imagine him closing his eyes, counting. (Do they still count?) No matter how many times you have seen it before, Nod says, when you see rock explode it still surprises you.

He holds me tightly, we move around the floor. Night washes the Tesuque valley in cold shadow, the moon rises, the eyes of the men along the wall glint seductively behind their Camels. In the mountains the last snow of the year is falling. On the stage, the harmonica player's left hand flutters irritably, as if he were fanning smoke from his eyes; his mouth puckers and jumps along the perforated silver, anemone flow of sound rising and falling above the whine of the pedal steel. The lead singer is blonde and holds the microphone close to her teeth. She is wearing a blue satin shirt, the beaded fringe above the breasts causing her nipples to rise expectantly in dark ovals the size of wedding rings.

'Aren't they fine?' Nod says. He is pleased. He sweeps me around in a tight, stylish circle, my boots barely touching the floor. Around us women dance with their eyes closed, their fingernails curving against plaid or embroidered cowboy shirts, their thoughts—who can have thoughts, in this music?—barely whispered. At the end of the set couples separate from each other slowly. There is a smattering of applause. Everyone's face looks pale and slightly shocked. A couple in a corner near the band's platform continue dancing as if nothing had happened. The woman is several inches taller than the man, who is wearing, above his black bolo tie, a huge turquoise cut in the shape of Texas. The woman stares straight ahead into the air above the man's slick black hair. It is very quiet. Around us people are moving away, to tables, to the bar against the far wall. Nod takes me by the hand. Someone unplugs the cord of the microphone. The harmonica player is left standing alone in the light, talking to himself. He cleans the spit from his instrument with a white handkerchief so old it is nearly transparent.

In the parking lot Nod lets go of my hand. Around us headlights are coming on like the lamps of a search party—dust rising from white gravel, the sound of many car doors slamming in pairs. Nod turns me around, kissing me. Ahead of us a tall girl in a white skirt patterned with flamingos is walking awkwardly on pink platform shoes, singing to herself in a voice blurred with fatigue. The skirt blows apart around her thighs; she stumbles. Nod takes her gently by the elbow. The three of us walk together to the end of the parking lot, where there is a black van with the words 'Midnight Rider' painted in silver across the doors. The windows are round, and seem to be made of black glass; there is a sound of muffled drumming from within.

When Nod knocks, a man gets out of the van, taking hold of the tall girl—she is still singing, her head thrown back, her eyes now tightly closed. She seems indifferent to his grasp. The man nods to us; he has a light scar across one corner of his mouth which makes him seem to be smiling slightly, ironically. He balances against the van, shifting the weight of the girl against him so that she falls inside. The floor of the interior is covered with a dark red-and-black rug. The girl lies on her side; her voice is muffled by the blonde hair which has fallen across her face. The man shuts the door. He looks at us and touches the scar absent-mindedly, with one finger. 'She knows the song,' he says, 'but not the words.'

The cowboys had seen us leave together. There was this, which might have been considered an incident: a blond cowboy with a narrow moustache—it seemed to be slightly longer on one side of his mouth than the other—kissed me on the nape of the neck as I went by him on my way to the bathroom. It was a very fast kiss, and his expression never changed; it left a faint circle of evaporation on my skin, cold as a snowflake. It was, I understood, an experiment. In the other room, far away, the guitarist rasped out a few chords, tightened his strings, rasped again, fell silent. He seemed to be taking a long while tuning his guitar. The woman hummed comforting sounds into the microphone: one, two, three, foah—

We stood for a moment, staring at each other. This always happens to me when I am confronted with a cowboy in a shadowed hallway; it has to do with having watched too many Lone Ranger matinées during a long and otherwise uninteresting midwestern adolescence. I thought of those Saturday afternoons, looking at him; I thought of the long white mane foaming against those gleaming black gloves, the eyes barely visible behind the mask, the steely composure in the face of evil and uncertainty. I tried for a few moments to summon my own steely composure. The cowboy leaned against the wall, cocking one shoulder jauntily. My steely composure had been abandoned somewhere between the second tequila sunrise and the third, and now it was hopelessly lost. The cowboy stared at me; I hoped that I emanated a kind of cool innocence. I understood that cool innocence ran a poor second to steely composure. His eyes were grey, his fingers in his jeans, knuckles riding the ridge of the hip bone, no wedding ring (good sign). Coors belt buckle (bad sign; cliché). Boots of dark suede with tall slanting heels (good sign). Grey eyes (neutral). Slight smile (very good sign: he is not pressing the issue, neither is he willing just to let it drop). I stood there, thinking about it.

He looked at me. I looked at him. My shoulders—one shoulder only if I am to be utterly truthful—lifted of its own accord: a shrug.

He watched me as I walked away. Out of the corner of my eye I could still see him; he shook his head vaguely, stood and strolled down to the end of the hall, walking with real grace on his tall, scuffed heels. The jukebox was indigo and silver and there was a framed photograph of Loretta Lynn on the wall above it. He stood and looked at Loretta Lynn for a few moments, cocking his head like a bank clerk trying to decipher a blurred cheque. Loretta Lynn, it was clear, would not have refused him. He eased a quarter from his pocket, pressed several of the numbered buttons, and paused. When nothing happened, he leaned slightly forward and nudged the jukebox suddenly with his hip. I could hear the coin drop from where I stood.

The door to the women's room says 'Fillies'. Inside there was a fat lady powdering her nose; the powder in her tortoise-shell compact was the colour of band-aids. She watched me from the corner of her eye. Tonight, I thought, everyone is watching everyone from the corners of their eyes. I closed the door and latched it. I could hear the fat woman sigh deeply as she clicked her compact shut. As I sat down, I neighed.

Nod would have been a diamond miner if there had been any diamonds in New Mexico: he only missed it by a continent. He could have been in South Africa, supervising the long-fingered black men in the dank caverns, if his father hadn't been a physicist in Los Alamos. But he was, and Nod regrets it. Diamonds, he says, think of that, coming out of the earth, thinking hard, now that would be *something*, the first human being to touch a *diamond*. Of course they don't look like diamonds right away, but you can tell. In South Africa the men dig hunched over—it is 'uneconomic', in the words of the mining companies, to dig away enough earth for the men to stand upright, the traditional vertical posture of *Homo sapiens,* but not, it seems, of miners. So the miners of diamonds remain for years in their position of enforced reverence, on their knees. The depths of the earth are open to them, the glinting, ancient lights buried within are retrieved and sold, only to end up on the fingers of virgins in fraternity house basements.

The night had clouded over, leaving only the moon, which followed us. Nod was driving. The Toyota jeep bucked in second gear over the narrow, stony road. Below us on the left was an abyss filled with the looming, lightning-struck tips of ponderosa, wind stroking through the heavy branches until they roared. Occasionally a single branch glittered in the moonlight. I stared down at my boots. I had placed them carefully, toe by toe, out of the way of the gear shift: now the toes seemed remote, indifferent as the pointed skulls of lizards. I was very tired. 'No,' Nod said, rubbing a clear space in the mist which covered the windshield. 'That light you see over there, *that's* the moon.' I looked. It was light as a flying saucer, cold and white, full of intelligent life.

When we got to the end of the road Nod parked the jeep, pulling out the handbrake. He stood at the entrance to the mine, his hands thrust into the pockets of his overalls, looking down. 'This whole mountain is honey-combed with mines,' he said. I did not feel reassured. He bent and threw a small stone into the interior. It made a very small chink, like a ring tapped against a mirror. 'This is one of the oldest,' Nod said. 'Look how they cut the wood from those braces: look at the craftsmanship in those notches. Those fuckers are going to last a thousand years.' I looked. I could see nothing except darkness.

'Smell the coal,' Nod said.

He went back to the jeep for a light. Nod always carries rare and useful things in his jeep: a bottle of Algerian wine, a blanket, a light. He drove the jeep a few more feet forward so that the headlights glared down into the entrance of the mine: this was so we could find our way out. The light grew hazy only a few feet from the front of the jeep. The jeep itself seemed mystically beautiful: a lost island, an airplane after you have just jumped out.

'Minotaur,' I sang out. 'Come home. Ally-ally-ox-in-free.'

Nod laughed. I was more than a little drunk. 'We always said it

different,' he said. 'We always used to say, "Ally-ally-in-come-free".'
He ran the light down the curved walls. The walls were dark and
seemed to have been chiselled; the light barely touched them. We did
not go far. 'Here,' Nod said. He got down on his knees. The earth at
the floor of the shaft seemed raw and gemmy, as if it had never quite
healed. Nod's shadow swept along the walls. He took off his overalls
and stepped away from them lightly. Barefoot, he swung the beam of
the flashlight in my direction.

'Nod,' I said. 'Take the damn light out of my eyes.'

'I love you,' he said. He turned the light off. I could hear nothing.
No sound from Nod. No matches in the pockets of my jeans. I cursed
heatedly: the cowboy, Nod, the darkness, the mine, Algerian wine,
the full moon, Calvin Klein.

'Find me,' he said, out of the darkness.

I wished for a long moment that I was with the cowboy, fucking in
the back of his International on an old Mexican blanket smelling of
dog hair, between bales of pink-yellow hay.

'Nod,' I said. 'It's dark, it's cold. I'm tired. Do you want to make
love or do you want to fuck around all night?'

(The idea suddeny of his agile two-hundred-pound mass moving
naked down the gleam-wet corridors forever and ever.)

I lay down on the blanket. I took off my boots. 'Ally-ally-in-
come-free,' I said. He was very drunk: suppose he got lost, how would
I ever find him? 'Ally-ally-come-home-free,' I called. The wine bottle
tipped cool against my spine. I lifted it, held it against my cheek for
the comfort of a solid object in the darkness. 'You damn well better
get your ass *over* here,' I screamed. I waited. If he was anywhere near
at all he could hear my crying.

When he came from the darkness he was different: he had small
curved horns, yellow tipped with ebony, and his eyes were dark in the
centres, ringed all the way around with startled white, his forehead
covered with ringlets damp as a rock star's. He stared at me. I stared
at him.

For a long while neither of us moved. In the light from the
headlights small motes of dust danced around his motionless horns.

'It's a lovely trick, Nod,' I said. 'How long have you had that thing
hidden down here?'

I stood up and pulled down my jeans, tripping slightly in the process. I laid them in the corner of the blanket near my cowboy boots, feeling for the bottle again in the darkness. I held it up for him to see. He stood with his mouth half open.

'What the hell is the matter with you?' I said. 'Haven't you ever seen a naked woman before?'

He took a small step toward me. I undid my shirt, one button at a time. 'I want you, okay?' I said. 'Nod, is that what you wanted me to say? I want you. Come over here, Nod. I want you right now.' He came toward me, lowering his head. He was not clumsy: miners never are, in the dark.

Nod, like all true heroes, left in the morning for Austin. He had written down my address on the side of a carton packed full of old copies of *National Geographic*. His cat, asleep on a pile of dirty overalls in the back of the jeep, opened one eye and stared at me coldly. She was not jealous, Nod said. She just disliked being looked at while she was trying to sleep; anyone would. Nod had on a pair of immaculate white overalls over a striped T-shirt; there was a red ceramic heart pinned to the front of the overalls. He had curled the *Rand McNally Road Atlas* into a narrow tube in his left hand, and now he swung it idly as if it was a baseball bat. His eyes were veiled.

'I'll bring you a diamond,' Nod said. 'If I find any.'

Of course, I thought he was lying.

I told this story to my analyst. Her hair is thick and curly and she sits in a white wicker chair in a sunny front room, listening to God knows what and nodding her head. In one corner of the room there is an old wooden carousel horse. When she first started practising in her own house, she thought of moving the horse into another room. The horse has faded blue eyes, a pure, vacant stare, small curved ears. Think of the dizzying moments that horse has known: small girls kissing its ears, caramel vomited across its flanks, a distant smell of mountains. Every single one of her clients protested when she moved the horse. She had to bring it back. These are crazy people? I thought. Once, when she thought I could not hear, she made a phone call. The conversation concerned another client. The session she had had with this client must have disturbed her. She whispered into the telephone.

'What is the professional term for someone who eats dirt?' she whispered. She wrote the word down on a small yellow pad.

She must have known it, and forgotten. Here is someone, telling her the story of how, as a child, he had eaten dirt, and here she is, in her white wicker chair, nodding gently, knowing she can't think of the word. When my husband calls from Oregon, the static sounds like sand blowing across glass; against the static I can make out a baby's crying. He asks how I am. I ask how he is. We are both fine. I count how many months it is that he has been gone; he pretends the baby crying is a Pampers commercial.

A small brown paper box from Austin. The delivery man who handed it to me looked at me queerly, because my face was painted. The neighbour's children had been here, and we all painted our faces together. Mine is gorgeous: dark gold, indigo. Silver false eyelashes. The little girl next door has promised to invest her allowance in a box of Fake Nails. The man does not know what to say, handing me his slate. The pencil is attached to the slate by a small beaded chain. His truck—the same colour as his uniform—ticks distantly in my driveway.

'Is it going to go off?' I ask.

He pretends not to get it. His name is stitched over his pocket, approximately where his left nipple would be, and below that, his heart. Alan. Alan leaves me the box. He shifts the gears in his truck and drives slowly away.

I open the box.

The earth inside smells dusky, rich. There is no message. I lift it, sifting the dirt between my fingers, sniffing. I even taste a little, hoping it will taste foreign and rare, like imported chocolate. It is only faintly sour. Perhaps a square foot of dirt. It will take me all night, I think. I dig through it softly, trying to feel with the insides of my fingers as well as the tips, the way I imagine a mole feels things with the damp pink skin of its nose, its body cloistered, remote. Certain nuns are not even allowed to see the priest, they receive the sacraments through tiny jewelled windows, in darkness. Only the hand, the whisper, the little piece of bread. 'Nod,' I whisper. The name goes no farther than the smoke from a match. The dirt feels good, it crusts against my fingers beneath the nails. I rub a small clod against my teeth, like a child toying with an aspirin, letting it dissolve into separate bitter grains. I lift two handfuls and finger the dry clumps, breaking the soft clods apart, watching them fall.

CREATIVE LITERATURE FROM CALDER

Best British

Trevor Hoyle's *The Man Who Travelled on Motorways* (paperback £3.95) combines erotic surrealist fantasy with the techniques of science fiction. The experience of long distance driving, the thoughts of the driver and the things that happen on the road, fuse into a new mythos of fascinating possibilities. Alexander Trocchi's *Young Adam* is a paperback reprint (£2.95) of his brilliant first novel, a psychological murder mystery set on a Scottish canal, that first gave a British voice to the beat movement. Howard Barker's play *Victory,* now playing at the Royal Court, is set in Restoration England and grimly portrays the causes of political reaction (£3.95). Steven Berkoff's amazing play *Decadence* (volume includes Greek), passionately shocking and running in London, is just published (£3.95).

Modern Classics

In Samuel Beckett's latest text *Worstward Ho* (cloth £5.50), the greatest word fashioner of our time works his magic once again, bringing forth reluctant life and then a whole world of poetic existance from deadland and void. His earlier *Ill Seen Ill Said* (£2.95), a ghostly parable of a half-seen 'She' in a lonely house is now in paperback. *Zazie in the Metro* Raymond Queneau's hilarious novel about a very adult girl's adventures in Paris is again available (cloth £7.95). Alain Robbe-Grillet's *Djinn,* mingling the ambiance of terrorism and the clandestine world of erotic masochism, arrives directly in paperback (£2.95), latest from the French master of the "new" novel, while Eugene Ionesco's only novel *The Hermit* (£2.95) is in the same series. *The Use of Speech* by Nathalie Sarraute (£3.95) like her *Tropisms* is about key words in our lives, their effect and their significance. "A tough, wholly pleasurable book" – TLS. New European plays are Obaldia's *Volume 3* with 3 amusingly different shorter plays (£4.95) and *Breakfast in Miami* by Reinhard Lettau (£3.95), discussions between dictators about the nature of power.

JOHN CALDER (PUBLISHERS) LTD
18 Brewer Street, London W1R 4AS

POETRY NATION REVIEW

the bi-monthly magazine of poetry, translation, essays, reviews and features

General Editor MICHAEL SCHMIDT
Editors DONALD DAVIE and C. H. SISSON

'I can't think of a current literary magazine that's more spirited, catholic, and distinguished.' – **Richard Wilbur**

'**PN Review** is a real poetry magazine: it is always interesting, it is hospitable to different kinds of poetry and to different points of view, and it prints work by most of the best practising British poets.' – **Thom Gunn**

'**Poetry Nation Review** both honours and belies its proud name. It *is*, today, the most incisive voice of a vision of poetry and the arts as central to national life – a vision with a vividly British quality. But it is *also* an international meeting-place, a denial of parochialism as are things deep-rooted.' – **George Steiner**

'. . . it is the liveliest magazine of poetry in the language.' – **Donald Hall**, *Parnassus*

_____

Annual subscription (six issues) £9.90 (£11.90 institutions) to PN Review, 208–212 Corn Exchange, Manchester M4 3BQ

Single copies @ £2.00 (trade terms apply)

I should like to subscribe to *PN Review* and enclose a cheque/ p.o. for £..............

Name: _____

Address: _____

_____

FREDERICK
BARTHELME
MONSTER DEAL

Frederick Barthelme was born in 1943. He is the editor of the *Mississippi Review* and director of the Center for Writers at the University of South Mississippi. His first collection of short stories, *Moon Deluxe,* will be published in August by Simon and Schuster in the United States.

T en o'clock Friday morning I'm on the porch in the landlord's burgundy robe, smiling at a tall woman who has clear blue eyes and slightly curly light brown hair—she looks like an athlete. She might be thirty-five. Her fingernails are glistening and perfect in the morning light. 'I'm a friend of Elliot's. Tina Graham—he didn't mention me?'

Elliot is the landlord. I tell her Elliot's out of the country until August, which is true.

'You must be Bergen, am I right?' She flaps open a legal-size suede-covered clipboard and reads, 'B-E-R-G-E-N', sliding a forefinger along under the letters as she spells my name.

'That's me,' I say.

'Sorry to bust in on you like this,' she says, closing the folder and stepping past me into the dark foyer. 'Elliot was supposed to tell you about me.' She smiles as if we've settled something. 'Maybe if we have some coffee I can explain—that's a pretty robe you've got.' She picks up the day-old newspaper.

'I just rent,' I say. 'The house, I mean.' Elliot's spending a year in Singapore on a cultural exchange. I leased the house—a forties bungalow done in lobster-pink stucco and trimmed with black wood and culvert tile—for the year. The neighbourhood is steep driveways and cars parked in yards, wood-frame houses, dirty white paint. Kids in striped shirts go by in groups of three or four, one of them always dragging a stick he uses to ward off dogs. Elliot told me he didn't care about the money.

Tina leads me into the kitchen. 'Listen, do you play squash? Maybe we could play later.' She drops the paper on the table and points at several different cabinets. 'Coffee?'

'Sure,' I say, showing her the coffee.

She takes off her jacket, rolls up her shirt sleeves, washes her hands with the Ivory. 'No beans?'

I shake my head. 'Sorry.'

'Doesn't matter,' she says. 'The grinder didn't work last time anyway.' She finds the filters in the cabinet above the coffee maker and glances at me while she puts eight or nine measures of coffee into the machine.

I rub my face. I start to say I'll make the coffee, but she playfully elbows me aside and takes the pot to the sink for water.

'Elliot should have explained this deal.' She gestures toward the coffee maker. 'I don't like to drink things I can't see through. How about yourself?'

The kitchen is small. I have to get out of the way as she moves from counter to cabinet, getting cups, starting the toast, collecting the silverware from the dishwasher. I sit at the breakfast table and play with the newspaper, spinning it absent-mindedly, thinking about the girl who delivers it. She's rough, young and sexy—I've only seen her up close once. Yesterday. After picking up the paper, I tripped on the front step trying to wave to her. She stopped to see if I was hurt. I invited her to dinner, but she told me she couldn't because she wasn't really a paper girl and she had to go to class. So I said what about Friday, and she said OK.

That awkward stuff has been happening to me. I bump into doorframes, hit my head on cabinet doors, trip on the legs of the bed—one morning last week I fell down trying to put the orange juice back into the refrigerator.

'They call you Jerry, right?' Tina says from the kitchen. 'OK if I call you Jerry?'

'Sure.' Through the French doors there's a courtyard filled with big-leafed plants and twisted vines that hang from a large tree. The court is paved with Mexican tile—blue, white, rose, yellow—and built around a bird fountain. The sun is bright but thin—a winter sun, even though it's May—and the courtyard is still shadowy and wet looking. There's a foot-high crucifix made of coloured glass embedded in the part of the garage wall I can see from the breakfast room.

Tina comes around the counter balancing two cups of coffee, one on top of the other, the way waitresses do at diners. In the other hand she's got a plate stacked with toast, and, on top of the toast, the butter dish out of the refrigerator. 'Sloppy,' she says, raising both hands slightly. 'But it gets the job done. You like toast?' She puts the cups and the toast on the table, then returns to the kitchen.

'Looks good,' I say, unstacking the coffees. 'What's this deal with Elliot?'

She comes back carrying my peach preserves and a big jar of Welch's grape jelly. 'Well, I'm here three, maybe four times a year, last couple of years, anyway. Always stay with Elliot. We were in school together—St Dominic's in Mobile. Same class with Snake Stabler, you know? The quarterback? Here, try this peach. It's really delicious.'

She spoons peach preserves on a slice of toast and pushes it across the linoleum tabletop on a napkin.

'I handle specialties, stuff you can't find ordinarily, stuff I pick up here and there. Right now it's housewares—Tupperware quality but no name, so it's cheap. Or I can go the other way, get you a thousand-dollar vacuum cleaner. Best damn vacuum cleaner you ever saw.' She shakes her head and stares over her raised coffee cup out into the courtyard. 'Absolutely vacuum you out of your socks—I demo'd it in Virginia and sucked up a cocker spaniel. Not the whole thing, just the tail. I got it out right away. I thought it'd be broken or something. It was cut up pretty good and didn't have much hair, but it was OK. I was scared to death. The woman took the demonstrator and gave me a cheque.'

She backs away from the table and takes off her shoes, using the toe of one foot on the heel of the other. 'Look,' she says. 'It's a terrible imposition, but do you mind if I stay? That's my deal with Elliot—I stay and buy the dinner.' She picks up her shoes, putting a finger in the heel of each. 'Tell you what, you check me out. Meanwhile, I'll catch some sleep.' She hooks the heels of her shoes on the table edge, folds a slice of toast in half, then dishes grape jelly into it. 'Sandwich,' she says, picking up the shoes again. 'Fair enough? Which bedroom do you want me in?'

I go to the office and call Larry, a friend of Elliot's. I tell him what's happened, and he tells me it's fine, he knows Tina. 'She's great,' he says.

'Good looking,' I say. 'But she's a monster. Six feet if she's an inch.'

'Six two,' he says. 'So wear boots and go to a monster movie.'

'Funny,' I say.

'I'm serious,' he says. 'She loves 'em. She'll make all the noises like the creatures, whatever noises they make—I saw an alligator movie with her once and she yawned menacingly all night.'

'I'm busy tonight, Larry.'

'So maybe I'll come over and take care of Tina. We can double up.'

'You come over and we'll discuss that.' When I hung up, Ruth, the woman who works for me, comes in and says we've got a report due Tuesday and she doesn't want to be typing all night Monday.

I yawn at her. It doesn't have any effect, so I tell her about Tina and she says, 'You want me to handle it or is this two-for-one week?'

Ruth is thirty-five, an ex-collegiate wrestler, conference champion in her division three years running. She and her boyfriend and her three kids from a previous marriage live in a trailer on the East side. I've been talking about the girl who throws the paper for several weeks, and yesterday, when I said I had a date with her, Ruth got annoyed.

'Tina's real pretty,' I say.

Ruth pushes her hair away from her face. 'So's Sylvester Stallone. So's a bazooka.' She reaches for the phone. 'Listen, I'll call her. You want me to call her?' She's wearing a blouse with a ruffle at the neck. The blouse is too sheer. She wiggles the telephone receiver in its cradle. 'Well?'

'Don't worry about it. Larry's coming over. Larry knows her. Anyway, she's probably sleeping. She's got to rest up.'

'Jesus, you're sick,' Ruth says. 'You know what I mean? You're so sick.'

It's three-thirty when I get home. Larry and Tina are sitting on the front step. The door to the house is open and the hall phone is on a chair in the doorway. I swing around the blue Cadillac Seville in the driveway and park in the garage. Tina's wearing red espadrilles, the pants to one of Elliot's suits, and a lilac Polo shirt. Her arms are tan and she's wearing a big round watch with a black band. Her hair is freshly washed, the curls tighter and darker than they were this morning.

'Hiya,' she says. 'Get lots of work done? I slept like a sweetheart.'

'Tina's got people she needs to see,' Larry says. 'She's got to be in Clifton tomorrow afternoon.'

'Yep,' Tina says. 'I've got a priest over there wants three hundred chickens for a church bazaar. My distributor in New Orleans gets me the birds and I bring 'em up myself, as soon as we nail the deal.'

'That's a bunch of chickens,' Larry says.

'I ought to get a refrigerator truck,' Tina says. 'But I might just load up the Caddy and save a few bucks. It depends on what I can do with Logan. He's the distributor. He gets these old fryers from A & P and shoots 'em to Hartz Mountain or somebody for fish food—maybe it's the wiener people, I don't know. If the chickens are bad I've got trouble. Even I can't sell bad chickens. We'll spray 'em, of course, but you can't be sure. Anyway, Logan takes a beating on the deal, so I come in and help him on the per pound, then turn around and save this priest in Clifton a bundle. Everybody's happy. The priest can't make this kind of a deal because Logan won't even talk to him.'

'Poor church,' Larry says. 'Lucky I quit going.'

'Cinnamon rolls and chocolate milk,' Tina says, stretching prettily. 'That's what I liked. Some Sundays I buy a pack of rolls and a quart of chocolate milk and get crazy—maybe if this deal works I'll do that.' She reaches to brush a gnat away from her forehead. 'And if the chickens don't go maybe I'll do it anyway. Sell him some of these flamingos Elliot's got all over the place.' She waves at the three plastic birds in the front garden and chuckles when Larry rolls his eyes back into his head. Tina has pretty teeth. 'Hey, Jerry,' she says. 'What're you doing about supper?'

'You mean supper? Or dinner?'

'Hell, I don't care what you call it, friend, I just want to know what you're doing about it.' Tina smiles and pokes Larry in the ribs. 'Tell you what,' she says, gesturing over her shoulder. 'I'm waiting on this call here, but soon as it comes in I'll take you out and buy you some food you'll never forget—how's that sound?'

'Sounds terrific,' Larry says.

'Nobody's talking to you, Larry,' she says. 'You had your chance years ago.'

The paper girl pulls up in her Jeepster. She waves, then gets out of the car and comes across the lawn toward us. She's fooling with a receipt book and a sheaf of carbons, carrying the rolled-up newspaper in her mouth.

'Hi,' I say.

She flips the paper end-over-end in my direction. 'You mind if I collect, Jerry? My envelope's in there'—she points to the paper—'but it'd be easier if I just go ahead and collect now.'

'Sure. That's OK. What is it?'

Frederick Barthelme

'Twenty-one,' she says. 'Three months, including this one.'

'Nice Jeep you got,' Tina says.

'Thanks,' Karen says. She twists to look at the car. 'My brother had one when I was a kid.'

'Who did the paint? Looks like pretty good paint from here.'

'I did it myself, and some of the body work—Bondo, mostly. A friend of mine did the running gear.' She has a husky voice that makes everything intimate, and the way she stands in my front yard, smiling just slightly, shifting her weight from one foot to the other, is very sexy.

'Sure is sharp', Tina says. She gets up and starts for the Jeepster. 'Mind if I take a look?'

Karen does an 'Aw, shucks' turn in the grass, then says, 'Help yourself.'

'I'm going to give you a cheque,' I say, making a writing motion in the air with my hand. 'That all right?'

She gives me her ballpoint. 'Who's the Amazon lady?' she says, gesturing toward Tina's back.

'You want to take her with you?' Larry says.

Karen grins and flicks her bangs away from her forehead. 'I don't think I'm going that direction.'

I finish filling out the stub in my chequebook and hand her the pen and the cheque together.

Larry says, 'Are you the same person who delivers my paper? On Crestmont, about six blocks over this way?' He tilts his head in the direction he's talking about.

'Nope. That's Carly. I know her, though. You got a problem?'

'I guess not,' he says.

Karen gives me a receipt and I walk with her back toward her car. 'We still going out later?'

'Sure,' she says. 'I shouldn't have said Amazon, should I?'

'It's OK. She's some friend of the landlord's.'

Tina's making a production out of the paint job, squatting to sight along the quarter panel, opening the doors to look at the jambs, checking the insides of the wheel wells. Karen looks patient and pretty following her around.

'All the carriers are women now,' Larry says when I get back to the porch. 'You notice that?'

100

'I don't know. There was a woman at the apartments where I used to live and now there's Karen—that's two.'

'And mine. I don't think I've missed a paper in a year. The phone installers and the cable people are women too. And the UPS delivery people. I've got this one UPS girl who always brings stuff to the house, you know? All decked out in that brown—she looks great. And my exterminator is a woman, a teenager. She hates it when I'm there alone and she has to spray. I make a lot of jokes, but that doesn't seem to help.' Larry rubs his eye socket with his palm. 'She doesn't crack a smile.'

Larry tells me he thinks it's fine to leave Tina in the house alone tonight, then he leaves. Inside, I leaf through a magazine and wait for her, wishing she'd let Karen get on with the paper route. I'm about ready to go see what's happening when they come in, each of them carrying a flamingo from the front yard. They're squawking like imaginary birds, and laughing about it.

'I'm helping Elliot to be a better person,' Tina says, standing the two birds in the corner of the living room. 'We're going to get a couple of highballs and then finish up Karen's route. I'm going to throw for her. You want to ride along?'

'I think I won't, thanks,' I say.

Karen asks about the bathroom and Tina points to the hall. 'Go back there, third door. I'll make the drinks.'

Karen smiles at me and heads off toward the bathroom. I follow Tina into the kitchen.

'Elliot still keep the booze up here?' she says, opening a cabinet above the dishwasher. She grabs a bottle of bourbon by its neck and puts it on the counter. 'Now, what we need is plastic glasses—I don't see any.' She looks at me. 'What the hell. Just go ahead and use glass glasses, right? You feeling OK, Jerry? Listen, you could do me a favour. You're going to be around, aren't you?'

'I think so.' I get a hard-boiled egg out of the refrigerator and toss it from hand to hand to crack the shell.

'You can catch my calls. Tell anybody who wants me I'll be around later.'

'I may go out. That's the only thing.'

'Don't do anything special, but if you're here I'd really appreciate it.' She stops what she's doing with the drinks and looks out the window. 'I've got a Code-A-Phone in the car, we could put that on.'

'I'll be here until you get back,' I say. 'Karen and I are going out later. Just for dinner.'

Tina nods. 'She told me that. Said you fell off the porch or something.'

I go back to the living room. Karen's standing in the foyer doorway with her arms crossed over her chest. She's wearing a bright green crew-neck sweatshirt and jeans. Her skin has a little sheen to it, as if she's just washed her face. 'Got a helper,' I say.

'What? Oh, right. She doesn't want to take No for an answer.' She frowns for a second, then swings her arms wide, palms open, and lifts her shoulders. 'Sorry,' she says. 'We'll be out of the way in a minute.'

'You're not in the way.' There's another silence, then I say, 'So, how's the paper business?'

She gives me a quick, odd stare and says, 'Fabulous.' Then she turns and scratches at the doorframe with a fingernail. 'Really, it's OK. It's not terrible. I used to be a night watchman at Clover Chemical—did I tell you this already? That was the pits. Now I party at night, sleep in the morning, deliver in the afternoon—it works out pretty good.'

'Doesn't sound bad,' I say.

'No. It's all right.' She waves a hand at the living-room. 'It's nice in here.'

'What time do you think you'll be finished?'

'I don't know,' she says. 'I'm running late. We can make the arrangements when I bring Tina back.'

I nod and watch Tina come out of the kitchen carrying two drinks, one in each hand. She's got the bourbon bottle under her arm and an ice-filled Baggie clamped in her teeth.

Karen grabs the Baggie and says, 'Open,' then takes one of the drinks.

'Thought we might need a refill somewhere along the way,' Tina says, putting the bottle down on the floor. 'Let me get some real shoes and I'm ready to bomb out of here. Jerry's going to handle my calls.'

Karen nods at me. 'That's nice of him,' she says.

When they're gone I go to the back bathroom for a sinus tablet, then walk around the house, making a complete circuit of all the rooms. In the kitchen I sit down and read an article in *Newsweek* about video cassette recorders. When I've finished that, I make a bacon sandwich. I vacuum the living-room, then go out to the back porch and get a six-foot piece of one-by-eight pine and bring that inside. I use it as a comb for the carpet, holding the pine lengthwise, dragging it across the room. I do that a couple of times to get the pile even, and it works pretty well. I put the board back outside, then go around the house and come in the front door so I won't have to walk on the living-room carpet.

Ruth calls to see how it's going, and I tell her Karen and Tina left to finish Karen's route.

'You're doing a great job, tiger. You've got 'em right where you want 'em.'

'Larry said it was OK to leave Tina here,' I say.

'Great,' she says. 'Good stuff.'

'I'll just wait and then go to dinner with Karen later—what's wrong with that?'

'That's a good plan,' she says. 'You stick with it. See you Monday.'

Saturday morning at nine-thirty I'm sitting in the kitchen in Elliot's robe when Tina starts banging on the front door. 'Hey. Open up in there. What in the goddamn hell is this, anyway?' Going to the door I can hear Tina giggling and Karen trying to hush her up.

'Sleep,' Tina says, when I open the door. She thrusts a forefinger ceremonially into her chest. Then she starts giggling. Both of them are slumped against the wall by the door, giggling.

'We've been in the woods all night,' Karen says, making a straight face and handing me a newspaper. 'I'm early today.'

'How's that for service?' Tina says. She stumbles over the doorsill and I reach out to steady her. 'Camping is'—she turns to Karen—'what is camping? I forgot.'

'Not your style,' Karen says. And they break up again.

'The woods have not been good to us,' Tina says, holding the lapel of my robe. 'Now, if you'll excuse us'—she sweeps an arm towards the bedrooms—'Smokey the Bear and myself will retire.'

They stagger down the hallway together, arm in arm, and, after a lot of manoeuvring and laughing, get into the bedroom and shut the door.

At noon I put a frozen strip steak in a frying pan and open the kitchen window to let out the smoke. I'm standing next to the sink buttering raisin toast when Tina leans on the counter between the kitchen and the breakfast area. She looks all brushed and groomed.

'Hey, Jerry,' she says. 'Listen, I'm really sorry we didn't get back last night. Karen's sorry too. We got drunk and threw papers all over the place. Then we went to a cowboy bar and teased the locals, but we got lost after. I get any calls? I've got to get moving here.'

'There weren't any calls,' I say.

'Damn that looks good,' she says, eyeing the toast. 'Nobody called? You sure?'

'I was here all night. No calls.'

I offer her a piece of toast. She gets the grape jelly out of the refrigerator and spreads a half-inch layer on one slice, then closes a second slice on top. 'Got a paper towel?' she asks, taking a bite out of the sandwich.

I pull two towels off the roll attached to the underside of the cabinet.

'She's still asleep,' Tina says. 'I didn't want to bother her. She feels really bad about your date and everything. She tried to call you, I think.' Tina puts the last quarter of the sandwich in her mouth. 'Anyway, I'm overdue in Clifton, you know? Got to power on.'

'Chickens,' I say.

'Yep. Sounds bad, doesn't it? A grown woman selling chickens.' She chews and looks at the frying pan. 'What've you got going here? What's this, steak?'

'Breakfast,' I say.

She nods at me, wiping her mouth with the towels. 'Gotcha. That rug sure looks good in the living-room—how'd you do that? You going to paint or something? I can get you a monster deal on thirty gallons of grey—good quality stuff. First-rate. How about spray equipment? Compressors—the whole business. Knock that room off quick.'

'I don't think so. Thanks anyway.'

She shrugs, balls the towels, and throws them toward the trash can. 'I guess grey's a bad idea. Who wants a grey house? Listen, I've got to go.' She reaches behind the counter and picks up her bag and the two flamingos they brought in yesterday. 'I'll just swing out the back here.'

I follow her through the garage to her car. Karen's Jeepster is parked behind the Cadillac. There's a lot of pumpkin-coloured mud on the tyres and splattered up on the side panels.

Tina holds the car door open and tosses the birds and her bag into the back seat. She crosses the yard and pulls the third flamingo out of the ground, and puts that in the car too. Then she pulls me into a quick, awkward hug. 'You're OK, Jerry. Thank Karen for me, will you? And look, let me give you a tip—take her someplace dancing, OK? Last night she would've killed to dance.'

After Tina leaves I stand around in the drive for a few minutes, then go back inside through the front door, through the living-room, into the kitchen. My steak is still cooking. I pour a fresh cup of coffee and start to read the newspaper, but then I don't want to read, I just want to look at the headlines.

Bobbie Ann Mason
Still Life With
Watermelon

Bobbie Ann Mason

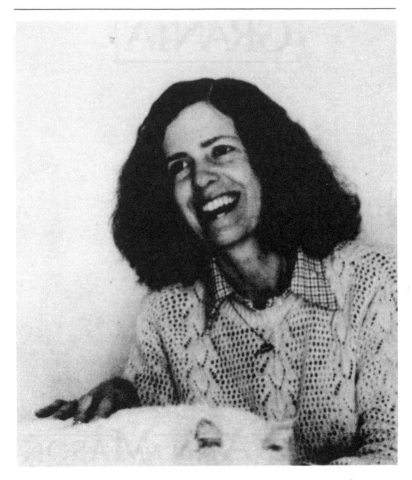

Bobbie Ann Mason was born in 1941, and was raised on a farm near Mayfield, Kentucky. She was educated at the University of Kentucky and the State University of New York at Binghamton, and holds a Phd from the University of Kentucky. Bobbie Ann Mason is the author of two books of non-fiction, *Nabokov's Garden* and the *Girl Sleuth*, and her short stories have appeared in the *Atlantic*, the *New Yorker*, the *New American Review*, and the *Virginia Quarterly Review*. 'Still Life with Watermelon' will be among the stories in her first collection, *Shiloh and Other Stories*, to be published in August by Chatto and Windus.

For several weeks now, Louise Milsap has been painting pictures of watermelons. The first one she tried looked like a dark-green basketball floating on an algae-covered pond. Too much green, she realized. She began varying the backgrounds, and sometimes now she throws in unusual decorative objects—a few candles, a soap dish, a pair of wire pliers. She tried including other fruits, but the size of the melons among apples and grapes made them appear odd and unnatural. When she saw a photograph of a cornucopia in a magazine, she imagined a huge watermelon stuck in its mouth.

Louise's housemate, Peggy Wilson, insists that a rich collector from Paducah named Herman Priddle will buy the pictures. Peggy and her husband, Jerry, had rented an apartment from him, but Jerry ran away with Priddle's mistress and now Peggy lives with Louise. Peggy told her, 'That man's whole house is full of them stupid watermelons.' When Peggy said he would pay a fortune for anything with a watermelon in it, Louise bought a set of paints.

Peggy said, 'He's got this one cute picture of these two little coloured twins eating a slice of watermelon. One at each end, like bookends. I bet he paid at least thirty dollars for it.'

Louise has lost her job at Kroger's supermarket, and she lies to the unemployment office about seeking a new job. Instead, she spends all day painting on small canvas boards in her canning room. Her husband, Tom, is in Texas with Jim Yates, a carpenter who worked for him. A month before, Tom suddenly left his business and went out West to work on Jim's uncle's ranch. Louise used to like Tom's impulsiveness. He would call up a radio programme and dedicate love songs to her, knowing it both embarrassed and pleased her to hear her name on the radio. Tom never cared about public opinion. Before he went to Texas, he bought a cowboy hat from Sam's Surplus. He left in his pickup, his 'General Contracting' sign still painted on the door, and he didn't say when he would return.

Louise said to him, 'If you're going to be a born-again cowboy, I guess you'll want to get yourself all bunged up on one of them bull machines.'

'That ain't necessarily what I'm aiming to do,' he said.

'Go ahead. *See* if I care.'

Louise, always a practical person, is determined to get along without Tom. She should look for a job, but she doesn't want to. She paints a dozen pictures in a row. She feels less and less practical. For two dollars and eighty-nine cents she buys a watermelon at Kroger's and paints a picture of it. It is a long, slender melon the colour of a tobacco worm, with zigzag stripes. She went to Kroger's from force of habit, and then felt embarrassed to be seen at her old checkout lane.

'Old man Priddle would give you a hundred dollars for that,' says Peggy, glancing at the painting when she comes home from work. Louise is just finishing the clouds in the background. Clouds had been a last-minute inspiration.

Peggy inserts a Dixieland tape into Louise's tape deck and opens a beer. Beer makes Peggy giggly, but Dixieland puts her in a sad mood because her husband once promised to take her to New Orleans to hear Al Hirt in person. Louise stands there with her paintbrush, waiting to see what will happen.

Peggy says, 'He's got this big velvet tapestry on his wall? It's one big, solid watermelon that must have weighed a ton.' Laughing, she stretches her arms to show the size. The beer can tilts, about to spill. Three slugs of beer and Peggy is already giggly.

Louise needs Peggy's rent money, but having her around is like having a grown child who refuses to leave home. Peggy reads Harlequin romances and watches TV simultaneously. She pays attention when the minister on *The 700 Club* gives advice on budgets. 'People just aren't *smart* about the way they use credit cards,' she informs Louise. This is shop talk from her job in customer services at the K Mart. Peggy keeps promising to call Herman Priddle, to make an appointment for Louise to take her paintings to Paducah, but Peggy has a thing about using the telephone. She doesn't want to tie up the line in case her husband tries to call. She frowns impatiently when Louise is on the telephone. One good thing about living with Peggy—she does all the cooking. Sometimes she pours beer into the spaghetti sauce—'to give it a little whang,' she says.

'You shouldn't listen to that tape,' Louise says to Peggy, later. The music is getting to Peggy by now. She sits in a cross-legged, meditative pose, the beer can balanced in her palm.

'I just don't know what he sees in a woman who's twenty years older than him,' says Peggy. 'With a face-lift.'

110

'How long can it last, anyhow?'

'Till she needs another face-lift, I reckon.'

'Well, that can't be long. I read they don't last,' says Louise.

'That woman's so big and strong, she could skin a mule one-handed,' says Peggy, lifting her beer.

Louise puts away her paints and then props the new picture against a chair. Looking at the melon, she can feel its weight and imagine just exactly how ripe it is.

While she paints, Louise has time to reflect on their situation: two women with little in common whose husbands are away. Both men left unconscionably. Sudden yearnings. One thought he could be a cowboy (Tom had never been on a horse); the other fell for an older woman. Louise cannot understand either compulsion. The fact that she cannot helps her not to care.

She tried to reason with Tom—about how boyish his notion was and how disastrous it would be to leave his business. Jim Yates had lived in Denver one summer, and in every conversation he found a way to mention Colorado and how pure the air was there. Tom believed everything Jim said. 'You can't just take off and expect to pick up your business where you left it when you get back,' Louise argued. 'There's plenty of guys waiting to horn in. It takes *years* to get where you've got.' That was Louise being reasonable. At first Tom wanted her to go with him, but she wouldn't dream of moving so far away from home. He accused her of being afraid to try new things, and over a period of weeks her resistance turned to anger. Eventually Louise, to her own astonishment, threw a Corning Ware Petite Pan at Tom and made his ear bleed. He and Jim took off two days later. The day they left, Tom was wearing a T-shirt that read: 'You better get in line now 'cause I get better-looking every day.' Who did he think he was?

Peggy does not like to be reminded of the watermelon collector, and Louise has to probe for information. Peggy and her husband, Jerry ('Flathead') Wilson, had gone to live in Paducah, forty miles away, and had had trouble finding work and a place to live, but an elderly man, Herman Priddle, offered them three identical bedrooms on the third floor of his house. 'It was a mansion,' Peggy told Louise. Then Priddle hired Jerry to convert two of the rooms into a bathroom and a kitchen. Peggy laid vinyl tiles and painted the walls. The old man, fascinated, watched them work. He let Peggy and Jerry watch his TV and he invited them to eat with him. His mistress, a beautician named Eddy Gail Moses, slept with him three nights a week, and while she was there she made enough hamburger-and-macaroni casseroles to last him the rest of the week. She lived with her father, who disapproved of her behaviour, despite her age.

Before Peggy knew what was happening, her husband had become infatuated with the woman, and he abruptly went to live with her and her father, leaving Peggy with Herman Priddle. Although Peggy grew suspicious of the way he looked at her, she and Priddle consoled each other for a while. Peggy started making the casseroles he was used to, and she stayed in Paducah for a few months, working at a pit barbecue stand. Gradually, Peggy told Louise, the old man began collecting pictures of watermelons. He looked for them in flea markets, at antique shops, and in catalogues; and he put ads in trade papers. When he hung one of the pictures in her bedroom, Peggy moved out. The watermelon was sliced lengthwise and it resembled a lecherous grin, she said, shuddering.

'Peggy's still in shock from the way Jerry treated her,' Louise tells Tom in a letter one evening. She writes him, care of a tourist home in Amarillo, Texas. She intends to write only perfunctory replies to his postcards so he will know she is alive, but she finds herself being more expressive than she ever was in the four years they were face to face. Hitting him seemed to release something in her, but she won't apologize. She won't beg him to come back. He doesn't know she has lost her job. And if he saw her paintings, he would laugh.

When Louise seals the letter, Peggy says to her, 'Did I tell you I heard Jim Yates is queer?'

'No.'

'Debbie Potts said that at work. She used to know Jim Yates back in high school.'

'Well, I don't believe it. He's too overbearing.'

'Debbie Potts has been to Europe,' says Peggy, looking up from the kitchen counter, where she is making supper. 'Did you know that?'

'Hooray for her.'

'That don't mean she's an expert on anything,' Peggy says

apologetically. 'I'm sure she doesn't know what she's talking about.'

'For crying out loud.'

'I'm sorry, Louise. I'm always putting my big foot in it. But you know, a lot of guys are coming right out now and saying they're gay? It's amazing.' She laughs wildly. 'They sure wouldn't be much use where it counts, would they? At least Flathead ran off with a woman—knock on wood.' Peggy taps a wooden spoon against the counter.

'How can you love a guy called Flathead?' says Louise, irritated. Apparently Jerry Wilson's nickname has nothing to do with his appearance. Louise has read that the Flathead Indians used to tie rocks to their heads to flatten them—why, she cannot imagine.

Peggy says, 'It's just what I know him by. I never thought about it.'

Peggy is making a casserole, probably one of Eddy Gail Moses's recipes. The Dixieland tape is playing full blast. Peggy says, 'The real reason he run off with that floozy was she babied him.'

'I wouldn't baby a man if my life depended on it,' says Louise.

She rummages around for a stamp. Too late, she wonders if she should have told Tom about the trouble with the air conditioner. He will think she is hinting for him to come home. Tom was always helpful around the house. He helped choose the kitchen curtains, saying that a print of butterflies she wanted was too busy and suggesting a solid colour. She always admired him for that. It was so perceptive of him to say the curtains were busy. But that didn't mean anything abnormal. In fact, after he started hanging out with Jim Yates, Tom grew less attentive to such details. He and Jim Yates had a Space Invaders competition going at Patsy's Dairy Whip, and sometimes they stayed there until midnight. Jim, who hit six thousand long before Tom, several times had his name on the machine as high scorer of the day. Once Tom brought Jim over for supper, and Louise disliked the way Jim took charge, comparing her tacos to the ones he'd had in Denver and insisting that she get up and grate more cheese. It seemed to Louise that he was still playing Space Invaders. Tom didn't notice. The night, weeks later, when Louise threw the Corning Ware at Tom, she knew she was trying to get his attention.

Late one evening, Peggy tells Louise that she saw her husband at the K Mart. He didn't realize that Peggy worked there. 'He turned all shades when he saw me,' Peggy says. 'But I wasn't surprised. I had a premonition.'

Peggy believes in dreams and coincidences. The night before she saw him, she had read a romance story about a complicated adoption proceeding. Louise doesn't get the connection and Peggy is too drunk to explain. She and Jerry have been out drinking, talking things over. Louise notices that Peggy already has a spot on her new pants suit, which she managed to buy even though she owes Louise for groceries.

'Would you take him back?' Louise wants to know.

'If he's good,' Peggy laughs loudly 'He's coming over again one day next week. He had to get back to Paducah tonight.'

'Is he still with that woman?'

'He *said* he wasn't.' Peggy closes her eyes and does a dance step. Then she says exuberantly, 'Everything Flathead touches turns to money. He cashed this check at the K Mart for fifty dollars. He sold a used hot-water heater and made a twenty-dollar profit on it. Imagine that.'

When Peggy sees Louise polishing her toenails, she says abruptly, 'Your second toe is longer than your big toe. That means you dominate your husband.'

'Where'd you get that idea?'

'Didn't you know that? Everybody knows that.'

Louise says, 'Are any of them stories you read ever about women who beat up their husbands?'

Peggy laughs. 'What an idea!'

Louise is thinking of Tom's humiliation the night she struck him with the pan. Suddenly in her memory is a vague impression that the lights flickered, the way it was said the electricity used to do on certain midnights when the electric chair was being used at the state penitentiary, not far away.

If Peggy goes back to her husband, Louise will have to earn some extra money. It dawns on her that the paintings are an absurd idea. Childish. For a few days she stays out of the canning room, afraid to look at the pictures. Half-heartedly she reads the want ads. They say: salesclerk, short-order cook, secretarial assistant, salesclerk.

On the day she is scheduled to sign up for her weekly unemployment cheque, Louise arranges the paintings in the living-room, intending to decide whether to continue with them. The pictures are startling. Some of the first ones appear to be optical illusions—watermelons disappearing like black holes into vacant skies. The later pictures are more credible—one watermelon is on a table before a paned window, with the light making little windows on the surface of the fruit; another, split in half, is balanced against a coffee percolator. Louise pretends she's a woman from Mars and the paintings are the first things she sees on earth. They aren't bad, but the backgrounds worry her. They don't match the melons. Why would a watermelon be placed against a blue sky? One watermelon on a flowered tablecloth resembles a blimp that has landed in a petunia bed. Even the sliced melons are unrealistic. The red is wrong—too pale, like a tongue. Tom sent her a picture postcard of the Painted Desert, but Louise suspects the colours in *that* picture are too brilliant. No desert could look like that.

On her way to the unemployment office, Louise picks up a set of acrylics on discount at Big-D. Acrylics are far more economical than oils. In the car, Louise, pleased by the prospect of the fresh tubes of paint, examines the colours: scarlet, cobalt blue, Prussian blue, aquamarine, emerald, yellow ochre, orange, white, black. She doesn't really need green. The discovery that yellow and blue make green still astonishes her; when she mixes them, she feels like a magician. As she drives towards the unemployment office, she wonders recklessly if the green of the trees along the street could be broken down by some scientific process into their true colours.

At the unemployment office the line is long and the building stuffy. The whole place seems wound up.

A fat woman standing behind Louise says, 'One time it got so hot here I passed out, and not a soul would help. They didn't want to lose their place in line. Look at 'em. Lined up like cows at a slaughterhouse. Ever notice how cows follow along, nose to tail?'

'Elephants have a cute way of doing that,' says Louise, in high spirits. 'They grab the next one's tail with their trunk.'

'Grab,' the woman says. 'That's all people want to do. Just grab.' She reaches inside her blouse and yanks her bra strap back on to her shoulder. She has yellow hair and blue eyes. She could turn green if she doesn't watch out, Louise thinks. The line moves slowly. No one faints.

When Louise arrives at home, Peggy's husband is there, and he and Peggy are piling her possessions into his van. Peggy has happy feet, like Steve Martin on TV. She is moving to Paducah with Jerry. Calmly Louise pours a glass of iced tea and watches the ice cubes crack.

'I already up and quit work,' Peggy calls to Louise from her bedroom.

'I got us a place in a big apartment complex,' says Jerry, with an air of satisfaction.

'It's got a swimming pool,' says Peggy, appearing with an armload of clothes on hangers.

'I saved twenty dollars a month by getting one without a dishwasher,' says Jerry. 'I'm going to put one in myself.'

Peggy's husband is tall and muscular, with a sparse moustache that a teenager might grow. He looks amazingly like one of the Sha Na Na, the one in the sleeveless black T-shirt. Louise notices that he can't keep his hands off his wife. He holds on to her hips, her elbows, as she tries to pack.

'Tell what else you promised,' Peggy says.

'You mean about going to New Orleans?' Jerry says.

'Yeah.'

Louise says, 'Well, don't you go off without setting me up with that watermelon man. I was counting on you.'

'I'll give him a call tomorrow,' says Peggy.

'Could you do it right now, before I lose track of y'all?'

Louise's sharp tone works. Peggy pulls away from Jerry and goes to the telephone.

While she is trying to find the number, she says, 'I hate to mention it, Louise, but I gave you a whole month's rent and it's only been a week. Do you think...?'

While Peggy is on the telephone, Louise writes a cheque for seventy-five dollars. She writes boldly and decisively, with enlarged numbers. Her new bank balance is twelve dollars and eleven cents. If Flathead Wilson were *her* husband, she would show him the road.

'He said come over Tuesday afternoon,' says Peggy, taking the cheque. 'I just know he's going to love your pictures. He sounded thrilled.'

After Peggy and Jerry leave, Louise notices the mail, which Peggy has left on a lamp table—a circular, the water-and-light bill, and a letter from Tom, postmarked ten days before. Louise laughs with relief when she reads that Jim Yates went to Mexico City with a woman he met in Amarillo. Jim plans to work in adobe construction. 'Can you imagine going to Mexico to work?' Tom writes. 'Usually it's the other way around.'

Happily Louise plays a Glen Campbell tape and washes the dishes Peggy has left. Peggy gave Louise all her cooking utensils—the cracked enamel pans and scratched Teflon. 'Flathead's going to buy me all new,' she said. Louise wishes Peggy hadn't left before hearing the news from Tom. But she's glad to be alone at last. While Glen Campbell sings longingly of Galveston, Louise for the first time imagines Tom doing chores on a ranch. Something like housework, no doubt, except out of doors.

She paints through the weekend, staying up late, eating TV dinners at random. It thrills her to step back from a picture and watch the sea of green turn into a watermelon. She loves the way the acrylics dry so easily; they are convenient, like Perma-Press clothing. After finishing several pictures, she discovers a trick about backgrounds: if she makes them hazier, the watermelons stand out in contrast, look less like balloons floating in space. With the new paints, she hits upon the right mix for the red interiors, and now the watermelon slices look good enough to eat.

On the day of Louise's appointment with Herman Priddle, Tom suddenly walks in the door. Louise freezes. She's standing in the centre of the living-room, as though she had been standing there all during his absence, waiting for his return. She can tell how time has passed by the way his jeans have faded. His hair has grown shaggy and he has a deep tan.

'Surprise!' he says with a grin. 'I'm home.'

Louise manages to say, 'What are you doing back here?'

'And why ain't you at work?' Tom says.

'Laid off.'

'What's going on here?' he asks, seeing the pictures.

Suddenly Louise is ashamed of them. She feels confused. 'You picked a *fine* time to show up,' she says. She tries to explain about the paintings. Her explanation makes no sense.

For a long time Tom studies her pictures, squatting to see the ones on the floor. His jeans strain at the seams. He reaches out to touch one picture, as though for a moment he thought the watermelon might be real. Louise begins taking the paintings to her car, snatching them from under his gaze. He follows her, carrying some of the paintings.

Tom says, 'I couldn't wait to get back home.'

'You didn't have to go off like that.'

'I've been thinking things over.'

'So have I.' She slams the rear hatch door of her car. 'Where's the pickup?'

'Totalled it north of Amarillo.'

'What? I thought all the roads were flat and straight out there.'

He shrugs. 'I reckon they are.'

'Where'd you get that junk heap?' she asks. The car he has brought home is a rusted-out hulk.

'In Amarillo. It was the best I could do—cost me two hundred dollars. But it drives good.'

He opens the door of his car and takes out a McDonald's sack from the front seat. 'I brought you a Big Mac,' he says.

Later, when he insists on driving her in her car to Paducah, Louise doesn't try to stop him. She sits still and glum beside him, like a child being escorted to a school recital. On the way, she says, 'That postcard you sent of the Painted Desert was mailed in Amarillo. I thought the Painted Desert was in Arizona.'

'I didn't mail it till I got back to Amarillo.'

'I thought maybe you hadn't even been there.'

'Yes, I was.'

'I thought maybe you sent it just to impress me.'

'Why would I do that?'

'So I wouldn't think the West was just dull, open spaces.'

'Well, it wasn't. And I did go to the Painted Desert.'

'What else did you do out there?'

'Different things.'

'Look—John Wayne's dead. Don't think you have to be the strong, silent type just 'cause you went out West.'

Louise wants to know about the colours of the Painted Desert, but she can't bring herself to ask Tom about them. Tom is driving the car with his forearms loosely draped over the wheel and his elbows sticking out. He drives so casually. Louise imagines him driving all the way to Texas like this, as if he had nothing better to do.

'I did a lot of driving around,' Tom says finally, after smoking a cigarette all the way down. 'Just to see what there was to see.'

'Sounds fascinating.' Louise doesn't know why she wants to give him such a hard time. She realizes that she is shaking at the thought of him wrecking his pickup, alone in some empty landscape. The ear she hit is facing her—no sign of damage. His hair is growing over it and she can't really see where she hit him. His sideburn, shaped like the outline of Italy, juts out on to his jaw. Tom is home and she doesn't know what that means.

Herman Priddle's house has a turret, a large bay window, and a wrap-around porch, which a woman is sweeping.

'Would you say that's a mansion?' Louise asks Tom.

'Not really.'

'Peggy said it was.'

Louise makes Tom wait in the car while she walks up to the house. She thinks the woman on the porch must be Eddy Gail Moses, but she turns out to be Priddle's niece. She has on a turquoise pants suit and wears her hair up in sculptured curls.

When Louise inquires, the woman says, 'Uncle Herman's in the hospital. He had a stroke a-Sunday and he's real bad, but they pulled him off the critical list today.'

'I brought some pictures for him to see,' says Louise nervously.

'Watermelons, I bet,' says the woman, eyeing Louise.

'He was supposed to buy my pictures.'

'Well, the thing of it *is*—what are we to do with the ones he's got? He'll have to be moved. He can't stay by hisself in this big old place.' The woman opens the door. 'Look at these things.'

Louise follows her into the dim room cluttered with antiques. The sight of all the watermelons in the room is stunning. The walls are filled, and other paintings are on the floor, leaning against the wall.

Louise stands and stares while the woman chatters on. There are so many approaches Louise has not thought of—close-ups, groupings, unusual perspectives, floral accompaniments. All her own pictures are so prim and tidy. The collection includes oils, drawings, watercolours, even a needlepoint chair cover and a china souvenir plate. The tapestry Peggy described is a zeppelin floating above the piano. Louise has the feeling that she is witnessing something secret and forbidden, something of historical importance. She is barely aware that Tom has entered and is talking to Herman Priddle's niece. Louise feels foolish. In sixth grade the teacher had once pointed out to the class how well Louise could draw, and now—as if acting at last on the basis of that praise—Louise has spent two months concocting an elaborate surprise for an eccentric stranger. What could she have been thinking of?

'Looks like somebody's crazy about watermelons,' Tom is saying politely.

'They won't bring a thing at auction,' the woman replies with a laugh. In a hushed voice then, she says, 'He sure had me fooled. He was here by hisself so much I didn't know whatall was going on. Now it seems like he was always collecting these things. It suited him. Do you ever have people do you that way? You think things are one way and then they get turned around and you lose track of how they used to be?'

'I know what you mean,' says Tom, nodding with enthusiasm.

On the way home Louise is in tears. Tom, perplexed, tries to console her, telling her that her pictures are as good as any of the old man's watermelons.

'Don't worry about him,' he says, holding her hand. 'It won't matter that you lost your job. I thought I'd go see about getting a small-business loan to get started again. We'll get straightened out somehow.'

Louise, crying, cannot reply. She doesn't feel like arguing.

'I didn't even know you could draw,' Tom says.

'I'm not going to paint any more watermelons,' she says.

'You won't have to.'

Louise blows her nose and dries her eyes. Tom's knuckles are tapping a tune against the steering wheel and he seems to be driving automatically. His mind could be somewhere else, like someone in an out-of-body experience. But Louise is the one who has been off on a crazy adventure. She knows now that she painted the watermelons out of spite, as if to prove to Tom that she could do something as wild as he was doing. She lost her head during the past weekend when she was alone, feeling the glow of independence. Gazing at the white highway line, she tries to imagine the next steps: eating supper with Tom, going to bed together, returning to old routines. Something about the conflicting impulses of men and women has got twisted around, she feels. She had preached the idea of staying home, but it occurs to her now that perhaps the meaning of home grows out of the fear of open spaces. In some people that fear is so intense that it is a disease, Louise has read.

A t the house, Louise reaches the door first, and she turns to see Tom coming up the walk. His face is in shadow against the afternoon sun. His features aren't painted in; she wouldn't recognize him. Beyond him is a vacant lot—a field of weeds and low bushes shaped like cup-cakes. Now, for the first time, Louise sees the subtle colours—amber, yellow, and deep shades of purple—leaping out of that landscape. The empty field is broad and hazy and dancing with light, but it fades away for a moment when Tom reaches the doorway and his face thrusts out from the shadow. He looks scared. But then he grins slowly. The coastline of Italy wobbles a little, retreats.

TOBIAS WOLFF
THE BARRACKS
THIEF

Tobias Wolff

Tobias Wolff was born in Alabama in 1945 and grew up in Washington State. He was educated at Oxford and Stanford universities, and is currently teaching at Syracuse University in New York. He is the author of one collection of short stories, *Hunters in the Snow*, that was published in Picador this year, and is the editor of an anthology of fiction from the United States entitled *Matters of Life and Death*. His fiction has appeared in the *Atlantic*, *Antaeus*, and *Vanity Fair*. He has won a number of awards, including the Mary Roberts Rinehart Foundation Award for Fiction, the National Endowment of Arts Award for fiction, and the O'Henry Prize.

W hen his boys were young, Guy Bishop formed the habit of stopping in their room each night on his way to bed. He would look down at them where they slept, and then he would sit in the rocking chair and listen to them breathe. He was a man who had always gone from one thing to another, place to place, job to job, and, even since his marriage, woman to woman. But when he sat in the dark between his two sleeping sons he felt no wish to move.

Sometimes, because it seemed unnatural, this peace he felt gave him fears. The worst fear he had was that by loving his children so much he was somehow endangering them, putting them in harm's way. At times he knew for a certainty that some evil was about to overtake them. As the boys grew older he had this fear less often, but it still came upon him from time to time. Then he tried to imagine what form the evil might take, from which direction it might come. When he had these thoughts Guy Bishop would close his eyes, give his head a little shake, and turn his mind to some more pleasant subject.

He was seeing a woman off and on. They had good times together and that was all either of them wanted, at least in the beginning. Then they began to feel miserable when they were away from each other. They agreed to break it off, but couldn't. There were nights when Guy Bishop woke up weeping. At one point he considered killing himself, but the woman made him promise not to. When he couldn't hold out any longer he left his family and went to live with her.

This was in October. Keith, the younger of the boys, had just begun his freshman year in high school. Philip was a junior. Guy Bishop thought that they were old enough to accept this change and even to grow stronger from it, more realistic and adaptable. Most of the worry he felt was for his wife. He knew that the break-up of their marriage was going to cause her terrible suffering, and he did what he could to arrange things so that, except for his leaving, her life would not be disrupted. He signed the house over to her and each month he sent her most of his salary, holding back only what he needed to live on.

Philip did learn to get along without his father, mainly by despising him. His mother held up, too, better than Guy Bishop had expected. She caved in every couple of weeks or so, but most of the time she was cheerful in a determined way. Only Keith lost heart. He could not stop grieving. He cried easily, sometimes for no apparent reason. The two boys had been close; now, even in the act of comforting Keith, Philip looked at him from a distance. There was only a year and a half between them, but it began to seem like five or six. One night, coming in from a party, he shook Keith awake with the idea of having a good talk, but after Keith woke up Philip went on shaking him and didn't say a word. One of the cats had been sleeping with Keith. She arched her back, stared wide-eyed at Philip, and jumped to the floor.

'You've got to do your part,' Philip said.

Keith just looked at him.

'Damn you,' Philip said. He pushed Keith back against the pillow. 'Cry,' he said. 'Go ahead, cry.' He really did hope that Keith would cry, because he wanted to hold him. But Keith shook his head. He turned his face to the wall. After that Keith kept his feelings to himself.

In February Guy Bishop lost his job at Boeing. He told everyone that the company was laying people off, but the opposite was true. This was 1965. President Johnson had turned the bombers loose on North Vietnam and Boeing had orders for more planes than they could build. They were bringing people in from all over, men from Lockheed and Convair, boys fresh out of college. It seemed that anyone could work at Boeing but Guy Bishop. Philip's mother called the wives of men who might know what the trouble was, but either they hadn't heard or they weren't saying.

Guy Bishop found another job but he didn't stay with it, and just before school let out Philip's mother put the house up for sale. She gave away all but one of her five cats and took a job as cashier in a movie theatre downtown. It was the same work she'd been doing when Guy Bishop met her in 1945. The house sold within a month. A retired Coast Guard captain bought it. He drove by the house nearly every day with his wife and sometimes they parked in front with the engine running.

Philip's mother took an apartment in West Seattle. Philip worked as a camp counsellor that summer, and while he was away she and Keith moved again, to Ballard. In the fall both boys enrolled at Ballard High. It was a big school, much bigger than the one where they'd gone before, and it was hard to meet people. Philip kept in touch with his old friends, but now that they weren't in school together they found little to talk about. When he went to parties with them he usually ended up sitting by himself in the living-room, watching television or talking to some kid's parents while everyone else slow-danced in the rec. room downstairs.

After one of these parties, Philip and the boy who'd brought him sat in the car and passed a paper cup full of vodka back and forth and talked about things they used to do. At some point in their conversation Philip realized that they weren't friends any more. He felt restless and got out of the car. He stood there, looking at the darkened house across the street. He wanted to do something. He wished he were drunk.

'I've got to go,' the other boy said. 'My dad wants me in early tonight.'

'Just a minute,' Philip said. He picked up a rock, hefted it, then threw it at the house. A window broke. 'One down,' Philip said. He picked up another rock.

'Jesus,' the other boy said. 'What are you doing?'

'Breaking windows,' Philip said. At that moment a light came on upstairs. He threw the rock but it missed and banged against the side of the house.

'I'm getting out of here,' the other boy said. He started the car and Philip got back inside. He began to laugh as they drove away, though he knew there was nothing funny about what he'd done. The other boy stared straight ahead and said nothing. Philip could see that he was disgusted.

'Wait a minute,' Philip said, grabbing the sleeve of the Nehru jacket the other boy had on. 'I don't believe it. Where did you get the Nehru jacket?' When the other boy didn't answer Philip said, 'Don't tell me—it's your dad's. That's why your dad wants you home early. He likes to know where his Nehru jacket is.'

When they got to Philip's apartment building they sat for a moment without talking. Finally Philip said, 'I'm sorry,' and put out his hand. But the other boy looked away.

Philip got out of the car. 'I'll give you a call,' he said, and when he got no response he added: 'I was just kidding about the Nehru jacket. It must have looked really great about twenty years ago.'

P hilip had always wanted to go to Reed College, but by the time he finished high school that year his grades were so bad he was lucky to graduate at all. Reed sent him a form rejection letter and so did the University of Washington, his second choice. He went to work as a bus boy in a motel restaurant and tried to stay out of the apartment. Keith was always there, playing records or just lying around, his sadness plain to see though he had begun to affect a breezy manner of speech. Philip suspected that he was stoned a lot of the time, but he didn't know what to do about it, or if he should do anything at all. Though he felt sorry for Keith, Philip was beginning to dislike him. He wanted to avoid anything that might cause trouble between them and add to the dislike he felt. Besides, he had a smoke now and then himself. It made him feel interesting—witty, sensitive, perceptive.

Sometimes the owner of the theatre where she worked gave Philip's mother a ride home. One night, coming home late himself, he saw them kissing. Philip turned around and went back up the street. The next day he refused to speak to her, and refused to tell her why, though he knew he was being theatrical and unfair. Finally it drove her to tears. As he sat reading Philip heard her cry out in the kitchen. He jumped up, thinking she must have burned herself. He found her leaning on the sink, her face in her hands. What had happened to them? Where were they? Where was her home, her cats, her garden? Where was the regard of her neighbours, the love of her family? Everything was gone.

Philip did his best to calm her. It wasn't easy, but after a time she agreed to go for a walk with him and she managed to collect herself. Philip knew he had been in the wrong. He told his mother that he was sorry, and that his moodiness had nothing to do with her—he was just a little on edge. She squeezed his arm. This won't go on for ever, Philip thought. In silence, they continued to walk the circular path around the small park. It was August and still warm, but the benches were empty. Now and then a pigeon landed with a rush of wings, looked around, and flew away again.

T heir parish priest from the old neighbourhood had friends among the local Jesuits. He succeeded in getting Philip a probationary acceptance to Seattle University. It was a good school, but Philip wanted to get away from home. In September he moved to Bremerton and enrolled at the junior college there. During the day he tried to keep awake in his classes and at night he worked at the Navy Yard, doing inventory in warehouses and dodging forklifts driven by incompetents.

Philip didn't get to know many people in Bremerton, but sometimes when he got off work at midnight he went drinking with a few of the marine guards. Bremerton was a soft berth for them after a year in Vietnam. They'd been in the fighting, and some of them had been wounded. They were all a little crazy. Philip didn't understand their jokes, and if he laughed anyway they gave him mean looks. They talked about 'asshole civilians' as if he weren't there.

The marines tolerated Philip because he had a car, an old Pontiac he'd bought for fifty dollars at a police auction. He ferried them to different bars and sometimes to parties, then back to the Yard through misty wet streets, trying to keep his eyes open, while they laughed and yelled out the window and threw beer on each other. If one of them got into a fight all the others piled in immediately, no questions asked. Philip was often amazed at their brutishness, but there were times, after he'd let them off and watched them go through the gate together, when he envied them.

At Christmas Philip's mother asked him to talk to Keith. Keith was doing badly in school, and just before vacation one of his teachers had caught him smoking a joint in a broom closet. He'd been alone, which seemed grotesque to Philip. When he thought of Keith standing in the dark surrounded by brooms and cleanser and rolls of toilet paper, puffing away all by himself, he felt disgusted. Only by going down to the school and pleading with the principal, 'grovelling', as she put it, had Philip's mother been able to dissuade him from reporting Keith to the police. As it was, he'd been suspended for two weeks.

'I'll talk to him,' Philip said, 'but it won't do any good.'

'It might,' she said. 'He looks up to you. Remember the way he used to follow you around?'

They were sitting in the living-room. Philip's mother was smoking and had her feet on the coffee table. Her toenails were painted red. She caught Philip staring at them and looked down at her drink.

'My life isn't going anywhere,' Philip said. He got up and walked over to the window. 'I'm going to enlist,' he said. This was an idea he'd had for some time now, but hearing himself put it in words surprised him and gave him a faint sensation of fear.

His mother sat forward. 'Enlist? Why would you want to enlist?'

'In case you haven't heard,' Philip said, 'there's a war on.' That sounded false to him and he could see it sounded false to his mother as well. 'It's just something I want to do,' he said. He shrugged.

His mother put her glass down. 'When?'

'Pretty soon.'

'Give me a year,' she said. She stood and came over to Philip. 'Give me six months, anyway. Try to understand. This thing with Keith has got me coming and going.'

'Keith,' Philip said. He shook his head. Finally he agreed to wait the six months.

They spent Christmas Day in the apartment. Philip gave Keith a puzzle that he worked on all afternoon and never came close to solving, though it looked simple enough to Philip. They had dinner in a restaurant and after they got back Keith went at the puzzle again, still with no success. Philip wanted to help, but whenever he offered a suggestion Keith went on as if he hadn't heard. Philip watched him, impatiently at first, then thoughtfully; he wondered what it was in Keith that found satisfaction in losing. If he went on the way he was, losing would become a habit, and he would never be able to pull his weight.

They had their talk but it went badly, as Philip knew it would. Though he tried to be gentle, he ended up calling Keith a coward. Keith laughed and made sarcastic remarks about Philip going into the service. He had suddenly decided that he was against the war. Philip pointed out that it had taken Keith seven tries to pass his driving test and said that anyone who had that much trouble driving a car, or solving a simple puzzle, had no right to an opinion on any subject.

'That's it,' Philip told his mother afterwards. 'Never again.'

A few nights later, Philip came back from a movie and found his mother in tears and Keith trying to soothe her, though it was obvious that he was close to the breaking point himself. Oh, hell, Philip thought, but it wasn't what he had assumed. They weren't just feeling sorry for themselves. Philip's father had come by and when they refused to open the door to him he had tried to break in. He'd made a scene, yelling at them and ramming the door with his shoulder.

Philip left Keith with his mother and drove out to his father's place in Bellevue, an efficiency apartment near the lake. Guy Bishop had moved to Bellevue a few months earlier when the woman he'd been living with went to Sarasota to visit her family, and decided to stay there.

He still had his windbreaker on when he opened the door. 'Philip,' he said. 'Come in.'

Philip shook his head.

'Please, son,' his father said, 'come in.'

They sat at a counter that divided the kitchen from the rest of the room. There were several pairs of gleaming shoes lined up along the wall, and the air smelled of shoe polish. On the coffee table there was a family portrait taken at Mount Rushmore in 1963. Keith and Philip were in the middle, grinning because the photographer, a Canadian, had just said 'aboot' for 'about'. The four presidents, eyes blank, seemed to be looking down at them. Next to the picture a stack of magazines had been arranged in a fan, so that a strip of each cover was visible.

Philip told his father to stay away from the apartment. That was where the family lived, Philip said, and Guy Bishop wasn't part of the family.

Suddenly his father reached out and put his hand on Philip's cheek. Philip stared down at the counter. A moment later his father took his hand away. Of course, he said. He would call first thing in the morning and apologize.

'Forget the apology,' Philip said. 'Just leave her alone, period.'

'It's not that simple,' his father said. 'She called me first.'

'What do you mean, she called you first?'

'She asked me to come over,' he said. 'When I got there she wouldn't let me in. Which is no excuse for acting the way I did.' He folded his hands and looked down at them.

'I don't believe you,' Philip said.

His father shrugged. A moment later he looked over at Philip and smiled. 'I've got something for you. It was meant to be a graduation present, but I didn't have a chance to give it to you then.' He went over to the closet and pulled out a suitcase. 'Come on,' he said.

Philip followed him out of the room and down the steps into the parking lot. It had rained. The pavement shone under the lights, and the cars gleamed. Philip's father bent down and unzipped the suitcase. It was full of what looked like silver pipes. He lifted them out all at once, and Philip saw that they were connected. His father arranged them, tightening wing-nuts here and there until finally a frame took shape with prongs at each end. He got two wheels from the suitcase and fastened them between the prongs. Then he bolted a leather seat to the frame. It was a bicycle, a folding bicycle. He put down the kick-stand and stepped back.

'*Voilà!*' he said.

They looked at it.

'It works,' he said. He put up the kick-stand and straddled it, searching with his feet for the pedals. He pushed himself around the parking lot, bumping into cars, wobbling badly. With its little wheels and elevated seat the bicycle looked like the kind bears ride in circuses. The chrome frame glittered. The spokes caught the light as they went around and around.

'You'll never be without transportation,' Philip's father said. 'You can keep it in the trunk of your car. Then, if something breaks down or you run out of gas, you won't be forced to hitchhike.' He almost fell taking a turn but managed to right himself. 'Or say you go to Europe. What better way,' he said, and then the bicycle caught the fender of a car and he pitched over the handlebars. He fell heavily. The bicycle came down with him and he lay there, all tangled up in it.

'My God,' he said. 'Give me a hand, son.' When Philip didn't come to him he said, 'I can't move. Give me a hand.'

Philip turned and walked towards his car.

The next morning Philip got up early and took a bus downtown. The Marine recruiting office was closed. He wandered around, and when it still hadn't opened two hours later he walked up the street and enlisted in the army. That night, when he knew his mother would be at work, he called home from Fort Lewis. At first Keith thought he was joking. Then the idea took hold. 'You're really in the army,' he said. 'What a trip. Jesus. Well, good luck. I mean that.'

Philip could tell he was serious. It touched him, and he did something he came to regret. He gave Keith his car.

Five months later, Keith disappeared. I was in jump school at Fort Benning when it happened, at the tail end of a training course that proved harder than anything I had ever done. When I got the message to call home we had just come back from our third of five parachute jumps. We'd been dropped after heavy rain and landed in mud to our ankles, struggling against a wind that pulled us down and dragged us through a mess of other men, scrub pine, tangled silk and rope. I was still spitting out mud when we got back to camp.

My mother told me that Keith had been gone for three days. He had left no message, not even a goodbye. The police had a description of the car and they'd talked to his friends, but so far they seemed no closer to finding him. We agreed that he had probably gone to San Francisco.

'No doubt about it,' I said. 'That's where all the losers are going now.'

'Don't take that tone,' she said. 'It breaks my heart to hear you talk like that. Is that what you're learning in the army?'

It had started to rain again. I was using an unsheltered pay phone near the orderly room and the rain began to melt the caked mud on my uniform. Brown streams of it ran off my boots. 'What do you want me to do?' I asked.

'I want you to go to San Francisco and look for Keith.'

I couldn't help laughing. 'Now how am I supposed to do that?' I said. 'This is Georgia, remember?'

'I've talked to a man at the Red Cross,' she said. 'You could get emergency leave. They'll even lend you money.'

'That's ridiculous,' I said, though I realized what she was saying was true. I could go on leave. But I didn't want to. It would mean missing the last two jumps, dropping out of the course. If I came back I would have to start all over again. I doubted I had the courage to do that; jump school was no day at the beach and I'd only made it this far out of ignorance of what lay ahead. I wanted those wings. I wanted them more than anything.

And if I did go, where would I look? Who would help me in San Francisco, me with my head shaved to the bone in a city full of freaks?

'You have to,' she said. 'He's your brother.'

'I'm sorry,' I told her. 'It's just not possible.'

133

'But he's so young. What is happening to us? Will somebody please tell me what is happening to us?'

I said that the police would find Keith, that he'd be glad to get home, that a taste of the real world would give him a new angle on things. I didn't believe what I was saying, but it calmed her down. Finally she let me go.

On our last jump, a night jump in full field equipment, a man was killed. His main chute didn't open. I heard him yell going down but it only lasted a moment and I paid no attention. Some clown was always yelling. It ended and there was no sound save the rhythmic creaking of my shoulder straps. I felt the air move past my face. The full moon lit up the silk above me, above the hundred other men falling in silence overhead and below and all around me. It seemed that every one of us fell under his own moon. Then a tree stabbed up to my right and I braced and hit the ground rolling.

The dead man was carried to the side of the road and left there for the ambulance. They didn't bother to cover him up. They wanted us to take a good look, and remember him, because he had screwed up. He had forgotten to pull his reserve parachute. As our truck went past him a sergeant said, 'There's just two kinds of men in this business—the quick and the dead.'

The fellow across from me laughed. So did several others. I didn't laugh, but I felt the impulse. The man lying by the road had been alive an hour ago, and now he was dead. Why did that make me want to smile? It seemed wrong. Someone was passing around a number. I took a hit and gave it to the man next to me. 'All right!' he said. 'Airborne!'

Two black guys started a jump song. I leaned back and looked up at the stars and after a while I joined in the song the others were singing.

After jump school I was sent to the 82nd Airborne Division at Fort Bragg. Most of the men in my company had served together in Vietnam. Like the marines I'd known in Bremerton, they had no use for outsiders. I was an outsider to them. So were the other new men, Lewis and Hubbard. The three of us didn't exist for the rest of the company. For days at a time nobody spoke to me except to give me orders. Because we were the newest and lowest in rank we got picked to pull guard duty on the Fourth of July while everyone else scattered to Myrtle Beach and the air-conditioned bars in Fayetteville.

That's where I'd wanted to spend the Fourth, in a bar. There was one place in particular I liked. Smitty's. They had a go-go dancer at Smitty's who chewed gum while she danced. Prostitutes, Fayettecong, we called them, sat in the booths with pitchers of beer between them. Car salesmen from the lots down the street figured out ways to unload monster Bonnevilles on buck privates who made seventy-eight dollars a month before taxes. The bartender knew my name.

The last way I wanted to spend my Fourth was pulling guard with Lewis and Hubbard. We had arrived on the same day and avoided each other ever since. I could see that they were as lonely as I was, but we kept our distance; if we banded together we would always be new.

So when I saw the duty roster and found myself lumped together with them it made me bitter. Lewis and Hubbard were bitter, too. I could feel it in the way they looked at me when I joined them outside the orderly room. They didn't greet me, and while we waited for the duty officer they stared off in different directions. It was late afternoon but still steaming. The straight lines of the camp—files of barracks, flagpoles, even the rocks arranged in rows—wavered in the heat. Locusts sawed away in frantic bursts.

Lewis, gaunt and red-faced, began to whistle. Then he stopped. Our uniforms darkened with sweat. The oil on our rifles stank. Our faces glistened. The silence between us grew intense and I was glad when the first sergeant came up and began to shout at us.

He told us that we were little girls, piglets, warts. We were toads. We didn't belong in his army. He lined us up and inspected us. He said that we should be court-martialled for our ugliness and stupidity. Then he drove us to an ammunition dump in the middle of a pine forest thirty miles from the post and made us stand with our rifles over our heads while he gave us our orders and filled our clips with live rounds. We were to patrol the perimeter of the ammunition dump until he relieved us. He didn't say when that would be. If anyone so much as touched the fence we should shoot to kill. *Shoot to kill,* he repeated. No yakking. No grabass. If we screwed up he would personally bring grief upon us. 'I know everything,' he said, and he

135

ordered us to run around the compound with our rifles still over our heads. When we got back he was gone, along with the three men whose places we had taken.

Lewis had the first shift. Hubbard and I sat in the shade of an old warehouse weathered down to bare grey boards with patches of green paint curling off. It had no windows. On the loading ramp where we sat two sliding doors were padlocked together and plastered with prohibitions, *No Smoking* and so on, with a few strange ones thrown in, like *No Hobnailed Boots.*

There were five other buildings, all in bad repair. Weeds grew between the buildings and alongside the chain-link fence. In places the weeds were waist-high. I don't know what kind of ammunition was inside the buildings.

Hubbard and I put our ponchos under our heads and tried to sleep. But we couldn't lie still. Gnats crawled up our noses. Mosquitoes hung in clouds around our heads. The air smelled like turpentine from the resin oozing out of the trees.

'I wish I was home,' Hubbard said.

'Me too,' I said. There didn't seem to be much point in ignoring Hubbard out here, where nobody could see me do it. But the word 'home' meant nothing anymore. My father was in Southern California, looking for work. Keith was still missing. The last time I'd spoken to her, my mother's voice had been cold, as if I were somehow to blame.

'If I was home,' Hubbard said, 'I'd be out at the drags with Vogel and Kirk. Don't ask me what I'm doing here because I sure don't know.' He took off his helmet and wiped his face with his sleeve. He had a soft, square face with a little roll of flesh under his chin. It was the face he'd have for the rest of his life. 'Look,' he said. He took out his wallet and showed me a picture of a '49 Mercury.

'Nice,' I said.

'It isn't mine.' Hubbard looked at the picture and then put it away. 'I was going to buy it before Uncle got me. I wouldn't race it, though. I'd take it out to the track and sit on the hood with Vogel and Kirk and drink beer.'

Hubbard went on talking about Vogel and Kirk. Then he stopped and shook his head. 'How about you?' he asked. 'What would you be doing if you were home?'

'If I were home,' I said, remembering us all together, 'we would drive up to the fair at Mount Vernon. Then we'd have dinner at my grandfather's place—he has this big barbecue every year—and afterwards we'd stay in a motel with a swimming pool. My brother and I would swim all night and watch the fireworks from the water.'

We had not been to Mount Vernon since my grandfather died when I was fourteen, so the memory was an old one. But it didn't feel old. It felt fresh and true, the starry night, the soft voices from the open doorways around the pool, the water so warm you forgot about it, forgot your own skin. Shaking hands with Keith underwater and looking up from the bottom of the pool at the rockets flaring overhead, the wrinkled surface of the water all a-shimmer with their light. My father on the balcony above, leaning over the rail, calling down to us. That's enough, boys. Come in. It's late.

'You like it, don't you?' Hubbard asked.

'Like what?'

'All this stuff. Marching everywhere. Carrying a rifle. The army.'

'Come off it,' I said. I shook my head.

'It's true,' he said. 'I can tell.'

I shook my head again but made no further denials. Hubbard's admission that the car in the picture wasn't his had put me in an honest mood. And I was flattered that he had taken the trouble to come to a conclusion about me. Even this one. 'The army has its good points,' I said.

'Name me one.' Hubbard leaned against the ramp. He closed his eyes. I could hear Lewis whistling as he walked along the fence.

I couldn't explain why I liked the army because I didn't understand the reason myself. 'Travel,' I said. 'You can go all over the world.'

Hubbard opened his eyes. 'You know where I've been to? South Carolina, Georgia, and North Carolina. All I've seen is a lot of hicks. And when they do send us overseas it will just be to kill slopes. You know the first sergeant? They say he killed over twenty of them. I could never do that. I shot a squirrel once and I cried all night.'

We talked some more and Hubbard told me that he hadn't been drafted, as I'd assumed. Like me, he had enlisted. He said that the army had tricked him. They'd sent a recruiter to his high school just before graduation to talk to the boys in Hubbard's class. The recruiter got them together in the gym and ran movies of soldiers being massaged by girls in Korea, and drinking beer in Germany out of steins. Then he visited the boys in their homes and showed each of them why the army was the right choice. He told Hubbard that anyone who could drive a tractor automatically got to drive a tank, which turned out not to be true. Hubbard hadn't even set foot in a tank, not once. 'Of course he didn't mention Vietnam,' Hubbard said.

When I asked Hubbard what he was doing in the Airborne he shrugged. 'I thought it might be interesting,' he said. 'I should have known better. Just more of the same. People running around yelling their heads off.'

He waved his hand through a swarm of mosquitoes overhead. 'We'll be getting orders pretty soon,' he said. 'Are you scared?'

I nodded. 'A little. I don't think about it much.'

'I think about it all the time. I just hope I don't get killed. They can shoot my dick off as long as they don't kill me.'

I didn't know what to say. The sound of Lewis's whistling grew louder.

'Nuts,' Hubbard said. 'I don't know what he's so cheerful about.'

Lewis came around the corner and climbed the ramp. 'Shift's up,' he said. 'Best watch how you go along that fence. There's nettles poking through everyplace.' He held out his hand for us to see. It was swollen and red. He leaned his rifle against the warehouse and began to unlace his boots.

'I'm allergic to nettles,' Hubbard said. 'I could die out there.' He stood and put on his helmet. 'Wish me luck. If I don't make it back tell Laura I love her.'

Lewis watched Hubbard go, then turned to me. 'I never saw so many bugs in my life,' he said. 'Wish I was at the beach. You ever been to Nag's Head? Those girls up there just go and go.'

'Never been there,' I said.

'I had one of those girls almost tore my back off,' Lewis said. 'Still got the marks.' He leaned towards me and for a moment there I thought he was going to take his shirt off and show me his back as he'd shown me his hand.

'Ever been to Kentucky?' he asked.

I shook my head.

'That's where I'm from. Lawton. It's a dry town but I've been drinking since I was thirteen. Year after that I started on intercourse. Now it's got to where I can't go to sleep anymore unless I ate pussy.'

'I'm from Washington,' I said. 'The state.'

Lewis took off his helmet. He had close-cropped hair, red like his face. He could have worn it longer if he'd wanted, now that we were out of training. But he chose to wear it that way. It was his style.

He studied me. 'You never been to Lawton,' he said. 'You ought to go. You won't want to leave and that's a guarantee.' He took off one of his socks and started doing something to his foot. It seemed to require all his concentration. He sucked in his long cheeks and stuck the tip of his tongue out of the side of his mouth. 'There,' he said and wiggled his toes. 'I guess you know about what happened the other day,' he said. 'It wasn't the way you probably heard.'

I didn't know what Lewis was talking about, but he gave me no chance to say so.

'I just didn't have the rope fixed right,' he said. 'I wasn't afraid. You ought to see me go off the high dive back home. I wanted to straighten out the rope, that's all.'

Now I understood. Our company had practised rappelling the week before off a fifty-foot cliff and someone had refused the descent. I'd heard the first sergeant raising hell but I was at the base of the cliff and couldn't make out what he was saying or see who he was yelling at.

'He called me Tinkerbell,' Lewis said.

'He calls everybody that,' I said. He did, too. Tinkerbell and Sweety Pie.

'You go ask around home,' Lewis told me. 'Just talk to those girls back there. They'll tell you if I'm a Tinkerbell.'

'He didn't mean anything.'

'I know what he meant,' Lewis said, and gave me a fierce look. Then he put his sock back on and stared at it. 'What's the matter with these fellows here, anyway? Pretty stuck on themselves if you ask me.'

'I guess so,' I said. 'Look, don't mind me. I'm going to get some sleep before my shift.' I closed my eyes. I hoped that Lewis would be quiet. He was starting to get on my nerves. It wasn't just his loud voice or the things he said. He seemed to want something from me.

'There's not one of these fellows would last a day in Lawton,' he

139

said. 'We've got a guard in the bank that bit a man's tongue out of his head.'

I opened my eyes. Lewis was watching me. 'It's just because we're new,' I said. 'They'll be friendlier when we've been around for a while. Now if you don't mind I'm going to catch some sleep.'

'What burns me,' Lewis said, 'is how you meet one of them in the PX or downtown somewhere and they look past you like they never saw you.'

Off in the distance a siren wailed. The sound was weak, only a pulse in the air, but Lewis cocked his head at it. He squinted. When the siren stopped Lewis held his listening attitude for a moment, then gave a little shake. 'I'm just as good as them,' he said. 'Look here. You got family?'

I nodded.

'I'm the only one left,' Lewis said. 'It was me and my dad, but now he's gone too. Heart attack.' He shrugged. 'That's all right. I get along just fine.'

Another siren went off, right in my ear it seemed. The sound made me wince. Then everything went quiet. Lewis's eyes were pink.

Hubbard came around the side of the building and started up the ramp. I was glad to see him. He waved and I waved back. He gave me an odd stare then and I realized he'd only been flapping mosquitoes out of his face.

'There's a man out by the gate who wants to talk to us,' he said.

Lewis started lacing up his boots. 'Officer?'

Hubbard shook his head. 'Civilian.'

'What does he want?' I asked, but Hubbard had already turned away. I followed him and Lewis came after me, muttering to himself and trying to tie his boots.

There was a car parked in the turn-around outside the gate. It had a decal on the door and a blinker flashing on top. It was early evening but still light. A man was sitting in the front seat. Another man leaned against the fence. He was tall and stooped. He wiped at his face with a red bandanna which he put in his back pocket when he saw us coming.

'Okay, mister,' Hubbard said, 'we're all here.'

'Bet you'd rather be some place else, too.' He smiled at us. 'Terrible way to spend the holiday.'

None of us said anything.

The man stopped smiling. 'We have a fire,' he said. He pointed to the east, at a black cloud above the trees. 'It's an annual event,' the man said. 'A couple of kids blew up a pipe full of matches. Almost took their hands off.' He turned his head and barked twice. He might have been laughing or he might have been coughing.

'So what?' Lewis said.

The man looked at him, then at me. I noticed for the first time that his eyes were blinking steadily. 'This isn't the best place to be,' he said.

I knew what he meant—the dry weeds, the warped ramshackle buildings, the ammunition inside. 'That fire's a mile off at least,' I said. 'Can't you put it out?'

'I think we can,' he said. He tugged at his pants. It must have been a habit. They were already high on his waist, held there by leather suspenders. 'The problem is,' he said, 'if you catch one spark in there that's all she wrote.'

Hubbard and I looked at each other.

The man leaned against the fence. 'You boys just come with us and I'll see that someone takes you back to Bragg.'

'That's a good way to get dead,' said Lewis. He cocked his rifle. The bolt slid forward with a sharp, heavy smack, a sound I'd heard thousands of times since joining the army but never so distinctly. It changed everything. Everything became vivid, interesting.

The man froze. His eyes stopped their endless blinking.

'You heard me,' Lewis said. 'Let loose of that fence or you're dog meat.'

The man stepped back. He stood with his arms at his sides and watched Lewis. I could hear the breath pass in and out of his mouth. A few minutes earlier I had been glad to see him. He was worried about me. He didn't want me to get blown up and that spoke well of him. But when I looked at him now, without weapon, without uniform, without anyone to back him up, I felt hard and cold. Nobody had the right to be that helpless.

None of us spoke. Finally the man turned and went back to the car.

'God Almighty,' Hubbard said. He turned to Lewis. 'Why did you do that?'

'He touched the fence,' Lewis said.

'You're crazy,' Hubbard said. 'You're really crazy.'

'Maybe I am and maybe I'm not.'

'You are,' Hubbard said. 'Take my word for it. Crazy hick.'

'You calling me a hick?' Lewis said.

Out in the car I could see the two men talking. The one Lewis had scared off kept shaking his head.

'Tell me something, hick,' Hubbard said. 'Tell me what we're supposed to do if this place goes up.'

'That's no concern of mine,' Lewis said.

'Jesus,' Hubbard said. He looked at me, appealing for help. I disappointed him. 'What are you grinning at?' he said.

'Nothing,' I said. But I might just as well have said 'Everything.' I liked this situation. It was interesting. It had a last-stand quality about it. But I didn't really believe that anything would happen, not to me. Getting hurt was just a choice some people made, like bad luck, or growing old.

'I don't believe this,' Hubbard said.

'If you don't like it here,' Lewis said, 'you can go somewhere else. Won't nobody stop you.'

Hubbard stared at the hand Lewis was shaking at him. It was beet-red and so bloated that you couldn't see his knuckles any more. It looked like an enormous baby's hand, even to the crease around the wrist. 'God Almighty,' Hubbard said. 'Those must have been some killer nettles you ran into. With plants like that I don't know what they need us for.'

'Look,' I said. 'We've got a visitor.'

The other man had got out of his car and was walking up to the fence. He smiled as he came towards us. 'Hello there,' he said. He took off his sunglasses as if to show us he had nothing to hide. His face was dark with soot. 'I'm Deputy Chief Ellingboe,' he said. He held up a card. When we didn't look at it he put it back in his shirt pocket. He glanced over at the man sitting in the car. 'You certainly gave old Charlie there something to talk about,' he said.

'Old Charlie about got his ears peeled,' Lewis said.

'There's no call for that talk,' the man said. He came up to the fence and looked at Lewis. Then he looked at me. Finally he turned to Hubbard and started talking to him as if they were alone. 'I know you think you're doing your duty, following orders. I appreciate that. I was a soldier myself once.' He leaned towards us, fingers wound through the iron mesh. 'I was in Korea. Men dropped like flies all around me but at least they died in a good cause.'

'Back off,' Lewis said.

The man went on talking to Hubbard. 'Nobody would expect you to stay in there,' he said. 'All you have to do is walk out and no one will say a thing. If they do I will personally take it up with General Paterson. Word of honour. I'll shake on it.' He wiggled the fingers of his right hand.

'Back off,' Lewis said again.

The man kept his eyes on Hubbard. He said, 'You don't want to stay in there, do you?'

Hubbard looked over at Lewis. A fat bug flew between them with a whine. They both flinched. Then they smiled at each other. I was smiling too.

'You're a smart boy,' the man said. 'I can see that. Use the brains God gave you. Just put one foot in front of the other.'

'You've been told to back off,' Hubbard said. 'You won't be told again.'

'Boys, be reasonable.'

Hubbard swung his rifle up and aimed it at the man's head. The motion was natural. The other man leaned out the car window and shouted, 'Come on! Hell with 'em!' The deputy chief looked at him and back at us. He took his hands away from the fence. He was shaking all over. A grasshopper flew smack into his cheek and he threw up his arms as if he'd been shot. The car horn honked twice. He turned and walked to the car, got inside, and the two men drove away.

We stood at the fence and watched the car until it disappeared around a curve.

'It's no big deal,' I said. 'They'll put the fire out.'

And so they did. But before that happened there was one bad moment when the wind shifted in our direction. We had our first taste of smoke then. The air was full of insects flying away from the fire, all kinds of insects, so many it looked like rain falling sideways. They rattled against the buildings and pinged into the fence.

Hubbard had a coughing fit. He sat on his helmet and put his head between his knees. Lewis went over to him and started pounding him on the back. Hubbard tried to wave Lewis off, but he kept at it. 'A little smoke won't hurt you,' Lewis said. Then Lewis began to cough. A few minutes later so did I. We couldn't stop. Whenever I took another breath it got worse. I ached from it, and began to feel dizzy. For the first time that day I was afraid. Then the wind changed again, and the smoke and the bugs went off in another direction. A few minutes later we were laughing.

The black smudge above the trees gradually disappeared. It was gone by the time the first sergeant pulled up to the gate. He only spoke once on the drive home, to ask if we had anything to report. We shook our heads. He gave us a look, but didn't ask again. Night came on as we drove through the woods, headlights jumping ahead of us on the rough road. Tall pines crowded us on both sides. Overhead was a ribbon of dark blue. As we bounced through the potholes I steadied myself with my rifle, feeling like a commando returning from a suicide mission.

The first sergeant let us out at company headquarters. He said, 'Sweet dreams, toads,' and went off down the street, gunning the engine and doing racing-shifts on the gears.

We turned in our rifles and lingered outside the orderly room. We didn't want to go away from each other. Without saying so, we believed that we had done something that day, that we were proven men. We weren't, of course, but we thought we were and that was a sweet thing to believe for an hour or two. We had stood our ground together. We knew what we were made of now, and the stuff was good.

We sat on the steps of the orderly room, sometimes talking, mostly just sitting there. Hubbard suddenly threw his hands in the air. In a high voice he said, 'Boys, be reasonable,' and we all started laughing. I was in the middle. I didn't think about it, I just reached out and put my arms on their shoulders. We were in a state. Every time we stopped laughing one of us would giggle and set it off again. The yellow moon rose above the mess hall. Behind us the poker-wise desk clerk, 'Chairborne' we called him, typed steadily away at some roster or report or maybe a letter to the girl he dreamed of—who, if he was lucky, kept a picture of him on her dresser, and looked at it sometimes.

The three of us fooled around together for the next couple of days. One night we went to a movie in town, but Lewis spoiled it by talking all the time. You'd think he had never seen a movie before. If an airplane came on the screen he said, 'Airplane'. If someone got hit he said 'Ouch!' The next night we went bowling and he spoiled that, too. He had to use his left hand because his right hand was still swollen up, and his ball kept bouncing into the gutter. The people in the next lane thought it was funny, but it got on my nerves.

I was in a bad mood anyway. My mother had called the day after the Fourth to tell me that my car had been located in Bolinas, California. Two hippies were living in it. They said that Keith had sold it to them but they had no idea where he was now. They'd met him by chance in a crash pad in Berkeley. When my mother said 'crash pad', I thought, Good God. I could see the whole thing.

She was beside herself. She said that she was going to quit her job and take a bus to San Francisco. Keith could be in trouble. He could be hungry. He could be sick. For a moment she didn't say anything, and I thought, He could be dead. I'm sure that's what she was thinking, too. I told her to stay home. When Keith got hungry he'd be in touch. There was no point in her wandering around a strange city, she'd never find him that way.

'Someone has to look for him,' she said.

'Someone like me, you mean.' I hadn't wanted to sound so rough. Before I had a chance to soften my words, though, my mother said, 'How far away you are. Nothing reaches you.'

We patched it up as well as we could. I told her I'd be getting my orders for Vietnam any day now, and promised to look around for Keith while I was in Oakland waiting to ship out.

On Monday the rest of the company returned to duty. Almost everyone had been drinking all weekend, and looked it. Some of the men had been in fights. The ones who'd gone to the beach had terrible sunburns and were forced to walk stiff-legged because they couldn't bend their knees. As they marched they swayed from side to side like penguins. There were over thirty of them in this condition and when we moved out together it was something to see.

Two days later our company was detailed for crowd control. A group of protesters had camped out on the main entrance to the post, on either side of the road. We were supposed to keep them from moving past the gate.

At first it was friendly enough. The protesters waved and threw us sandwiches which we were forbidden to touch. Some of the women were good-looking in a soulful way and that didn't hurt their cause. The men were something else. They were all decked out in different costumes and seemed pleased with themselves in a way that I found disagreeable. There was one in particular I had my eye on. He was always chanting something, and he was the one who finally rounded everybody up and got them on the road.

They stood there for a while. With their arms joined they sang songs. Then they moved towards us. They stopped just short of the gate and began to talk to us. There was a tired-looking blonde girl across from me and next to her was the fellow I'd been watching. I didn't care for him. He was prettier than the girl, and his long black hair curled up at the ends. He looked like Prince Valiant.

The girl said hello, and told me her first name. 'What's yours?' she said.

I didn't answer. We'd been told not to, but I wouldn't have anyway.

Prince Valiant shook his head. 'You're not allowed to talk,' he said. 'Doesn't that strike you as paradoxical? Here you are supposed to be defending freedom and you can't talk.'

'Why do you want to kill your brothers?' the girl said.

The man next to me began swearing under his breath.

Prince Valiant smiled at him. 'Speak up,' he said loudly. 'Haven't you ever heard of the First Amendment?'

The girl kept talking to me. 'Your brothers and sisters in Vietnam don't want a war,' she said. 'If you didn't go, there wouldn't be any war.'

'Don't be a CIA robot,' Prince Valiant said.

'Cocksucker,' said the man next to me.

Prince Valiant smiled at him. He looked at me. 'I think your friend's got a problem,' he said.

I was trembling. I wanted to take my rifle to that smile of his and put it down his gullet. The sun was overhead, baking our helmets, and sweat ran down my forehead into my eyes. Everything got quiet. All along the line I could feel the tautness of something about to break.

At that moment the highway patrol pulled up, four cars with lights flashing. The patrolmen got out and started clearing the protesters off the road. There was no resistance. Prince Valiant backed away. 'You should get some help with that problem of yours,' he said to the man beside me, who stepped forward out of line.

The blonde girl looked at us. 'Please,' she said, 'please don't.' She was pulling on Prince Valiant's arm. The first sergeant yelled at the man beside me to get back in line. He hesitated. Then he stepped back. Prince Valiant laughed and gave us the finger.

The protesters sang more songs, then broke up. After they left we were relieved by another company. I was still trembling. The other men were upset, too. We got back in time for dinner, but hardly any of us went to the mess hall. Instead we sat around and talked about what had happened, and what would have happened if they'd turned us loose. It was the first time I'd joined in a general conversation. While we were talking, Lewis came in. He'd been on KP that day so he'd missed the excitement. He listened for a while, then asked me in a loud voice if I wanted to go see the Bob Hope movie that was playing in town.

Everyone stopped talking.

I told Lewis no, I wasn't in the mood.

He looked at the other men. He stood there for a moment. Then he shrugged and walked outside again.

The stealing began a few days after the protest. A corporal had his wallet taken from under his pillow. It was found beneath the barracks steps, empty. The corporal swore that he'd had over a hundred dollars in it, which was probably a lie. Nobody in the company owned that much money except the clerk-typist, who regularly cleaned everyone out at marathon poker games in the mess hall.

Nothing like this had ever happened before in our company, not in anyone's memory, and everybody assumed that the thief must be from another unit—maybe even a civilian. Our platoon sergeants told us to keep our eyes open. That was all that was said about it.

The next night a man had his fatigue pants stolen while he slept. The thief balled them up and stuffed them into a trash can in the latrine, along with his empty wallet. There was something intimate about this theft. Now we all knew, as these things are known, that the thief was one of us.

After the second theft our first sergeant went through all the barracks and made a speech. He had a vivid red scar that ran from the corner of one eye across his cheek and down under his collar. He had been badly wounded in Vietnam, so badly wounded that the army was forcing him to take early retirement. He had just a few weeks left to go.

The scar gave weight to everything the first sergeant said. He spoke with painful slowness and agitation, as if each word was a fish he had to catch with his hands. He said that to his mind an infantry company was like a family, a family without any women in it, but a family. He wanted the thief to think about that, and then ask himself one question: What sort of a man would turn his back on his own kind?

'Think about it,' the first sergeant said. Then he went to the barracks next door where through the open window we could hear him saying exactly the same thing.

Because the stealing was something new, and I was new, I felt accused by it. No one said anything, but I felt in my heart that I was suspected. It made me furious. For the first time in my life I was spoiling for a fight, just waiting for someone to say something so I could swing at him and prove my innocence. I noticed that Lewis carried himself the same way—swaggering and glaring at everyone all the time. He looked ridiculous, but I thought I understood. We were all breathing poison in and out. It was a bad time.

Hubbard was different. He seemed to wilt. He walked around with his hands in his pockets and his eyes on the ground, and I could hardly get a word out of him. Later I discovered that it wasn't the stealing that got him down, or the suspicion, but pure grief. His friends Vogel and Kirk had been killed, along with their dates, in a car smash-up on the Fourth.

We all had our suspicions. My suspicions lay with a man who had never given me any reason to think badly of him. To me he just looked like a thief. I suppose that someone even suspected Hubbard, miserable as he was. If so, Hubbard got clear of suspicion four days after the second theft.

It happened like this. He had left the mess hall early to take a shower. At some point he apparently looked up and saw someone lift his pants off the hook where he'd hung them. He shouted and whoever it was hauled off and hit him dead on the nose. He hadn't seen the thief's face because of the steam in the shower stall, and the blow knocked him down so he had no chance to give chase. His nose was broken, mashed flat against one cheek.

As soon as the story got around, the barracks emptied out. Everyone wanted to get away from the company that night. So did I. But I wanted to see Hubbard even more, partly out of concern and partly for some need that was not clear to me. So I sat on the orderly room steps and waited for him. Men from another company were playing softball on the parade ground. They yelled insults at each other until it got dark and they quit. Then I heard the smaller sounds, moths rustling against the bare light bulb overhead, frogs croaking, one of the Puerto Rican cooks in the mess hall singing happily to himself in that beautiful language that set him apart from us, and made him a figure of fun.

Hubbard came back from the hospital in a white jeep. He was wearing a shiny metal cast over his nose, held by two strips of tape that went across his face. The first sergeant met him and I waited while they talked. When Hubbard finally turned and started towards the barracks, I came up to him. We walked together without speaking for a moment, then I said, 'Who was it?'

'I don't know,' he said.

I followed him inside and sat on the next bunk while he took his boots off and stretched out, hands behind his head. He stared up at the ceiling. The cast gleamed dully.

'You really didn't see him?' I asked.

He shook his head.

'Well, I didn't do it,' I said. 'I swear I didn't.' Without thinking about it, I put my hand over my heart. I could feel my heart beating.

Hubbard looked at me. His lips were pressed together. He was utterly dejected. I could not imagine him pointing a rifle at someone's head. He looked back up at the ceiling. 'Who said you did?' he asked.

'Nobody. I just wanted you to know.'

'Fine,' he said. 'I never thought it was you anyway.' Suddenly he turned his head and looked at me again. It made me uncomfortable.

'Just between us,' I said, 'who do you think it was?'

He shrugged. 'I don't know. I'd like to be alone right now if that's all right with you.'

'Whatever you want,' I said. 'If I can do anything, let me know. That's what friends are for.'

At first he didn't answer. Then he said, 'That was stupid, what we did out at the ammo dump. You probably think it was some big deal, but if you want to know the truth I almost throw up every time I think of it. We nearly got ourselves killed. Don't you ever think about that?'

'Sure I do.'

'About being dead? Do you think about being dead?'

'Not exactly.'

'Not exactly,' he said. 'Boy, you're really something. No wonder you like the army so much.'

I waited for Hubbard to go on, and when he didn't I stood up and looked down at him. His eyes were closed. 'I'm sorry about what happened to you,' I said. 'That's why I came by.'

'Thanks,' he said, and touched the cast on his nose curiously, as if I had just reminded him of it. 'It isn't only this,' he said. Then, with his eyes still closed, he told me about his friends getting killed.

It spooked me. It was like a ghost story, the way Hubbard had talked about them so much on the day it happened. I thought I should say something. 'That's tragic,' I said, the word used in my family for all deaths, and as soon as it was out of my mouth I regretted it. I didn't know then it is nearly impossible to talk to other people about their own suffering. Instead of giving up, I tried again. 'I know how you feel,' I said. 'I'd feel the same way if I lost my best friends.'

'You don't have any,' Hubbard said, 'not like Vogel and Kirk, anyway.' He rolled on to his side so that he was facing away from me. 'Nobody that close,' he said.

'How do you know?' I said.

'I just know.'

I understood that Hubbard wanted me to leave. And I was glad to get away from him. It was too late to go anywhere so I went back to my own building. It was empty. I sat down on my bunk. I thought about what Hubbard had said, that I had nobody close. It got to me, coming from Hubbard, because we should have been close after what we'd been through together, he and Lewis and I.

Anyway, it just wasn't true.

I tried to read, but it took an effort in that big quiet room full of bunks. While I stared at the book, I thought of other things. I wondered how I would hold up if I got wounded. I'd only been hurt once before, when I was eight, in a fall from a tree. My leg had been broken and I wasn't very brave about it. For several months everyone knew exactly how uncomfortable I was at any given moment. Keith was following me in those days. After I got out of the cast I walked with a limp, and Keith began to limp, too. It drove me crazy. I used to scream at him. Once I shot him with my B-B gun, trying to make him go away—but he kept limping after me, bawling his eyes out.

The door banged open and two men came in, a little drunk. Though taps hadn't been sounded yet they turned off all the lights and went to bed. I had no choice but to do the same.

For a long while I lay in the dark with my eyes open. My unhappiness made me angry, and as I became more angry I began to brood about the thief. Who was he? What kind of person would do a thing like that?

Lewis shuffles along the road leading out of Fort Bragg, muttering to himself and trying to hitch a ride, but he is so angry that he glares at all the drivers and they pass him by. He's angry because he couldn't talk his friends into going to the pictures with him. Bob Hope is his favourite actor but it's not as much fun going alone. He thinks they owed it to him to come.

When he gets to the bottom of Smoke Bomb Hill someone in a convertible stops for him. The driver of the convertible is a teacher who works at the elementary school on post. He is nervous, shy. Lewis leans over the side of the convertible and asks him something which he can't understand because Lewis's voice is so loud and thick. The teacher just keeps looking straight ahead and gives a little nod.

Lewis gets in. He tells the teacher that a fellow in Lawton had a car like this one and drove it across someone's yard one night and got his head cut off by a metal clothes line. They never did find the head, either. Lewis says he figures one of the dogs on the street got ahold of it and buried it somewhere.

He takes out a package of gum and crams four sticks in his mouth, dropping the wrappers on the floor of the car. He has unwrapped the last stick and is about to put it in his mouth when he remembers his manners and holds the gum out to the teacher. The teacher shakes his head, but Lewis stabs it at him until he takes it. When he starts to chew on it, Lewis smiles and nods.

They leave the post and head towards town. The road is lined with drive-in restaurants and used-car lots advertising special deals for servicemen. American flags hang limp above the air-conditioned trailers where terms are struck, and salesmen in white shirts stand around in groups. In the early dusk their shirts seem to glow. The air smells of burgers.

The teacher sneaks a look at Lewis. Lewis says something incomprehensible and the teacher looks away quickly and nods. Lewis turns the radio on full blast and starts punching the buttons. When he doesn't get anything he wants he spins the tuning-knob back and forth. Finally, he settles on a telephone call-in show. People are calling in their opinions as to whether we should drop an atomic bomb on North Vietnam.

A man says we should, right away. Then a woman gets on the line and says that she believes the average person in North Vietnam is probably a lot like the average person here at home, and that their leaders are the ones making the trouble. She thinks we should be patient, and if that doesn't work then we should figure out a way to just bomb the leaders. Lewis chews up a storm. He watches the radio as if listening with his eyes.

He reminds the teacher of one of his students. It's the unfinished face, the way he stares, his restlessness. He asks Lewis to turn down the radio, and as Lewis reaches for the knob the teacher notices his hand—puffed-up and livid. In the five days since Lewis's brush with the nettles the swelling has hardly gone down at all. The teacher asks Lewis what happened to it.

Lewis holds it up in front of his face and turns it back and forth. Nettles, he says. Hurts like hell, too, and that's no lie.

What did you put on it? the teacher asks.

Nothing, Lewis says.

Nothing?

I'm in the army, Lewis says.

The teacher is going to say that Lewis should go on sick call, but he decides that they've probably bullied him into thinking there's something wrong with that. His father was an army officer and he knows how they do things. He feels sorry for Lewis, for being helpless and in the army and having his hand so hideously swollen. You really should put some calamine lotion on it, he says.

Never heard of it, Lewis says.

It's what you do for nettles, the teacher says. It eases the pain and makes the swelling go down.

I don't know, Lewis says. I just as soon wait and see. Every time you go to the doctor they end up sticking a needle in you.

You don't have to go to a doctor, the teacher says. You can buy it in a drugstore. Lewis nods and looks off. The teacher can tell that he has no intention of spending his money on calamine lotion. He can almost see that hand throbbing away, getting worse and worse, and the boy doing nothing about it. Everybody uses it, he says. We've always got a bottle around.

The teacher is not inviting Lewis to his home. He just wants him to comprehend that calamine lotion is no big undertaking. But Lewis misunderstands. What the hell, he says, I'll try anything once. Long as I get to the pictures by eight.

The teacher turns to explain. But there's no way to do it without sounding like he's backing out. Just before they reach town he pulls off on a side street bordered with pines. Almost immediately the sound of traffic dies. The nasal voice coming out of the radio seems unbearably loud and stupid. It embarrasses the teacher to belong to a species that can think such things. When he stops the car in front of the house he sits for a moment, letting the silence calm him.

They go in through a redwood gate in the back. Lewis whistles when he sees the pool, a piano-shaped pool designed by the teacher's father, who also designed the house. The house has sliding doors everywhere with rice-paper panels. All the drawers and cabinets have brass handles with Japanese ideograms signifying 'Long Life', 'Good Luck', 'Excellent Health'. The teacher's father was stationed in Japan after the war and fell in love with Japanese culture. There's even a rock garden in the front yard.

The house is empty. The teacher's mother is visiting friends in California. His father died two years ago. The teacher leads Lewis to the living-room and tells him to sit down. The chairs are heavy and ornately carved. The arms are dragons and the legs are bearded old men with their arms raised to look like they're holding the seats up. Lewis hesitates, then lowers himself into the smallest chair as if that is the polite thing to do.

The teacher goes to the medicine cabinet and takes out the calamine lotion. He comes back to the living-room, shaking the bottle. He gives the bottle to Lewis, but Lewis can't open it because of his bad hand, so the teacher takes it back and twists off the cap. He gives the bottle to Lewis again, then sees that Lewis doesn't know what to do with it. Here, the teacher says. Look. He sits in the chair across from Lewis. He pulls the chair close. He pours some lotion into his palm, then takes Lewis's hand by the wrist and starts to work it in, over the swollen, dimpled knuckles, between the thick fingers. Lewis's hand is unbelievably hot.

Hey! Lewis says. That feels fine. I wish I had some before.

The burning skin drinks up the lotion. The teacher shakes more out, directly on to the back of Lewis's wrist. Lewis leans back and closes his eyes. The room is cool, blue. A cardinal is singing outside, one of three birds the teacher can identify. He rubs the lotion into Lewis's hand, feeling the heat leave little by little, the motions of his own hand circular and rhythmic. After a time he forgets what he is doing. He forgets his stomach which always hurts, he forgets the children he teaches who seem bent on becoming brutes and slatterns, he forgets his hatred of the house and his fear of being anywhere else. He forgets his sense of being absolutely alone.

So does Lewis.

Then the room is silent and grey. The teacher has no idea when the bird stopped singing. He looks down where his hand and Lewis's are joined, fingers interlaced. For once Lewis is still. He breathes so peacefully and deeply that the teacher thinks he is asleep. Then he sees that Lewis's eyes are open. There is a thin gleam of light upon them.

The teacher unclasps his hand from Lewis's hand.

I have to admit that stuff is all right, Lewis says. I might just go and buy me a bottle.

The teacher screws the cap on and holds the bottle out. Here, he says. Keep it. Go on.

Lewis takes it. Thanks, he says.

The teacher stands and stretches. I guess we'd better go, he says.

You don't want to miss that movie.

Lewis follows him out of the house. He stops for a moment by the pool, which the teacher walks past as if it isn't there. The moon is full. It looks like a big silver dish floating on the water. Lewis puts his hands in his pockets and jingles the change.

He and the teacher don't talk on the way to town. Lewis leans into the corner, one arm hanging over the car door and the other on top of the seat. He strokes the leather with just that tenderness his dog used to feel. In town the sidewalks are crowded. Recruits with shaved heads, as many as fifteen or twenty in a group, walk from bar to bar, pushing each other and laughing too loudly, the ones in the rear almost running to keep up. They fall silent when they come up to the clusters of prostitutes, but when they are well past they call things over their shoulders. Different groups shout at each other back and forth across the street. The lights are on over the bars, in the tattoo parlours and clothing stores, in the gadget shops that sell German helmets and Vietcong flags, Mexican throwing knives, lighters that look like pistols, fancy condoms, fireworks and dirty books. The lights flash on the hood of the convertible and along the sides of the cars they pass.

The teacher stops in front of the movie theatre. He tells Lewis to be sure and use that lotion and Lewis promises he will. They wave to each other as the convertible pulls away.

The previews are just beginning. Lewis buys a jumbo popcorn and a jumbo coke and a Sugar Daddy. He sits down. A giant tarantula towers over a house. From inside a woman looks out and sees the hairy legs and screams. Lewis laughs. That's some spider, he says out loud. The previews end and the first cartoon begins, a Tom and Jerry. Every time the cat runs into a wall or sticks his tail into a light plug Lewis cracks up. Now and then he shouts advice to the mouse. The couple in front of him move across the aisle and down. The next cartoon is a Goofy. Tinkerbell does the credits, flying from one side of the screen to the other, bringing the names out of her sparkling wand.

Tinkerbell, Lewis says. When he hears the word his stomach clenches. He gets up and walks outside. He stands under the marquee for a moment, just breathing, then runs down the sidewalk in the direction the convertible went, pushing people out of his way without regard. He runs three, four, five blocks to where the downtown ends. His eyes burn from the sweat running into them and his shirt is soaked through. He takes the bottle of calamine lotion out of his pocket and throws it into the road. It shatters. I'm no Tinkerbell, he says. He watches the cars go by for a while, balling and unballing his fists, then turns and walks back into Fayetteville to find a girl.

It is too loud, too bright. One of the women on the street smiles at him but he keeps going. He has never paid for it and he's not about to start now. He's never had it free either, but he came really close once at Nag's Head and has almost managed to forget that he failed. He turns off Combat Alley and heads down a side street. The bars give out. It is quiet here. He passes the public library, a red brick building with white pillars and high windows going dark one by one. A woman holds the door as people leave, mostly old folks. Just before she locks up two girls come out, a fat one in toreador pants and another girl in shorts, her legs white as milk. They both light cigarettes and sit on the steps. Lewis walks to the corner and turns back up the street. He stops in front of the girls. This here the library? he says.

It's closed, the fat one says.

Is that a fact, Lewis says, without looking at her. He watches the one in shorts, who is staring at her own feet and doing the French inhale with her cigarette. He can't see her face very well except for her lips, which are so red they seem to be separate from the rest of her. Shoot, Lewis says, I wanted to get this book.

What book? the fat one asks.

Just a book, Lewis says. For college.

The two girls glance at each other. The one in shorts straightens up. She walks down the steps past Lewis and looks up the street, leaning forward and lifting up one of her long legs like a flamingo.

You're from the post, the fat one says.

Here comes Bo, says the one in shorts. Give me another weed.

Both girls light fresh cigarettes. A car pulls up in front of the library, a '57 Chevvy full of boys. The girl in shorts sticks her head in the window. She backs away, holding a beer and laughing. The door opens. She gets in and the car peels off.

The fat girl says, She is so loose, and grinds out the cigarette under her shoe.

The car stops at the end of the block and comes back in reverse, gears screaming. The door opens again and the fat girl gets in and the car pulls away.

Lewis walks the side streets. He meets no girls, but once, passing an apartment building, he looks in a window and sees a pretty blonde woman in nothing but her panties and bra watching television. He is about to rap on the glass when a little boy comes into the room pulling a wooden train behind him and yelling his head off. The train is on its side. Without taking her eyes off the screen the woman puts the train on its wheels.

Lewis heads back to Combat Alley. There are still a couple of women on the street, but he doesn't know how to go up to them, or what they will expect him to say. And there are all these other people walking by. Finally he goes into the Drop Zone, a bar with a picture of a paratrooper painted on the window.

Most of the prostitutes in town are reasonable women. Their reasons are their own and they aren't charitable, but they aren't crazy either. Mainly they want to do something easier than what they were doing before, so they try this for a while until they find out how hard it is. Then they go back to waitressing, or their husbands, or the bottling plant. Sometimes they get caught in the life, though, and there's a time right after they know they're caught when some of them do go crazy.

Lewis picks out the crazy one in a bar filled with reasonable girls. She is older than the others and not the best looking, and the trouble she's in shows plainly. She hasn't brushed her hair all day and her dark eyes are ringed with circles like bruises. She is sitting by herself at the bar. The ice has melted in her ginger ale, which she pushes back and forth and never picks up. In a few years she will be talking to herself.

Lewis doesn't even look at any of the others. He is going to do something bad and she is the one to do it with. He goes straight to her and sits on the stool next to her. He avoids the bartender's gaze because he is not sure that he has enough money to pay for liquor and women both. 'Liquor and women' are the words that come to his mind. He is really going to do it. Tonight, with her. He swivels on his stool and says, You come from around here?

She can't believe her ears. She stares at him and he looks down. His face is in motion, jerking and creasing and knotting. You want something? she says.

Lewis wants to look at her, but can't.

Well? she says.

No, he says. I mean, maybe I do.

Well do you or don't you?

I don't know, he says. I never paid for it before.

Then go beat your meat, she says, and turns her shoulder to him.

The calamine lotion has dried pink on Lewis's hand and is starting to flake off. He picks at it with a fingernail. How much? he says.

She turns on him. Her eyes are raking his face. What are you trying to pull? she says. You trying to get me jugged or something?

All I said—

I know what you said. Jesus Christ. She dips into her shiny white bag and pulls out a cigarette. She glances around, lights it, and blows smoke toward the ceiling. Drop dead, she says.

Lewis doesn't know what he's done wrong, but he will have a woman and this is the woman he will have. Hey, he says, you ever been to Kentucky?

Kentucky, she says to herself. She grabs her purse and gets off the stool and walks out of the bar. Lewis follows her. When they get outside she whips around on him. Damn you, she says. What do you want?

I want to go with you.

She looks up and down the street. People move past them and no one pays them any attention. You don't give a shit, she says. I get jugged, it's all the same to you.

You asked me did I want anything, Lewis says. What are you all mad about?

She says, I had enough of you, and turns away down the sidewalk. Lewis follows her. After a while he catches up and they walk side by side. I'll show you a time, Lewis says. That's a guarantee.

She doesn't answer.

Right down the street from where Lewis threw the bottle of calamine there is a motel with separate little bungalows. She stops in front of the last one. Ten dollars, she says.

How about eight?

Damn you, she says.

It's all I got.

She looks at him for a while, then goes up the steps and unlocks the door and backs into the bungalow. Let's have it, she says, and holds out her hand.

But there are only six ones in Lewis's wallet. He had forgotten the popcorn and the coke and the Sugar Daddy. He hands the money to her. That's six, he says. I'll give you the rest on payday.

Drop dead, she says, and starts to close the door.

Lewis says, Hey! He gets his foot in and pushes with his shoulder. Hey, he says, give me my money back. She pushes back from the other side. Finally he hits the door with his whole weight and it gives. She backs away from him. He goes after her. Give me my money back, he says. Then he stops. Put that knife away, he says. I just want my six dollars is all.

She doesn't move. She holds the knife like a man, not raised by her ear but in front of her chest, wrist up. Her breathing is hoarse but steady, unhurried.

All right, Lewis says. Look here. You keep the six dollars and I'll bring the rest tomorrow. I'll meet you tomorrow, same place. Okay?

I don't care what you do, she says. Just get.

Tomorrow, he says. He backs out. When he's on the steps the door bangs shut and he hears the lock snap.

The next day Lewis steals the first wallet. It is not under a pillow as the owner later claims but lying on his bunk in plain sight. Lewis sees it on his way to lunch and doubles back when everyone is in the mess hall. It holds two one-dollar bills and some change. Lewis takes the money and tosses the wallet under the barracks steps. He is mad the whole time, mad at the corporal for leaving it out like that and for being so stuck on himself and never saying hello, mad at how little money there is, mad at not having any money of his own.

He doesn't think of borrowing a few dollars from his friends. He has never borrowed anything from anyone. To Lewis there is no difference between borrowing and begging. He even hates to ask questions.

Later, when he hears that the corporal is telling everyone he had a hundred dollars stolen, Lewis gets even madder. That evening at dinner he stares at the corporal openly but the corporal eats without looking up. On his way out of the mess hall, Lewis deliberately bumps against the corporal's chair, hard. He stops at the door and looks back. The man is eating icecream like nothing happened. It burns Lewis up.

It also burns him up the way everybody just automatically figures the wallet was stolen by an outsider. They are so high and mighty they think nobody in the company could ever do a thing like that. *I'm no outsider,* he thinks. He gets so worked up he can't sleep that night.

The next day Lewis is assigned to a detail at the post laundry, humping heavy bags across the washroom. The air swirls with acrid steam. Figures appear and vanish in the mist, never speaking. It is useless to try and talk over the whining and thumping of the big machines, but now and then someone shouts an order at someone else. Lewis takes one short break in the morning but gets so far behind that he never takes another. All day he thinks about the woman in Fayetteville, how she looks, how bad she is. Doing it for money and carrying a knife. He is sure that nobody he knows has ever had a woman pull a knife on him. He thinks of different people and pictures to himself how they would act if they found out. It makes him smile.

When he gets back to the company he takes a shower and lies down for a while to catch his breath. Everyone else is getting ready for dinner, joking around, snapping each other with towels. Lewis watches them. His eyes sting from the fumes he's been working in and he closes them for a moment, just for a rest, and when he opens them again the barracks is dark and filled with sleeping men.

Lewis sits up. He hasn't eaten since breakfast and feels hollow all through. Even his legs seem empty. He remembers the woman in town, but it's too late now and anyway he doesn't have the money to pay her with. He imagines her sitting at the bar, sliding her glass back and forth.

It starts to rain. The drops rattle on the tin roof. A flash of lightning flickers on the walls and the thunder follows a while after, a rumble like shingle turning in a wave, more a feeling than a sound. Lewis gets up and walks between the bunks until he finds a pair of fatigue pants lying on a footlocker. He picks them up and goes to the latrine and takes the money out of the wallet. A five-dollar bill. Then he stuffs the wallet and pants into the trash can and goes back to bed.

He thinks about the woman again. At first he was sorry that he didn't meet her when he said he would, but now he's glad. It will teach her something. She probably thought she had him and it's best she know right off the kind of man she is dealing with. The kind that will come around when he gets good and ready. If she says anything he will just give a little smile and say, Honey, that's how it is with me. You can take it or leave it.

He wonders what she thinks happened. Maybe she thinks she scared him off with that knife. *That's a good one,* he thinks, him afraid of some old knife like you'd buy at a church sale. Kitchen knife. He remembers it pointed at him with the dim light moving up and down the blade, worn and wavy-edged from too many sharpenings, and it's true that he feels no fear. None at all.

As he dresses in the morning Lewis looks over at the man he stole from. The man is sitting on his bunk and staring at the floor.

The whole company knows about it by breakfast. And this time they know it's not an outsider but one of their own. Lewis can tell. They eat quietly instead of yelling and stealing food from one another, and nobody really looks at anybody else. Except Lewis. He looks at everyone.

That night the first sergeant comes through and makes a speech. It's a lot of crap about how an infantry company is like a family blah blah blah. Lewis makes himself deaf and leaves for town as soon as it's over.

In town Lewis looks for the woman in the same bar. But she isn't there. He tries all the bars. Finally he walks down to the bungalow. The windows are dark. He listens at the door and hears nothing. A TV on a window sill across the street makes laughing noises. He sits and waits.

He waits for two hours and more and then he sees her coming down the sidewalk with the tiniest little man he has ever seen. You could almost say he's a midget. She's walking fast, looking at the ground just in front of her, and when they get close he can hear her muttering and him huffing to keep up. Lewis comes down the steps to meet them. Hey, says the little man, what the heck's going on?

Beat it, Lewis says.

Okay, okay, the little man says, and heads back up the street.

The woman watches him go. She turns to Lewis. Who do you think you are? she says.

Lewis says, I brought you the rest of the money.

She moves up close. I remember you, she says. You get out of my way. Get!

Here's the money, Lewis says, and holds it out to her.

She takes it, looks at it, drops it on the ground and walks past him up the steps. Four dollars, she says. You think I'd go for four dollars? Get yourself a nigger.

Lewis picks it up. I already gave you six, he says. This here is the rest.

You got a receipt? she says, and sticks her key in the lock.

Lewis grabs her arm and squeezes it. She tries to jerk away but he holds on and closes her hand around the money. That makes ten, he says. He lets go of her arm.

She gives him a look and opens the door. He follows her inside. She turns on the overhead light, kicks her shoes across the room, and goes into the bathroom. He can hear her banging around in there as he sits on the bed and takes off his shoes and socks. Then he stands and strips to his underwear.

She comes out naked. She is heavy in the ankles and legs and walks flat-footed, but her breasts are small, girlish. She drops her eyes as she walks toward him and he smiles.

All right, she says, let's have a look. She yanks his underpants to his knees and grabs him between her thumb and forefinger and squints down while she rolls him back and forth. Looks okay, she says, and drops him. You won't do any harm with that little shooter. Come on. She goes to the bed and sits down. Come on, she says again, I got other fish to fry.

Lewis can't move.

Okay, softy, she says, and goes to her knees in front of Lewis.

No, Lewis says.

She ignores him.

No! Lewis says, and pushes her head back.

Christ, she says. Just my luck. A homo.

Lewis hits her. She sprawls back on the floor. They look at each other. She is breathing hard and so is Lewis, who stands with his fists in front of him like a boxer. She touches her forehead where he hit her. There's a white spot. Okay, she says. She gives a little smile and reaches her hand out.

Lewis pulls her up. She leans into him and runs her hands up and down his neck and back and legs, dragging her fingernails. She stands on his feet and pushes her hips against his. Then she rises up on her toes, Lewis nearly crying out from the pain of her weight, and she presses her teeth against his teeth and licks his mouth with her tongue. She kisses his face and whenever he goes to kiss her back she moves her mouth somewhere else, down his throat, his chest, his hips. She puts her arms around his knees and takes him in her mouth and a sound comes out of Lewis like he has never heard another human make. He puts his hands along her cheeks and closes his eyes.

When he is close to finishing he tries to think about something else. He thinks about close-order drill. They are marching in review, the whole company on parade. The files flick past like rows of corn. He looks for a familiar face but finds none. Then they are gone. He opens his eyes and pulls back.

The regular way, he says. In bed.

He wants to hold her. He wants to lie quiet with her a moment, but she straddles him. She lowers herself on to him and digs her fingers into his flanks so that he rises up into her. He tries to move his own way, but she governs him. She puts her mouth on his and bites him. His foot cramps.

Then she rolls over and wraps her legs around his back and slides her finger up inside him. He shouts and bucks to be free. She laughs and tightens around him. She holds her mouth against his ear and presses with her teeth and murmurs things. Lewis can't make out what she's saying. Then she arches and stiffens under him, holding him so tightly he can't move. Her eyes are open halfway. Only the whites show. Lewis feels himself lift and dip as she breathes. She is asleep.

She sleeps for hours. Nothing disturbs her, not the argument in the street, not Lewis stroking her hair and saying things to her. Then he falls asleep, too.

When he wakes, her eyes are open. She is watching him. Hey there, he says. He reaches out and touches her cheek. He says the same words he was saying before he dozed off. I love you, he says.

She pushes his hand away. You garbage, she says. She slides off

163

the bed and finds her purse where she dropped it on the floor and takes out the knife. He gets up on the other side and stands there with the bed between them.

You talk to me like that, she says. You come here and mock me. You're garbage. I won't be mocked by you, not by you. You're just the same as me.

Let me stay, he says.

Get out of here, she says. Get! Get! Get!

Lewis dresses. I'll come back later, he says. He goes to the door and she follows him part way. I'll be back, he says. I'll bring you money.

She waves the knife. You'll get this, she says.

It's three o'clock in the morning. The last bus to camp left hours ago so Lewis has to make the trip on foot. The only cars on the road are filled with drunks. They yell things as they drive by. Once a bottle goes whistling past him and breaks on the shoulder. Lewis keeps going, feet sliding in his big square shoes. He doesn't even turn his head.

Just outside the base there is a tunnel with a narrow walkway along the side. The beams from the headlights of the cars glance off the white tiles and fill the tunnel with light. Lewis steadies himself on the handrail as he walks. One of the drivers notices him and leans on his horn and then the other drivers honk too, all together. The blare of the horns builds up between the tiles. It goes on in Lewis's head long after he leaves the tunnel.

He gets back to camp just after dawn and lies on his bunk, waiting for reveille. The man in the next bunk whistles as he breathes. Lewis closes his eyes, but he doesn't sleep.

The bugle blows and the men sit up and fumble their boots on, cigarettes dangling, eyes narrowed against the smoke. Lewis thinks that he was wrong about them, that they are an okay bunch of fellows, not really conceited, just careful who they make friends with. He can understand that. You never know with people. He thinks about what good friends they are to each other and how they held the line in Vietnam against all those slopes. He wishes he had got to know them better. He wishes he was not this way.

For the next three days he tries to find a wallet to steal. At night, when he is sure that everyone is asleep, he prowls between the bunks and pats the clothes left on footlockers. He skips meals and checks under pillows and mattresses. As the days pass and he finds nothing he gets reckless. Once, during breakfast, he tries to break into a wall locker where he saw a man put his camera, one of those expensive kind you look through the top of, worth something as pawn, but the lock won't give and the metal door booms like thunder every time Lewis hits it with his entrenching tool. He feels dumb but he keeps at it until he can see there's no point.

During dinner on the fourth night he searches through the barracks next to his. There is nothing. On his way back out he passes the latrine and hears the hiss of a shower. He stops at the door. In one of the stalls he sees a red back through the steam, and just outside a uniform hanging on a nail. The bulge of the wallet is clear.

Lewis comes in along the wall. The man in the shower is making odd noises and it takes Lewis a moment to realize that he is crying. Lewis slips the pants off the hook and takes out the wallet. He is just putting the pants back when the man in the shower turns around. His pink face floats in the mist. Hey! he says. Lewis hits him and the man goes down without a sound.

Outside the barracks Lewis falls in with the first group of men leaving the mess hall. He heads towards the parade ground and when he gets there he climbs to the top bench in the reviewing stands. He looks over in the direction of the company. No one has followed him, but men are drifting into small groups. They know that something has happened.

Lewis rubs his hand. It is still a little swollen and now it hurts like crazy from the punch he threw. He felt strange doing that, surprised and helpless and sad, like a bystander. What else will he watch himself do? He opens and closes his fingers.

There is a breeze. Halyards spank against the metal flagpole as the rope swings out and back.

He sees right away from the military ID that the wallet is Hubbard's. Lewis knows that he and Hubbard had a feeling once between them. He doesn't feel it now and can't recall it exactly, but he wishes he had not hit him. If there'd been any choice he'd have chosen not to. He pockets the money, three fives and some change, and looks through the pictures. Hubbard and a man who looks just like him standing in waders with four dead fish on the ground in front of them, one big one and three just legal. Hubbard in a mortarboard hat with a tassel hanging down. A car. Another car. A girl who looks exactly like Hubbard if Hubbard had a pony tail. An old man on a tractor. A white house. A piece of yellow paper folded up.

Lewis unfolds the paper and reads, 'Dear Son'. He looks away, then looks back.

Dear Son,

I have some very bad news. I don't think there is any way to tell you but just to write what happened. It was three days ago, on the Fourth. Norm and Bobby went down to Monroe to watch the drag races there. They were double-dating with Ginnie and Karen Schwartz. From what I understand they and some of the other kids did a little 'celebrating' at the track. Tom saw them and said they were not really drunk but you know how your brother is. Let's just say he isn't very observant. Norm was driving when they left for home.

They don't know for sure what happened but just the other side of Monroe the car went into a skid and hit a truck parked off the road. Norm and Bobby and Ginny were killed right away. Karen died in the hospital that night. She was unconscious the whole time.

Dear, I know I should have called you, but I was afraid I wouldn't be able to talk. Tom and I and Julie and even your father have been crying like babies ever since it happened. The whole town has. Everyone you see is just miserable. It is the worst thing to ever happen here.

This is about all I can write. Call collect when you feel up to it. Dear, don't ever forget that each and every person on this earth is a beautiful gift of God. Remember that always and you will never go wrong. Your loving Mother.

Lewis sits in the stands and shakes his head because Hubbard's mother is so wrong. She doesn't know anything. He would like to know what she thinks when she hears what just happened to Hubbard. Hubbard probably won't tell her. But if she knew, and if she knew about the woman in town and all the things Lewis has done, then she would know something real and give different advice.

He throws the wallet into the shadows under the stands. He starts to drop the letter after it but it stays between his fingers and finally he folds it up again and puts it in his pocket. Then he walks out to the road and hitches a ride to town.

She is not in any of the bars. Lewis goes to the bungalow and shakes the door. You in there? he says. The window is dark and he hears nothing, but he feels her on the other side. Open up, he says. He slams his shoulder against the door and the lock gives and he stumbles inside. From the light coming in behind him he can see the dark shapes of her things on the floor. He waits, but nothing moves. He is alone.

Lewis closes the door and without turning on the light walks over to the bed. He sits down. Breathing the bad air in here makes him light-headed. His arms ache from stacking oil drums all day in the motor pool. He's tired. After a time he takes off his shoes and stretches out on the twisted sheets. He knows that he has to keep his eyes open, that he has to be awake when she comes back. Then he knows that he won't be, and that it doesn't matter anyway.

It doesn't matter, he thinks. He starts to drift. The darkness he passes into is not sleep, but something else. *No,* he thinks. He pulls free of it and sits up. He thinks, *I have got to get out of here.*

Lewis can't tie his shoes, his hands are shaking so. With the laces dragging he walks outside and up the sidewalk towards town. He can hear everything, the trucks gearing down on the access road, the buzz of the streetlights, and from somewhere far away a steady, cold, tinkling noise like someone all alone breaking every plate in the house just to hear the sound. Lewis stops and closes his eyes. Dogs bark up and down the street, and as he listens he hears more and more of them. They're pitching in from every side of town. He wonders what they're so mad about, and decides that they're not really mad at all but just putting it on. It's something to do when they're all tied up. He lifts his face to the stars and howls.

The next morning Lewis wakes up feeling like a million dollars. He showers and shaves and puts on a fresh uniform with sharp creases. On his way to the mess hall he stands for a moment by the edge of the parade ground. They've got a bunch of recruits out there crawling on their bellies and lobbing dummy hand grenades at truck tyres. Sergeants are walking around screaming at them. Lewis grins.

At breakfast he eats two bowls of oatmeal and half a bowl of strawberry jam. He whistles on his way back to the barracks. Then the first sergeant calls a special formation and everything goes wrong.

Lewis falls in with the rest of the company. He knows what it's about. *Shoot,* he thinks. It doesn't seem fair. He's all ready to make a new start and he wishes that everybody else could do the same. Just wipe the slate clean and begin all over again. There's no point to it, this anger and fuss, the first sergeant walking up and down saying it gives him nerves to know there's a barracks thief in his company. Lewis wishes he could tell him not to worry, that it's all history now.

Then Hubbard goes to the front of the formation and Lewis sees the metal cast on his nose. *Oh Lord,* he thinks, *I didn't do that.* He stares at the cast. There was a man in Lawton who used to wear one just like it because his nose was gone, cut off in a fight when he was young. Underneath was nothing but two holes.

Hubbard follows the first sergeant up and down the ranks. Lewis meets his eyes for a moment and then looks at the cast again. *That hurts,* he thinks. He will make it up to Hubbard. He will be Hubbard's friend, the best friend Hubbard ever had. They'll go bowling together and downtown to the pictures. The next long weekend they'll hitch a ride to Nag's Head and rustle up some of those girls down there. At night they will go down on the beach and have a time. Light a fire and get drunk and laugh. And when they get shipped overseas they will stick together. They'll take care of each other and bring each other back, and afterwards, when they get out of the army, they will be friends for ever.

The first sergeant is arguing with someone. Then Lewis sees that the men around him are emptying their pockets into their helmets and unblousing their boots. He does the same and straightens up. Hubbard and the first sergeant are in front of him again and Hubbard bends over the helmet and takes out the letter that Lewis could not let go of, that he's forgotten does not belong to him.

Where's my wallet? Hubbard says.

Lewis looks down.

The first sergeant says, Where is this boy's wallet?

Under the stands, Lewis says. While they wait Lewis looks at the ground. He sees the shadows of the men behind him, sees from the shadows that they are watching him. The first sergeant is saying something.

Look at him, the first sergeant says again. He puts his hand under Lewis's chin and forces it up until Lewis is face to face with Hubbard. Lewis sees that Hubbard isn't really mad after all. It is worse than that. Hubbard is looking at him as if he is something pitiful. Then Lewis knows that it will never be as it could have been with the two of them, nor with anyone else. Nothing will ever be the way it could have been. Whatever happens from now on, it will always be less.

Lewis knows this, but not as a thought. He knows it as a distracted, restless feeling like the feeling you have forgotten something when you are too far from home to go back for it.

The sun is hot on the back of his neck. A drop of sweat slides down between his shoulder blades, then another. They make him shiver. He stares over Hubbard's head, waiting for the next drop. Out on the parade ground the flag whips in a gust, but it makes no noise. Then it droops again. The metal cast glitters. Everything is still.

The morning after Hubbard got his nose broken the first sergeant called a special formation. He walked up and down in front of us until the silence became oppressive, and then he kept doing it. There were two spots of colour like rouge on his cheeks. The line of his scar was bright red. I couldn't look at him. Instead I kept my eyes on the man in front of me, on the back of his neck, which was pocked with tiny craters. Finally the first sergeant began to talk in a voice that was almost a whisper. It was that soft, but I could hear each word as if he were speaking just to me.

He said that a barracks thief was the lowest thing there was. A barracks thief had turned his back on his own kind. He went on like that.

Then the first sergeant called Hubbard in front of the formation. With the metal cast and the tape across his cheeks, Hubbard's face looked like a mask. The first sergeant said something to him, and the two of them began to walk up and down the ranks, staring every man full in the face. I tasted something sour at the root of my tongue. I wondered how I should look. I wanted to glance around and see the faces of the other men but I was afraid to move my head. I decided to look offended. But not too offended. I didn't want them to think that this was anything important to me.

I composed my face and waited. It seemed to me that I was weaving on my feet, in tiny circles, and I made myself go rigid. All around me I felt the stillness of the other men.

Hubbard walked by first. He barely turned his head, but the first sergeant looked at me. His eyes were dark and thoughtful. Then he moved on, and I slowly let out the breath I'd been holding in. A jet moved across the sky in perfect silence, contrails billowing like plumes. The man next to me sighed deeply.

After they had inspected the company the first sergeant ordered us to take off our helmets and put them between our feet, open end up. Then he told us to empty our pockets into our helmets and leave the pockets hanging out. My squad leader, an old corporal with a purple nose, said 'Bullshit!' and put his helmet back on.

He and the first sergeant looked at each other. 'Do it,' the first sergeant said.

The corporal shook his head. 'You don't have the right.'

The first sergeant said, 'Do it. Now.'

'I never saw this before in my whole life,' the corporal said, but he took his helmet off and emptied his pockets into it.

'Unblouse your pants,' the first sergeant said.

We took our pantlegs out of our boots and let them hang loose. Here and there I heard metal hitting the ground, knives I suppose.

The first sergeant watched us. He had got his wounds during an all-night battle near Dak To in which his company had almost been overrun. I think of that and then I think of what he saw when he looked at us, bareheaded, our pockets hanging down like little white flags, open helmets at our feet. A company of beggars. Nothing worth dying for. He was clearly as disappointed as a man can be.

He looked us over. Then he nodded at Hubbard and they started up the ranks again. A work detail from another company crossed the street to our left, singing the cadence, spades and rakes at shoulder arms. As they marched by they fell silent, as if they were passing a funeral. They must have guessed what was happening.

Hubbard looked into each helmet as they walked up the ranks. I had a muscle jumping in my cheek. And then it ended. Hubbard stopped in front of Lewis and bent down and took a piece of paper from his helmet. He unfolded it and looked it over. Then he said, 'Where's my wallet?'

Lewis did not answer. He was standing two ranks ahead of me and I could see from the angle of his neck that he was staring at Hubbard's boots.

'Where is this boy's wallet?' the first sergeant said.

'The parade ground,' Lewis said. 'Under the stands.'

The first sergeant sent a man for the wallet. Nobody spoke or moved except Hubbard, who folded the paper again and put it in his pocket. All my veins opened up. I felt the rush of blood behind my eyes. I was innocent.

When the runner came back with the wallet Hubbard looked through it and put it away.

'You stole from this boy,' the first sergeant said. 'You look at him.'

Lewis did not move.

'Look at him,' the first sergeant said again. He pushed Lewis's chin up until Lewis was face to face with Hubbard. They stood that way for a time. Then from behind, I could see Lewis's fatigue jacket begin to ripple. He was shaking convulsively. Everyone watched him, those in the front rank half-turned around, those behind leaning out and craning their necks. Lewis gave a soft cry and covered his face with his hands. The sound kept coming through his fingers and he bent over suddenly as if he'd been punched in the belly.

The man behind me said, 'Jesus Christ!'

Lewis staggered a little, still bent over, his feet doing a jig to stay under him. He crossed his arms over his chest and howled, leaning down until his head almost touched his knees. The howl ended and he straightened up, his arms still crossed. I could hear him wheezing.

Then he dropped his arms to his sides and arranged his feet and tried to come to attention again. He raised his head until he was looking at Hubbard, who still stood in front of him. Lewis began to make little whimpering noises. He took a step forward and a step back and then he shrieked in Hubbard's face, a haunted-house laugh that went on and on. Finally the first sergeant slapped him across the face—not hard, just a flick of the hand. Lewis went to his knees. He bent over until his forehead was on the ground. He flopped on to his side and drew his knees up almost to his chin and hugged them and rolled back and forth.

The first sergeant said, 'Dismissed!'

Nobody moved.

'Dismissed!' he said again, and this time we broke ranks and drifted away, throwing looks back to where Hubbard and the first sergeant stood over Lewis, who hugged his knees and hooted up at them from the packed red earth.

For the rest of that day we did target duty at the rifle range, raising and lowering man-sized silhouettes while a battalion of recruits blazed away. The bullets zipped and whined over the pits where we huddled. By late afternoon it was clear that the targets had won. We boarded the trucks and drove back to the company in silence, swaying together over the bumps, thinking our own thoughts. For the men who'd been in Vietnam the whole thing must have been a little close to home, and it was a discouraging business for those of us who hadn't. It was discouraging for me, anyway, to find I had no taste for the sound of bullets passing over my head. And it gave me pause to see what bad shots those recruits were. After all, they belonged to the same army I belonged to.

Hubbard ate dinner by himself that night at a table in the rear of the mess hall. Lewis never showed up at all. The rest of us talked about him. We decided that there was no excuse for what he'd done. If the clerk had busted him at poker, or if someone in his family was sick, if he'd been in true need he could have borrowed the money or gone to the company commander. There was a special kitty for things like that. When the mess sergeant's wife disappeared he'd borrowed over a hundred dollars to go home and look for her. The supply sergeant told us this. According to him, the mess sergeant never paid the money back, probably because he hadn't found his wife. Anyway, Lewis wouldn't have died from being broke, not with free clothes, a roof over his head, and three squares a day.

'I don't care what happened,' someone said, 'you don't turn on your friends.'

'Amen,' said the man across from me. Almost everyone had something to say that showed how puzzled and angry he was. I kept quiet, but I took what Lewis had done as a personal betrayal. I had myself thoroughly worked up about it.

Not everyone joined in. Several men kept to themselves and ate with their eyes on their food. When they looked up they made a point of not seeing the rest of us, and soon looked down again. They finished their meals and left early. The first sergeant was one of these. As he walked past us a man at my table shouted 'Blanket party!' and we all laughed.

'I didn't hear that,' the first sergeant said. Maybe he was telling us not to do it, or maybe he was telling us to go ahead. What he said made no difference, because we could all see that he didn't care what happened any more. He was already in retirement. The power he let go passed into us and it was more than we could handle. That night we were loopy on it.

I went looking for Hubbard. A man in his platoon had seen him walking towards the parade ground, and I found him there, sitting in the stands. He nodded when he saw me, but he did not make me welcome. I sat down beside him. It was dusk. A light breeze blew into our faces. I smelled rain in it.

'This is where he went through my wallet,' Hubbard said. 'It was down there.' He pointed into the shadows below. 'What I can't figure out is why he kept the letter. If he hadn't kept the letter he wouldn't have got caught. It doesn't make any sense.'

'Well,' I said, 'Lewis isn't that smart.'

'I've been trying to picture it,' Hubbard said. 'Did you ever play "Picture It" when you were a kid?'

I shook my head.

'It was a game this teacher of ours used to make us play. We would close our eyes and picture some incident in history, like Washington crossing the Delaware, and describe what we were seeing to the whole class. The point was to see everything as if you were actually there, as if you were one of the people.'

We sat there. Hubbard unbuttoned his fatigue jacket.

'I don't know,' Hubbard said. 'I just can't see Lewis doing it. He's not the type of person that would do it.'

173

'He did it,' I said.

'I know,' Hubbard said. 'I'm saying I can't *see* him do it, that's all. Can you?'

'I'm no good at games. The point is, he stole your wallet and busted your nose.'

Hubbard nodded.

'Listen,' I said. 'There's a blanket party tonight.'

'A blanket party?' He looked at me.

For a moment I thought Hubbard must be kidding. Everyone knew what a blanket party was. When you had a shirker or a guy who wouldn't take showers you got together and threw a blanket over his head and beat the bejesus out of him. I had never actually been in on one but I'd heard so much about them that I knew it was only a matter of time. Not every blanket party was the same. Some were rougher than others. I'd heard of people getting beat up for really stupid reasons, like playing classical music on their radios. But this time it was a different situation. We had a barracks thief.

I explained all this to Hubbard.

'Count me out,' he said.

'You don't want to come?'

Hubbard shook his head. A dull point of light moved back and forth across the metal cast on his nose.

'Why not?'

'It's not my style,' he said. 'I didn't think it was yours, either.'

'Look,' I said. 'Lewis is supposed to be your friend. So what does he do? He steals from you and punches you out and then laughs in your face. Right in front of everyone. Don't you care?'

'I guess I don't.'

'Well, I do.'

Hubbard didn't answer.

'Jesus,' I said. 'We were supposed to be friends.' I stood up. 'Do you know what I think?'

'I don't care what you think,' Hubbard said. 'You just think what everyone else thinks. Beat it, okay? Leave me alone.'

I went back to the company and lay on my bunk until lights out. The wind picked up even more. Then it began to rain, driving hard against the windows. The walls creaked. When they played taps the notes faded and blared as the wind gusted. There should have been a real storm but it blew over in just a few minutes, leaving the air hot and wet and still.

After the barracks went dark we got up and made our way to the latrine, one by one. For all the tough talk I'd heard at dinner, in the end there were no more than eight or nine of us standing around in T-shirts and shorts. Nobody spoke. We were waiting for something to happen. One man had brought a flashlight. While we waited he goofed around with it, making rabbit silhouettes with his fingers, twirling it like a baton, sticking it in his mouth so that his cheeks turned red, and shining it in our eyes. In its light we all looked the same, like skulls. A man with a cigarette hanging out of his mouth boxed with his own shadow, which went all the way up the wall on to the ceiling so that it seemed to loom over him. He snaked his head from side to side and bounced from one foot to the other as he jabbed upwards. Two other men joined him. Their dog tags jingled and I suddenly thought of home, of my mother's white Persian cat, belled for the sake of birds, jumping on to my bed in the morning with the same sound.

The man with the flashlight stuck it between his legs and did a bump and grind. Then he made a circle on the wall and moved his finger in and out of it. Someone made panting noises and said, 'Hurt me! Hurt me!' A tall fellow told a dirty joke but nobody laughed. Then someone else told a joke, even dirtier. No one laughed at his, either, but he didn't care. He told another joke and then we started talking about various tortures. Someone said that in China there was a bamboo tree that grew a foot a day, and when the Chinese wanted to get something out of a person or just get even with him, they would tie him to a chair with a hole in the bottom and let the tree grow right through his body and out the top of his head. Then they would leave him there as an example.

Somebody said, 'I wish we had us one of those trees.'

No one made a sound. The flashlight was off and I could see nothing but the red tips of cigarettes trembling in the dark.

'Let's go,' someone said.

We went up the stairs and down the aisle between the bunks. The men around us slept in silence. There was no sound but the slap of our bare feet on the floor. When we got to the end of the aisle the man

175

with the flashlight turned it on and played the beam over Lewis's bunk. He was sitting up, watching us. He had taken off his shirt. In the glare his skin was pale and smooth-looking. The beam went up to his face and he stared into it without blinking. I thought that he was looking right at me, though he couldn't have been, not with the flashlight shining in his eyes. His cheeks were wet. His face was in turmoil. It was a face I'd never really seen before, full of humiliation and fear, and I have never stopped seeing it since. It is the same face I saw on the Vietnamese we interrogated, whose homes we searched and sometimes burned. It is the face that has become my brother's face through all the troubles of his life.

Lewis's eyes seemed huge. Unlike an animal's eyes, they did not glitter or fill with light. His face was purely human.

He sat without moving. I thought that those eyes were on me. I was sure that he knew me. When the blanket went over his head I was too confused to do anything. I did not join in, but I did not try to stop it either. I didn't even leave, as one man did. I stayed where I was and watched them beat him.

Lewis went into the hospital the next morning. He had a broken rib and cuts on his face. There was an investigation. That is, the company commander walked through the barracks with the first sergeant and asked if anyone knew who'd given Lewis the beating. No one said anything, and that was the end of the investigation.

When Lewis got out of the hospital they sent him home with a dishonourable discharge. Nobody knew why he had done what he'd done, though of course there were rumours. None of them made sense to me. They all sounded too familiar—gambling debts, trouble with a woman, a sick relative too poor to pay doctor bills. The subject was discussed for a little while and then forgotten.

The first sergeant's retirement papers came through a month or so later. He had served twenty years but I doubt if he was even forty yet. I saw him the morning he left, loading up his car. He had on two-tone shoes from God knows where, a purple shirt with pockets on the sleeves, and a pair of shiny black pants that squeezed his thighs and were too short for him. I was in the orderly room at the time. The officer of the day stood beside me, looking out the window. 'There goes a true soldier,' he said. He blew into the cup of coffee he was holding. 'It is a sorry thing,' he went on, 'to see a true soldier go back on civvy street before his time.'

The desk clerk looked up at me and shook his head. None of us had much use for this particular officer, a second lieutenant who had just arrived in the company from jump school and went around talking like a character out of a war movie.

But the lieutenant meant what he said, and I thought he was right.

The first sergeant wiped his shoes with a handkerchief. He looked up and down the street, and though he must have seen us at the window he gave no sign. Then he got into his car and drove away.

All this happened years ago, in 1967.

My father worked at Convair in San Diego, went East for a while to Sikorsky, and finally came back to San Diego with a woman he had met during some kind of meditation and nutrition seminar at a summer camp for adults. They had a baby girl a few weeks after my own daughter was born. Now the two of them run a restaurant in La Jolla.

Keith came home while I was in Vietnam. He lived with my mother off and on for twelve years, and when she died he took a room in the apartment building where he works as a security guard. The manager gave him a break on the rent. It's not a bad job. All the tenants know his name. They chat with him in the lobby when they come in late from parties, and they remember him generously at Christmas. I saw him dressed up in his uniform once, downtown, where there was no need for him to have it on.

Hubbard and I got our orders for Vietnam at the same time. We had a week's leave, after which we were to report to Oakland for processing. Hubbard didn't show up. Later I heard that he had crossed over to Canada. I never saw him again.

I never saw Lewis again, either, and of course I didn't expect to. In those days I believed what they'd told us about a dishonourable discharge—that it would be the end of you. When I thought of a dishonourable discharge I thought of a man in clothes too big for him standing outside bus terminals and sleeping in cafeterias, face down on the table.

Now I know better. People get over things worse than that. And Lewis was too testy to be able to take anyone's word for it that he was finished. I imagine he came out of it all right, one way or the other. Sometimes, when I close my eyes, his face floats up to mine like the face in a pool when you bend to drink. Once I pictured him sitting on the steps of a duplex. A black dog lay next to him, head between its paws. The lawn on his side was bald and weedy and cluttered with toys. On the other side of the duplex the lawn was green, well-kept. A sprinkler whirled rapidly, sending out curved spokes of water. Lewis was looking at the rainbow that hung in the mist above the sprinkler. His fingers moved over the dog's smooth head and down its neck, barely touching the fur.

I hope that Lewis did all right. Still, he must remember more often than he'd like to that he was thrown out of the army for being a thief. It must seem unbelievable that this happened to him, unbelievable and unfair. He didn't set out to become a thief. And Hubbard didn't set out to become a deserter. He may have had good reasons for deserting, perhaps he even had principles that left him no choice. Then again, maybe he was just too discouraged to do anything else; discouraged and unhappy and afraid. Whatever the cause of his desertion, it couldn't have been what he wanted.

I didn't set out to be what I am, either. I'm a conscientious man, a responsible man, maybe even what you'd call a good man—I hope so. But I'm also a careful man, addicted to comfort, with an eye for the safe course. My neighbours appreciate me because they know I will never give my lawn over to the cultivation of marijuana, or send my wife weeping to their doorsteps at three o'clock in the morning, or expect them to be my friends. I am content with my life most of the time. When I look ahead I see more of the same, and I'm grateful. I would never do what we did that day at the ammunition dump, threatening people with rifles, nearly getting ourselves blown to pieces for the hell of it.

But I have moments when I remember that day, and how it felt to be a reckless man with reckless friends. I think of Lewis before he was a thief and Hubbard before he was a deserter. And myself before I was a good neighbour. Three men with rifles. I think of a spark drifting up from that fire, glowing as the breeze pushes it toward the warehouses and the tall dry weeds, and the three crazy paratroopers inside the fence. They'd have heard the blast clear to Fort Bragg. They'd have seen the sky turn yellow and red and felt the earth shake. It would have been something.

ANGELA CARTER
SUGAR DADDY

I would say my father did not prepare me well for patriarchy; himself confronted, on his marriage with my mother, with a mother-in-law who was the living embodiment of peasant matriarchy, he had no choice but to capitulate, and did so. Further, I was the child of his mid-forties, when he was just the age to be knocked sideways by the arrival of a baby daughter. He was putty in my hands throughout my childhood and still claims to be so, although now I am middle-aged myself while he, not though you'd notice, is somewhat older than the present century.

I was born in 1940, the week that Dunkirk fell. I think neither of my parents was immune to the symbolism of this, of bringing a little girl-child into the world at a time when the Nazi invasion of England seemed imminent, into the midst of death and approaching dark. Perhaps I seemed particularly vulnerable and precious and that helps to explain the over-protectiveness they felt about me, later on. Be that as it may, no child, however inauspicious the circumstances, could have been made more welcome. I did not get a birthday card from him a couple of years ago; when I querulously rang him up about it, he said: 'I'd never forget the day you came ashore.' (The card came in the second post.) His turn of phrase went straight to my heart, an organ which has inherited much of his Highland sentimentality.

He is a Highland man, the perhaps atypical product of an underdeveloped, colonialized country in the last years of Queen Victoria, of oatcakes, tatties and the Church of Scotland, of four years' active service in World War One, of the hurly burly of Fleet Street in the twenties. His siblings, who never left the native village, were weird beyond belief. To that native village he competently removed himself ten years ago.

He has done, I realize, what every Sicilian in New York, what every Cypriot in Camden Town wants to do, to complete the immigrant's journey, to accomplish the perfect symmetry, from A to B and back again. Just his luck, when he returned, that all was as it had been before and he could, in a manner of speaking, take up his life where it left off when he moved south seventy years ago. He went south; and made a career; and married an Englishwoman; and lived in London; and fathered children, in an enormous parenthesis of which he retains only sunny memories. He has 'gone home', as immigrants do; he established, in his seventh decade, that 'home' has an existential significance for him which is not part of the story of his children's independent lives. My father lives now in his granite house filled with the souvenirs of a long and, I think, happy life. (Some of them bizarre; that framed certificate from an American tramp, naming my father a 'Knight of the Road', for example.)

He has a curious, quite unEnglish, ability to live life in, as it were, the *third person,* to see his life objectively, as a not unfortunate one, and to live up to that notion. Those granite townships on the edge of the steel-grey North Sea forge a flinty sense of self. Don't think, from all this, he isn't a volatile man. He laughs easily, cries easily, and to his example I attribute my conviction that tears, in a man, are a sign of inner strength.

He is still capable of surprising me. He recently prepared an electric bed for my boyfriend, which is the sort of thing a doting father in a Scots ballad might have done had the technology been available at the time. We knew he'd put us in separate rooms—my father is a Victorian, by birth—but not that he'd plug the metal base of Mark's bed into the electric-light fitment. Mark noticed how the bed throbbed when he put his hand on it and disconnected every plug in sight. We ate breakfast, next morning, as if nothing untoward had happened, and I should say, in the context of my father's house, it had not. He is an enthusiastic handyman, with a special fascination for electricity, whose work my mother once described as combining the theory of Heath Robinson with the practice of Mr Pooter.

All the same, the Freudian overtones are inescapable. However unconsciously, as if *that* were an excuse, he'd prepared a potentially lethal bed for his daughter's lover. But let me not dot the i's and cross the t's. His final act of low, emotional cunning (another Highland characteristic) is to have lived so long that everything is forgiven, even his habit of referring to the present incumbent by my first husband's name, enough to give anybody a temporary feeling.

He is a man of immense, nay, imposing physical presence, yet I tend to remember him in undignified circumstances.

One of my first memories is how I bust his nose. (I was, perhaps, three years old. Maybe four.) It was on a set of swings in a public park. He'd climbed up Pooterishly to adjust the chains from which the swings hung. I thought he was taking too long and set the swing on which I sat in motion. He wasn't badly hurt but there was a lot of blood. I was not punished for my part in this accident. They were a bit put out because I wanted to stay and play when they went home to wash off the blood.

They. That is, my father and my mother. Impossible for me to summon one up out of the past without the other.

Shortly after this, he nearly drowned me, or so my mother claimed. He took me for a walk one autumn afternoon and stopped by the pond in Wandsworth Common and I played a game of throwing leaves into the water until I forgot to let go of one. He was in after me in a flash, in spite of the peril to his gents' natty suiting (ever the dandy, my old man) and wheeled me dripping in my pushchair home to the terrible but short-lived recriminations of my mother. Short-lived because both guilt and remorse are emotions alien to my father. Therefore the just apportioning of blame is not one of his specialities, and though my mother tried it on from time to time, he always thought he could buy us off with treats and so he could and that is why my brother and I don't sulk, much. Whereas she—

She has been dead for more than a decade, now, and I've had ample time to appreciate my father's individual flavour, which is a fine and gamey one, but, as parents, they were far more than the sum of their individual parts. I'm not sure they understood their instinctive solidarity against us, because my mother often tried to make us take sides. Us. As their child, the product of their parenting, I cannot dissociate myself from my brother, although we did not share a childhood for he is twelve years older than I and was sent off, with his gas mask, his packed lunch and his name tag, as an evacuee, a little hostage to fortune, at about the time they must have realized another one was on the way.

I can only think of my parents as a peculiarly complex unit in which neither bulks larger than the other, although they were very different kinds of people and I often used to wonder how they got on, since they seemed to have so little in common, until I realized that was why they got on, that not having much in common means you've always got something interesting to talk about. And their children, far from being the raison d'être of their marriage, of their ongoing argument, of that endless, quietly murmuring conversation I used to hear, at night, softly, dreamily, the other side of the bedroom wall, were, in some sense, a sideshow. Source of pleasure, source of grief; not the glue that held them together. And neither of us more important than the other, either.

Not that I suspected this when I was growing up. My transition

182

from little girl to ravaged anorexic took them by surprise and I thought they wanted my blood. I didn't know what they wanted of me, nor did I know what I wanted for myself. In those years of ludicrously overprotected adolescence, I often had the feeling of being 'pawns in their game'...in *their* game, note...and perhaps I indeed served an instrumental function, at that time, rather than being loved for myself.

All this is so much water under the bridge. Yet those were the only years I can remember when my mother would try to invoke my father's wrath against me, threaten me with his fury for coming home late and so on. Though, as far as the 'and so on' was concerned, chance would have been a fine thing. My adolescent rebellion was considerably hampered by the fact that I could find nobody to rebel with. I now recall this period with intense embarrassment, because my parents' concern to protect me from predatory boys was only equalled by the enthusiasm with which the boys I did indeed occasionally meet protected themselves against me.

It was a difficult time, terminated, inevitably, by my early marriage as soon as I finally bumped into somebody who would go to Godard movies with me and on CND marches and even have sexual intercourse with me, although he insisted we should be engaged first. Neither of my parents were exactly overjoyed when I got married, although they grudgingly did all the necessary. My father was particularly pissed off because he'd marked me out for a career on Fleet Street. It took me twenty years more of living, and an involvement with the women's movement, to appreciate he was unusual in wanting this for his baby girl. Although he was a journalist himself, I don't think he was projecting his own ambitions on me, either, even if to be a child is to be, to some degree, the projective fantasy of its parents. No. I suspect that, if he ever had any projective fantasies about me, I sufficiently fulfilled them by being born. All he'd wanted for me was a steady, enjoyable job that, perhaps, guaranteed me sufficient income to insure I wouldn't too hastily marry some nitwit (a favourite word of his) who would displace him altogether from my affections. So, since from a child I'd been good with words, he apprenticed me to a suburban weekly newspaper when I was eighteen, intending me to make my traditional way up from there. From all this, given my natural perversity, it must be obvious why I was so hell-bent on getting married—not, and both my parents were utterly adamant about this, that getting married meant I'd give up my job.

In fact, it *did* mean that because soon my new husband moved away from London. 'I suppose you'll have to go with him,' said my mother doubtfully. Anxious to end my status as their child, there was no other option and so I changed direction although, as it turns out, I *am* a journalist, at least some of the time.

As far as projective fantasies go, sometimes it seems the old man is only concerned that I don't end up in the workhouse. Apart from that, anything goes. My brother and I remain, I think, his most constant source of pleasure—always, perhaps, a more positive joy to our father than to our mother, who, a more introspective person, got less pure entertainment value from us, partly, like all mothers, for reasons within her own not untroubled soul. As for my father, few souls are less troubled. He can be simply pleased with us, pleased that we exist, and, from the vantage point of his wondrously serene and hale old age, he contemplates our lives almost as if they were books he can dip into whenever he wants.

As for the books I write myself, my 'dirty books', he said the other day: 'I was a wee bitty shocked, at first, but I soon got used to it.' He introduces me in the third person: 'This young woman....' In his culture, it is, of course, a matter of principle to express pride in one's children. It occurs to me that this, too, is not a particularly English sentiment.

Himself, he is a rich source of anecdote. He has partitioned off a little room in the attic of his house, constructed the walls out of cardboard boxes, and there he lies, on a camp bed, listening to the World Service on a portable radio with his cap on. When he lived in London, he used to wear a trilby to bed but, a formal man, he exchanged it for a cap as soon as he moved. There are two perfectly good bedrooms in his house, with electric blankets and everything, as I well know, but these bedrooms always used to belong to his siblings, now deceased. He moves downstairs into one of these when the temperature in the attic drops too low for even his iron constitution, but he always shifts back up again, to his own place, when the ice melts. He has a ferocious enthusiasm for his own private space. My mother attributed this to a youth spent in the trenches, where no privacy was to be had. His war was the War to end Wars. He was too old for conscription in the one after that.

When he leaves this house for any length of time, he fixes up a whole lot of burglar traps, basins of water balanced on the tops of doors, tripwires, bags of flour suspended by strings, so that we worry in case he forgets where he's left what and ends up hoist with his own petard.

He has a special relationship with cats. He talks to them in a soft, chirrupping language they find irresistible. When we all lived in London and he worked on the night news desk of a press agency, he would come home on the last tube and walk, chirrupping, down the street, accompanied by an ever-increasing procession of cats, to whom he would say goodnight at the front door. On those rare occasions, in my late teens, when I'd managed to persuade a man to walk me home, the arrival of my father and his cats always caused consternation, not least because my father was immensely tall and strong.

He is the stuff of which sit-coms are made.

His everyday discourse, which is conducted in the stately prose of a thirties *Times* leader, is enlivened with a number of stock phrases of a slightly eccentric, period quality. For example. On a wild night: 'Pity the troops on a night like this.' On a cold day:

Cold, bleak, gloomy and glum,

Cold as the hairs on a polar bear's—

The last word of the couplet is supposed to be drowned by cries of outrage. My mother always turned up trumps on this one, interposing: 'Father!' on an ascending scale.

At random: 'Thank God for the navy, who guard our shores.'

On entering a room: 'Enter the fairy, singing and dancing.' Sometimes, in a particularly cheerful mood, he'll add to this formula: 'Enter the fairy, singing and dancing and waving her wooden leg.'

Infinitely endearing, infinitely irritating, irascible, comic, tough, sentimental, ribald old man, with his face of a borderline eagle and his bearing of a Scots guard, who, in my imagination as when I was a child, drips chocolates from his pockets as, a cat dancing in front of him, he strides down the road bowed down with gifts, crying: 'Here comes the Marquis of Carrabas!' The very words, 'my father', always make me smile.

But why, when he was so devilish handsome—oh, that photograph in battledress!—did he never marry until his middle

185

thirties? Until he saw my mother, playing tennis with a girlfriend on Clapham Common, and that was it. The die was cast. He gave her his card, proof of his honourable intentions. She took him home to meet her mother. Then he must have felt as though he were going over the top, again.

In 1967 or 1968, forty years on, my mother wrote me: 'He really loves me (I think).' At that time, she was a semi-invalid and he tended her, with more dash than efficiency, and yet remorselessly, cooking, washing up, washing her smalls, hoovering, as if that is just what he'd retired from work to do, up to his elbows in soapsuds after a lifetime of telephones and anxiety. He'd bring her dinner on a tray with always a slightly soiled traycloth. She thought the dirty cloth spoiled the entire gesture. And yet, and yet...was she, after all those years, still keeping him on the hook? For herself, she always applauded his ability to spirit taxis up as from the air at crowded railway stations and also the dexterous way he'd kick his own backside, a feat he continued to perform until he was well into his eighties.

Now, very little of all this has to do with the stern, fearful face of the Father in patriarchy, although the Calvinist north is virtually synonymous with that ideology. Indeed, a short-tempered man, his rages were phenomenal; but they were over in the lightning flash they resembled, and then we all had ice cream. And there was no fear. So that, now, for me, when fear steps in the door, then love and respect fly out the window.

I do not think my father has ever asked awkward questions about life, or the world, or anything much, except when he was a boy reporter and asking awkward questions was part of the job. He would regard himself as a law-and-order man, a law-abiding man, a man with a due sense of respect for authority. So far, so in tune with his background and his sense of decorum. And yet somewhere behind all this lurks a strangely free, anarchic spirit. Doorknobs fall from doors the minute he puts his hand on them. Things fall apart. There is a sense that anything might happen. He is a law-and-order man helplessly tuned in to misrule.

And somewhere in all this must lie an ambivalent attitude to the authority to which he claims to defer. Now, my father is not, I repeat, an introspective man. Nor one prone to intellectual analysis; he's always got by on his wits so never

186

felt the need of the latter. But he has his version of the famous story, about one of the Christmas truces during World War One, which was *his* war, although, when he talks about it, I do not recognize Vera Brittain's war, or Siegfried Sassoon's war, or anything but a nightmarish adventure, for, as I say, he feels no fear. The soldiers, bored with fighting, remembering happier times, put up white flags, moved slowly forward, showed photographs, exchanged gifts—a packet of cigarettes for a little brown loaf...and then, he says, 'Some fool of a First Lieutenant fired a shot.'

When he tells this story, he doesn't know what it *means*, he doesn't know what the story shows he really felt about the bloody officers, nor why I'm proud of him for feeling that; nor why I'm proud of him for giving the German private his cigarettes and remembering so warmly the little loaf of bread, and proud of him for his still undiminished anger at the nitwit of a boy whom they were all forced to obey just when the ranks were in a mood to pack it in and go home.

Of course, the old man thinks that, if the rank and file *had* packed it in and gone home in 1915, the Tsar would still rule Russia and the Kaiser Germany, and the sun would never have set on the British Empire. He is a man of grand simplicities. He still grieves over my mother's 'leftish' views; indeed, he grieves over mine, though not enough to spoil his dinner. He seems, rather, to regard them as, in some way, genetically linked. I have inherited his nose, after all; so why not my mother's voting patterns?

She never forgave him for believing Chamberlain. She'd often bring it up, at moments of stress, as proof of his gullibility. 'And, what's more, you came home from the office and said: "There ain't gonna be a war."'

See how she has crept into the narrative, again. He wrote to me last year: 'Your mammy was not only very beautiful but also very clever.' (Always in dialect, always 'mammy'.) Not that she did anything with it. Another husband might have encouraged her to work, or study, although, in the 1930s, that would have been exceptional enough in this first generation middle-class family to have projected us into another dimension of existence altogether. As it was, he, born a Victorian and a sentimentalist, was content to adore, and that, in itself, is sufficiently exceptional, dammit, although it was not good for her moral fibre. She, similarly trapped by historic circumstance, did not even know, I think, that her own vague discontent, manifested by sick headaches and complicated later on by genuine ill-health, might have had something to do with being a 'wife', a role for which she was in some respects ill-suited, as my father's tribute ought to indicate, since beauty and cleverness are usually more valued in mistresses than they are in wives. For her sixtieth birthday, he gave her a huge bottle of Chanel No. 5.

For what it's worth, I've never been in the least attracted to older men—nor they to me, for that matter. Why *is* that? Possibly something in my manner hints I will expect, nay, demand, behaviour I deem appropriate to a father figure, that is, that he kicks his own backside from time to time, and brings me tea in bed, and weeps at the inevitability of loss; and these are usually young men's talents.

Don't think, from all this, it's been all roses. We've had our ups and downs, the old man and I, for he was born a Victorian. Though it occurs to me his unstated but self-evident idea I should earn my own living, have a career, in fact, may have originated in his experience of the first wave of feminism, that hit in his teens and twenties, with some of whose products he worked, by one of whose products we were doctored. (Our family doctor, Helen Gray, was eighty when she retired twenty years ago, and must have been one of the first women doctors.)

Nevertheless, his Victorianness, for want of a better word, means he feels duty bound to come the heavy father, from time to time, always with a histrionic overemphasis: 'You just watch out for yourself, that's all.' 'Watching out for yourself' has some obscure kind of sexual meaning, which he hesitates to spell out. If advice he gave me when I was a girl (I could paraphrase this advice as 'Kneecap them'), if this advice would be more or less what I'd arm my own daughters with now, it ill accorded with the mood of the sixties. Nor was it much help in those days when almost the entire male sex seemed in a conspiracy to deprive me of the opportunity to get within sufficient distance. The old man dowered me with too much self-esteem.

But how can a girl have *too much* self-esteem?

Nevertheless, not all roses. He is, you see, a foreigner; what is more, a Highland man, who struck further into the heartland of England than Charles Edward Stewart's army ever did, and then buggered off, leaving his children behind to carve niches in the alien

188

soil. Oh, he'd hotly deny this version of his life; it is my own romantic interpretation of his life, obviously. He's all for the Act of Union. He sees no difference at all between the English and the Scots, except, once my mother was gone, he saw no reason to remain among the English. And his always unacknowledged foreignness, the extraversion of his manners, the stateliness of his demeanour, his fearlessness, guiltlessness, his inability to feel embarrassment, the formality of his discourse, above all, his utter ignorance of and complete estrangement from the English system of social class, make him a being I puzzle over and wonder at.

It is that last thing—for, in England, he seemed genuinely classless—that may have helped me always feel a stranger, here, myself. He is of perfectly good petty bourgeois stock; my grandfather owned a shoe shop although, in those days, that meant being able to make the things as well as sell them, and repair them, too, so my grandfather was either a shopkeeper or a cobbler, depending on how you looked at it. The distinction between entrepreneur and skilled artisan may have appeared less fine, in those days, in that town beside the North Sea which still looks as if it could provide a good turnout for a witchburning.

There are all manner of stories about my paternal grandfather, whom I never met; he was the village atheist, who left a fiver in his will to every minister in the place, just in case. I never met my Gaelic-speaking grandmother, either. (She died, as it happens of toothache, shortly before I was born.) From all the stories I know they both possessed in full measure that peculiar Highland ability, much perplexing to early tourists, which means that the meanest, grubbing crofter can, if necessary, draw himself up to his full height and welcome a visitor into his stinking hovel as if its miserable tenant were a prince inviting a foreign potentate into a palace. This is the courtly grace of the authentic savage. The women do it with an especially sly elegance. Lowering a steaming bowl on to a filthy tablecloth, my father's sister used to say: 'Now, take some delicious kale soup.' And it was the water in which the cabbage had been boiled.

It's possible to suspect they're having you on, and so they may be; yet this formality always puts the visitor, no matter what his or her status, in the role of supplicant. Your humiliation is what spares you.

189

When a Highlander grovels, then, oh, then, is the time to keep your hand on your wallet. One learns to fear an apology most.

These are the strategies of underdevelopment and they are worlds away from those which my mother's family learned to use to contend with the savage urban class struggle in Battersea, in the nineteen hundreds. Some of my mother's family learned to manipulate cynically the English class system and helped me and my brother out. All of them knew, how can I put it, that a good table with clean linen meant self-respect and to love Shakespeare was a kind of class revenge. (Perhaps that is why those soiled traycloths upset my mother so; she had no quarrel with his taste in literature.) For my father, the grand gesture was the thing. He entered Harrods like the Jacobite army invading Manchester. He would arrive at my school to 'sort things out' like the wrath of god.

This effortless sense of natural dignity, of his own unquestioned worth, is of his essence; there are noble savages in his heredity and I look at him, sometimes, to quote Mayakovsky, 'like an Eskimo looking at a train'.

For I know so little about him, although I know so much. Much of his life was conducted in my absence, on terms of which I am necessarily ignorant, for he was older than I am now when I was born, although his life has shaped my life. This is the curious abyss that divides the closest kin, that the tender curiosity appropriate to lovers is inappropriate, here, where the bond is involuntary, so that the most important things stay undiscovered. If I am short-tempered, volatile as he is, there is enough of my mother's troubled soul in me to render his very transparency, his psychic good health, endlessly mysterious. He is my father and I love him as Cordelia did, 'according to my natural bond'. What the nature of that 'natural bond' might be, I do not know, and, besides, I have a theoretical objection to the notion of a 'natural bond'.

But, at the end of *King Lear*, one has a very fair notion of the strength of that bond, whatever it is, whether it is the construct of culture rather than nature, even if we might all be better off without it. And I do think my father gives me far more joy than Cordelia ever got from Lear.

CAROLA HANSSON
AND KARIN LIDEN
MOSCOW WOMEN

I n contrast to virtually every other European country, the Soviet Union has been notable for its determination to give women a place in society equal to men's. The extent of the commitment is evident in the details of ordinary Soviet life. It is taken for granted, for instance, that all women should be educated and that they should be encouraged to take up a profession—fifty-one and a half percent of the Soviet labour force is made up of women—and women, like all Soviet citizens, are guaranteed employment. Moreover, the familiar images of women as sex objects are rarely seen in film or pornography or advertising: female sexuality is free from so many of the exploitative commercial practices evident in the west.

But while it is true that women form a crucial part of the work force, it is difficult to see them as being independent and equal in other aspects of society. Lenin is reported to have replied to the request to write about sexual and family education by saying, 'Further ahead—not yet! Now all my strength and time have to go into other issues. There are greater, more serious problems.' And Marx and Engels have been understood as believing that true liberation of women would only be possible with the abolition of personal property, allowing women to 'regain' the equality they originally possessed. But now, with private property abolished, with some of the more urgent economic needs met, what kind of liberation has actually taken place? Why, after such inspired beginnings, has this liberation appeared to have slowed down? And just how compatible are feminism and socialism? These are among the questions that Carola Hansson and Karin Liden address. Both have done a great deal of research in Soviet life and *Granta* publishes here some of their work, consisting of four fairly developed interviews, a number of rather startling statistics, and a brief selection of the highlights of some of the other interviews. All the interviews were conducted in the women's homes, in Russian, without an interpreter. There were no authorities involved and the women's names are pseudonyms. The tapes were left in Moscow once the interviews were completed, and, through secret channels, were passed on to Stockholm, arriving six months later.

Liza

We first meet Liza in her brother's home. She is wearing a long red robe with a deep décolletage, has blonde curly hair, wears black mascara. Her eyelids are pale blue and her lips a dark rose.

I'm twenty-eight. I have a degree in literature and work for a publisher. I have a son, Emil. I had a husband, who was an artist, but now he's gone. We got married in 1970 and divorced in 1975.

Does your former husband spend time with Emil?

No, he rarely sees his father. The situation is complicated. When the baby was born I gave him my surname. I decided that since I had had to carry the whole burden and I suffered the most, I wanted to give him my name. His father was very upset that the boy didn't have his name, and now they almost never see each other. Emil never gets anything from him.

You were born in Moscow?

Yes. Six of us lived in a room twenty square metres in size, which was part of a communal apartment. It was Mama's room. Papa wasn't born in Moscow and when he married my mother they settled down in that room. There was also Mama's sister, Grandmother, and I, and then my brother, Alyosha, was born. In 1937 Mama's father was put in prison. If my grandmother had divorced him she could have avoided going with him and could have stayed with her three children. But she didn't think it was right to divorce him after he was jailed, so she went to prison for eight years as a family member of an enemy of the people. When the children were left alone they were forced to leave their apartment, even though her husband had had an important position in the government. They were kicked out, and my mother, who was sixteen at the time, was left with two small children, eventually settling into the very same room where I grew up.

How do you remember your childhood?

I think I had a very happy childhood, so happy that...Marina Tsvetayeva writes that her childhood was so happy that when she reached sixteen she wanted to die. We did live under difficult circumstances. Papa was a poet and a writer, and used to block himself off in a corner to work, which gave the room a cramped look; he wrote some of his most important works right there in that corner. It was a terrible life, and still Papa kept on writing....We had nothing. When I was born they had only potatoes on the table to celebrate my birth. They didn't have the money for a baby carriage, so they put me in a basket that Papa hung outside the window and that boys would sometimes throw stones at, thinking it was fruit or something. On the whole I remember my childhood as very happy—especially my relationship with my father.

Do you think that women and men have the same goals in life?

Yes, but I think that women are more honest than men. For example, in the thirties, when the whole country was a mass of lies and betrayals, the women lied less. Akhmatova and Tsvetayeva were only 'fragile creatures', but they didn't lie. They could be broke, they could starve—Tsvetayeva went so far as to hang herself—but they didn't lie.

When we were forbidden to believe in God, the soldiers came to the villages brandishing their pistols, asking, 'Are you believers?' 'No,' everyone answered. But still the women went to church, and it's they who have kept religion alive.

Would you have chosen another profession if you had been a man?

I don't know. Had I been a man I would have travelled around Russia, and also would have been able to change jobs often. As a woman, that's hard to do.

Are there typically female professions in Russia?

Of course. Textile workers, for instance, are mostly women. Doctors and physiotherapists are also mostly women. Almost all teachers are women. At day-care centres practically all employees are women. People who clean are usually women. As a matter of fact, most service work is done by women, at home and in the community. In the country women work mostly on the *kolkhoz*.*

Why do you think that's so?

Because the salaries are low. It's terribly sad. Our women have a horrible time and of course prestige also plays a part. A man won't do household or household-related chores. Here, dishwashers are always women. Teachers are also very badly paid, and that's why they're mostly women. Women aren't readily accepted in important posts.

Could you imagine a man working at a day-care centre?

Yes, I can imagine it, but one doesn't often find men suitable for that. Here there are very few responsible fathers; they all drink too much.

To change the subject to sexuality. Do you have contraceptives in the Soviet Union?

We have the IUD, although it isn't used very much. Women who want one have to queue for a long time. We try not to use the pill because of the possible danger to a future foetus. Some also use aspirin, but that's also considered to be dangerous.

---

*A *Kolkhoz* is a state-owned farm.

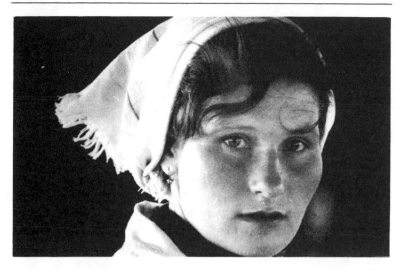

But above all we have many abortions. They're horrible, absolutely horrible. But what's the answer? Our contraceptives aren't any good. There are condoms, but they're so repulsive and bad that we would rather go through an abortion....The first Christians copulated only in order to procreate. In my opinion abortions are punishments for our sins.

Have you ever had an abortion?

Yes, many—seven. It's hard both physically and psychologically. Now that it's done with drugs there's no pain, but it's hard on the psyche.

How did you react when you discovered that you were pregnant the first time?

I was hysterical. It was totally unexpected, since I didn't believe...I couldn't imagine that children were conceived that quickly. No one had told me anything. We don't learn anything about sex in school, and no one in the family talks about it. I got together with my husband, and I got pregnant immediately. It was so strange that I had an abortion. I went through with the second pregnancy but the

197

delivery was very difficult. I begged for a Caesarean, howled like an animal, screamed so much that they finally had to give me something to induce labour, and I had terrible contractions and kept on screaming until there was blood in my mouth. My baby was born in a special clinic, but still....During the delivery I was badly torn, and they didn't even sew me up.

As a woman, what do you find the most difficult problems to cope with?

My main problem is that the man I love is married and has a child. Sometimes when things are most difficult I long for the presence of a man who is strong, a *bogatyr**...who would shelter me so that I wouldn't have to think about anything.

What, according to you, are women's most pressing problems here?

Their husbands' low salaries, and the limited time they have left for their children. Most women aren't wildly enthusiastic about their work; they'd like to bring up their children in a normal way, but they're too busy trying to make money. It seems to me that our women suffer from equality.

What do you mean by equality?

Here equality consists of the women carrying the heaviest burden. Here a woman's life just fades away without her being aware of it. She's young, then suddenly she's old, and she's buried without knowing why she ever lived.

Are you familiar with the women's movement in the West?

Yes, I'm familiar with the movement to legalize abortion, and women's rights, but where the right to vote is concerned...here all women have the right to vote. We don't need a women's movement.

---

*The supernaturally strong hero of Russian folk legends.

Here we're all convinced that everything is the way it ought to be. But I think when women were emancipated, it actually amounted to man's liberation from the family.

Is there anything you wish to add?

Yes—it's terrifying when a woman speaks. The truth comes out, and a very real pain emerges.

Women in the Work Force

E arly Soviet industry expanded rapidly, and to keep up with expansion workers were needed: women were brought into the labour force really for reasons of economy, not ideology. By 1928, twenty-four percent of skilled labourers were women; by 1972 it had risen to fifty-one and a half percent.

In the Soviet Union the right to work has been written into the constitution, and officially there has been no unemployment since 1930. Equal pay for equal work is established by law. Nevertheless, the Soviet woman is obviously discriminated against in the work place. The same

sex roles exist as in other countries: the women perform the service and routine jobs, while the men perform the upper-echelon and management jobs. In addition, the job categories dominated by women are supervised by men. Women generally constitute the majority in light industry (textiles, ready-made clothing, the food industry), medicine, teaching and services. The following list of women's professions was compiled in 1970. The picture has not changed appreciably since then.

Profession	Percentage of Women
Nurses	99
Typists	99
Day-care personnel	98
Pediatricians	98
Secretaries	95
Librarians	95
Cashiers	94
Clothing industry	88
Laboratory personnel	85
Midwives	83
Telephone operators	83
Managerial personnel in institutions	82
Computer operators	77
Doctors	74
Workers in food industries	74
Teachers	72
Textile workers	72

These professions are among the lowest paid.

Sonya

Sonya is twenty-three. She lives with her husband, and their newborn daughter in one of Moscow's newest suburbs. Volodya teaches biology at the university. Sonya has studied French and Spanish and graduated six months ago.

How do you manage on Volodya's salary and your stipend?

With the help of our parents. It's impossible to get an apartment here. But when my grandmother moved in with my mother, we got her room. It was very complicated. The room is part of a communal apartment and there are several people living here—a single man in the adjacent room and an older woman in the third room. But in May the older woman expects to move, and then things may get worse. Just imagine another family in our tiny kitchen where you can hardly turn around. We live in 16.7 square metres, and that's almost as much as we have a right to. But getting something else is almost impossible. The waiting lists are enormous.

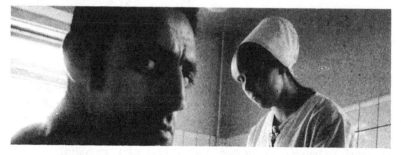

Do you plan to let your husband's career take precedence over your own?

Yes, if there's no other way out. But I'm gradually getting irritated with the way things are; he's doing something interesting and I'm not. It's a problem and people don't know *how* serious it is. It gnaws at a couple's relationship and leads to serious conflicts. One never hears women say that they got divorced because only their husband had time to write his dissertation, but that's the way it is. The frustration of never being able to do the things you want hollows a relationship the way drops of water hollow a stone.

Is this problem ever dicussed?

Very seldom—almost never. We don't think we can do anything about these problems. Change can only come from the top.

What other reasons can you give for the numerous divorces here?

In the newspapers they say that a bad sex life is an important factor. That's understandable, since there's no information on sex available anywhere. Most people get married very early, at seventeen or so; they're totally inexperienced. They have children immediately and become tired, dissatisfied and disappointed. I have many friends who have divorced after six months.

It seems very difficult to get hold of contraceptives.

Yes, it's really difficult.

You don't use the pill?

No, I never wanted to use the pill. It contains hormones, and it is harmful. I read that a pharmaceutical firm in West Germany—or perhaps it was the state—sold pills that caused dreadful birth defects, and a lot of disfigured babies were the result, without arms and legs. I would never even consider taking the pill.*

So most women live in constant fear of becoming pregnant?

Yes. There are lots of home remedies. Various creams and some kind of foam. My grandmother has told me that a little urine kills sperm. There are a lot of primitive methods, but one has to know how to apply them. I could never use any of them, so for me there's no solution to the problem.

Is abortion a solution?

For many women it is. Some do it ten or fifteen times. Often it's the only way out, especially since so many men absolutely refuse to use condoms. Then what does one do?

---

*Most women interviewed showed little understanding of modern birth control methods, and confused the pill with thalidomide.

Carola Hansson and Karin Liden

Did you ever consider an abortion when you became pregnant?

I had already had two.

Could you have imagined not having children?

Yes, but now that she's here, of course I've changed my mind!
The economic situation doesn't permit a family to have more than
one or at most two children. The day-care centres are another
problem. The groups are too large, the rooms are dirty, the staff is
constantly changing, and the children are always sick. It's horrible.
At work a father told me about his son's day-care centre. The boy is
three years old and his group is huge. To reduce the size of the group,
the staff opened the windows so that the children would catch cold.
I've heard of this happening several times.

We had also heard that story, which even if only apocryphal still suggests that day care is felt to be very inadequate. Are these abuses discussed in the press?

To a certain extent. But the whole system functions badly, and
usually nothing is said.

What do you wish for now?

It's very important to me that I don't lose my personality. All people
are different, but life here seems to pour them into the same mould. I
need to develop what I am, and to get to know *me*.

Do you think that the problems you have discussed with us are typical of women?

Officially, there *are* no women's problems here.

Do women discuss their situation with each other?

No, because we aren't taught to think independently or to express our
opinions about things and issues. We don't discuss our personal lives.

We don't look for reasons why we live the way we do, because it still isn't possible to change anything here.

Birth Control and Abortions

The official Soviet community is characterized by a reserve about sexual matters that verges on prudery. As a result, there is little information about sex available. Parents are rarely much of a help—statistics show that between ninety-four and ninety-three percent of young people learn about sex outside the home, usually from friends. Information about birth control is also scarce, perhaps because most birth control devices are either substandard or simply not available. Condoms are unreliable and clumsy. The pill isn't always easily available, and possible side effects are seen as a deterrent to its use. Diaphragms and intrauterine devices don't seem popular either, partly because of the unpleasantness of going to the gynaecologist. 'One has to have contacts,' many women say, and by that they mean that only then are they well treated and well cared for.

Abortions, which are entirely free during the first three months of pregnancy, are the most common method of birth control. Documentation shows that four out of every five pregnancies end in abortion.

The right to have an abortion has been the subject of discussion for a long time in the Soviet Union. When abortion became legal in 1920, it was intended as an attempt to put a stop to the illegal abortions that were so often fatal. In 1936, under Stalin, a new and rigorous family law was introduced that was meant to raise the birthrate. Although it prohibited abortion, the birthrate remained unchanged, and the number of accidents and deaths from illegal abortions increased. Only in 1968 did they again become legal for all women in the Soviet Union.

Elena Stepanovna

Elena Stepanovna is in her seventies. She receives a pension from her former position as a librarian and from time to time publishes an article. She doesn't want to talk about her life or answer personal questions. Instead we ask her to tell us how the woman's role has changed during her lifetime.

I remember vividly how, when I was a young girl after the revolution, women in my immediate circle—the big-city intelligentsia—accepted enthusiastically the world that was opening up. We could participate in everything. We felt completely equal to men—in every single aspect of life.

Co-education was established then; I always studied with boys. My school was good and there was a real feeling of camaraderie among us. Maybe it was the quality of the education: that the teachers were so inspired themselves that they inspired us to feel that men and women were equal, as regards not just the law but life itself—in capacity and talent. Yes, I think that the atmosphere in which I grew up *developed* our potential as much as the boys'. It was so tremendously exciting: we were interested in everything, fascinated by everything.

But then the situation changed. Suddenly the burdens got heavier because of what was happening in our country. There was the war, and women's lives became terribly difficult.

What effects did the war have on women?

In a way, women became stronger through their hardships, but in another way, they were destroyed. Women were forced to engage in work that was way beyond their strength. But it was women's innermost being that was damaged most: after the war there were so terribly many widows here who were forced to shoulder the responsibility of bringing up their children alone.

Today women are also forced to bring up children on their own, but that is because divorce seems to be very common.

When I was very young, the laws were instituted that simplified relationships in sexual matters. In a way they became *too* simple. A couple could get married on Thursday, and on Saturday one of the spouses could go to ZAGS* and get a divorce—even without the partner's knowledge. It was probably the very first expression of what freedom, complete freedom, ought to be. Then came the terrible period when abortions were forbidden. Imagine the woman's plight when she had to work, already had two children, and discovered that she was expecting a third, a fourth, a fifth...How was it possible to

*ZAGS are the civilian registration bureaux, the everyday name for Soviet 'marriage palaces'.

deny her an abortion? It was a dreadful time, a brutal time. I myself
saw the awful results. Many, having sought 'nonmedical' assistance,
lost their fertility. Many died. Now that we have free abortions, a
woman can decide for herself whether or not she wants to give birth,
and that's only for the better.

**There are, nevertheless, an extraordinary number of abortions among
young people.**

What we need today is better information about sex. Young people
ought to be more prepared when they enter marriage. There's an
abysmal ignorance about sexual matters, and very little literature. We
have to do something radical and we have to do it fast!

Oh, but on top of it all, there is such a double burden that the
woman carries today: she is expected to be part of the work force but
at the same time she is expected to be a traditional mother, caring for
the children, the husband, and the house.

Divorces

**When the Soviet Union was first established, a very radical
family law was passed. Among other things it
became easy to dissolve a marriage. It was sufficient for
either the husband or the wife to demand one; the formalities were over
in a few minutes. In 1936 the laws were amended to require that both
parties appear, and in 1944 a law was changed so that it was difficult,
unpleasant and expensive to be divorced. This law was slightly relaxed in
1965, but when children are involved, the divorce must be tried in court.
The court decides who remains in charge of the children, and almost
without exception rules in favour of the mother. The father is usually
ordered to pay twenty-five percent of his salary for one child, thirty-
three and one-third percent for two, and fifty percent for three or more.
It's still very expensive to get divorced; it costs between fifty and two
hundred rubles depending on the time and the method. (A marriage, on
the other hand, costs one ruble and fifty kopeks.)**

**Despite the expense, divorces are very common in the Soviet Union.
The statistics for 1977 and 1978 show that a third of all marriages end in
divorce. In large cities such as Moscow and Kiev, half of all marriages**

are dissolved. Most divorces occur during the first year of marriage. Why so many? In addition to the usual reasons—alcoholism, physical cruelty, infidelity—Soviet sociologists have found that about twenty percent of divorces are caused by friction between young couples and their parents and parents-in-law. Of those who divorced in 1977, seventy-nine percent had no place to live when they got married other than with parents or in a communal apartment.

Another contributing factor is the deplorable inadequacy of sex education in the schools. Moreover, it was not until the beginning of the seventies that the first marriage-counselling centre was opened in Leningrad. A doctor who worked at that centre said, 'I'm not exaggerating when I say that nine-tenths of the young people who are about to get married don't have even a rudimentary knowledge of sex.'

Alevtina Giorgievna

A few days later we are invited to have tea with Elena Stepanovna, who has just spent several hours travelling across Moscow to fetch her friend: 'I wanted you to meet the marvellous Alevtina Giorgievna. Alevtina Giorgievna was born in the Orlov district, in the country. She has lived in Moscow for a couple of years. She has had a very hard and difficult life, but she has been able to sustain a wonderful lightness of spirit, innate goodness, and inner calm. This is what I admire so much in her.'

I got married to a boy from the village when I was seventeen—that would have been 1924—and he was tall and handsome and he liked to sing. At that time I had had four years of school, and that was all I ever got.

When the war came everyone moved in together: my sister, who was a widow with three children; I with my three children; and my sister-in-law, who had five. My husband and my brother of course were off fighting the war. The Germans came and forced us to work for them. We had to build stables for their horses. During that winter my sister-in-law died of exhaustion, leaving five children. I took care of them.

We were evacuated for three years, but the whole time we lived quite close to our village, which was right at the front. Towards the end of the war there were terrible struggles all round us. We hid in our miserable mud huts, our only shelter, until finally our own soldiers came and helped us to get behind the front. We walked and walked until we got to a *sovkhoz** where we stayed for about a week. My husband had been killed and was buried in a mass grave right there. He had been recruited immediately at the outset of the war. He was wounded and died in a hospital in 1942.

What happened after the war?

After a couple of weeks we returned to our village. It had been completely destroyed, and there were bodies all over the place. The air was almost impossible to breathe. We tried to find places to sleep, and used grass as blankets, but we were almost devoured by flies. I remember how I tried to console my little Tonya, who was five. I caressed her and caressed her; that was all I could do for her. But we survived. Later, soldiers came and helped us bury all the dead. And we began to try to live there; a wall went up here and there. All that was left of our two brick houses were two corners, and we tried to build from there.

---

*A *sovkhoz* is a Soviet state-owned farm that pays wages to its workers.

Only women and children had returned. All the men had been taken by the war. Then a man came from the city to help us organize the work. We had to name a woman as chairwoman of the *kolkhoz*, and men as 'brigadiers', and so on. I was chosen as leader of the group. We worked around the clock. The war was hard on us.

What were your first tasks?

When spring came we had to walk to get seed—sixty kilometres back and forth—and we had to carry sixteen kilos each. It was early spring; we had tied rags around our feet and were wet the whole time. We carried the seed home, but all the fields were ruined because they had made trenches there. So the women had to till them up again. Look at my fingers; they're ruined from that work! They don't hurt, but it's not nice to have fingers like that. And then we had to plough, and we had to use spades. Everything was gone. Finally we managed to get three horses and ploughs, and later we got a tractor, too.

But there were mines everywhere. And so many children blown into bits! One woman lost both her little boys at the same time.

For three years I was leader of the *kolkhoz*. It was very difficult. Now it would be much easier, because all the necessary supplies are available—machines, everything. But at that time! If you knew how many difficult days I spent!

What changes have been the most important in women's lives here?

A lot has changed! I don't quite know how to say it, but before, women were so much better.

But aren't women much better off materially today?

Of course! Dear me, the way we looked after the war! We had no clothes—only rags. The *kolkhoz* was so poor everything had to go to the state. We couldn't buy a thing then, but now everyone is so well off!

But tell me, my dear, is it good for a child when its mother isn't at home? There's no nursery in our *kolkhoz* because there are so few children born nowadays. Women don't want to have any. It's very bad. Everyone ought to have two or three *at least*.

There is not room to represent the many women whom Carola Hansson and Karin Liden interviewed. But many of the observations in the other interviews are important and worth noting. These would include the following:

Natasha

Mornings are always the same. About seven o'clock the baby wakes up and Yura goes to work. Then I feed the baby. While he sits there and eats I clean our room, make the bed, and heat the water for the wash. Then I feed him what he didn't finish. He makes an awful mess when he eats, so I have to wash him afterwards. Then, since he's full and happy he plays nicely, and in the meantime I prepare breakfast. While the porridge is cooking I put myself in order. After that I do some washing and ironing, Yura comes home, and we eat. If Yura has things to do, he leaves. I wash the dishes, play with the baby, take him out, and do things around the house.

The evenings are the busiest time around here. Everyone comes home and has to be fed—at least eight people, because we often have guests. It's hard on me because I have to feed the baby and make dinner for everyone else. Then we take the baby for a walk, put him to bed, wash the dishes, and wash all over again. Things begin to calm down around nine. Then we study; I'm a student at the faculty of law, and somehow I intend to graduate this year...

Do you understand what I'm getting at? Women, like myself, who do research, or, who are at least *trying* to find the time to do research, to achieve the same kind of prestige as men, are bound to have problems in their marriages: we are bound to have difficulties with

our men who are used to having things done for them in a certain way. For men, work comes first, then friends and then the wife. But women have to put men first, then the children and finally their work. Men get prestige from the work; women are meant to enjoy prestige from their children if they are successful at keeping their children neat and clean.

In our family I believe we're equals. But of course, in a way, Yura is the head of the family...because...that's the way he wants it.

213

Would it be inconceivable to have a women's movement here of the type we have in the West?

We're so different from you. We aren't active. We've been taught to leave our problems to the government. The government thinks for us, takes care of us. Maybe we allow the government too much responsibility. It isn't God, after all, and can't be all-encompassing. Perhaps we ought to be a little more active, but I don't know how. We don't discuss our problems the same way you do. We can, of course, refer to our representatives. But you can hardly go to your representative and tell him that you want to write your dissertation but that you have two children who need to be cared for. There are more serious problems.

Nina

Can you describe your marriage for us? Is it happy? Unhappy?

Most things about marriage are fine. I'm glad that we share things equitably. Vova, my husband, cares a lot about our child, much more than before. If you had met me a while ago, I would have said that I wasn't very happy. There are, however, a few matters about which I'm not too happy. I don't think that sex is the most important part of our marriage. We have some problems, but that's probably because we got married quite recently, and also because we're working so hard. Both of us. And it's very important for me to be able to talk to Vova about my work, my personal ambitions. But I notice that he doesn't have an equally great need for this. He wants to work on his own projects and gets bored with all my plans and my talk.

I don't know. I really don't have any free time at all. There's so much to do and not enough time to do it in. Is it a uniquely feminine problem not to have any free time? Is the household a woman's responsibility? We all wish that household chores would take much less time, that there were well-stocked shops in the vicinity, and that service-places—for washing and things like that—were on the premises. We would also like to have more nurseries and day-care centres, or, at the least, day-care centres that were functional and efficient enough actually to meet the needs of parents.

As for women's problems...I don't really know whether they exist. Basically it's the government's problem.

Lida

You say that a husband ought to help his wife when she's tired. How do you think household work should be divided?

If I were married I would make absolutely sure that my husband never saw me washing. I would wash when he was out, or else early in the morning when he was still sleeping, so that I'd have time to have a shower and clean up before he got up. I would never want him to see me sweaty or sloppily dressed. I think that cooking should be done early in the morning or on Sundays, mostly while the husband is still in bed. The table should be set by the time he has got up, so that everything is ready when he appears for breakfast. The husband ought to help with lunch and the children. He can scrub the potatoes and the children can do the dishes while the wife makes sure that everything is in order.

How about washing the dishes and cleaning up?

I think the husband ought to help with that. He really should do the shopping, since it's hard and a heavy job. Planning the shopping, though, is entirely the woman's job, even if the husband is capable of buying a litre of milk or a kilo of meat. But since men hate to queue, shopping often gets delegated to women as well.

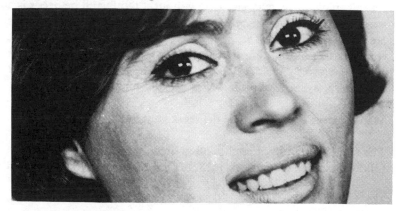

Carola Hansson and Karin Liden

Is the situation the same when both work full time?

Of course. At home a woman usually does everything. When the husband comes home he reads his paper and watches TV, contrary to what the newspapers say. They show men on March 8, the International Women's Day, cooking and cleaning and shopping and scrubbing floors. But it's really the women who do everything.

How do you feel about the future?

Actually, I think less and less about the future. It seems meaningless to dream if there's no chance of fulfillment. How can I explain the situation to you? I think you have to be passionately involved with life to be able to ignore all its inadequacies. But I don't have that involvement any more. I don't think you should look at life through rose-coloured glasses—it's all too grey—but you should be able to see clearly enough to recognize that your own dissatisfactions are mostly your own fault. To enjoy life you have to stop looking on the darker side, but I can't seem to do that. I don't feel any joy in just being alive.

Would you have chosen another career if you had been a man?

If I'd been a man? I don't know. I can't possible imagine myself as a man.

Do women and men have the same goal in life?

I don't think so. A man can live without a family; all he needs is a woman—to come from time to time to clean for him and do his laundry and, if he feels so inclined, he sleeps with her. Of course, a woman can adopt his life-style, but most women, I think, want their own home, family, children. From time immemorial, men provide for the family, women keep the home fires burning.

Whose career do you think is the most important?

The man's, naturally. Families often break up because women don't follow their men to their new jobs. It's hard for a man to live without

216

his family once he's used to being taken care of all the time. Of course there are men who can endure, who continue, for instance, to be faithful, but for most men it isn't easy. A woman ought to go where her husband goes.

Maysa

What would you say a happy marriage is?

A happy marriage is when you love each other and have your own apartment.

What dreams do you have for the future?

First of all, it's that private room....

How would you describe femininity?

To me, femininity encompasses a lot of things—delicacy, a little mystery, an ability to bring out the attractive qualities within oneself and to hide the bad ones. A woman mustn't lose her temper. And of course she has to take care of her appearance. A lot of women give up on that as soon as they're married.

As a mother, a woman has to have patience and be loving with the child. She ought to put her child before herself.

How about the father?

A father must really be firm and determined. Not unkind, but he ought to affirm his masculinity. To the child he should represent authority.

Nadezhda Pavlovna

Nadezhda Pavlovna, a Ph.D. and a member of the Party, has been a university professor for more than twenty-five years. She is currently teaching prospective teachers in Alma-Ata, the capital of the Soviet Republic of Kazakhstan.

What does equality between men and women mean to you?

I think that all this talk about equality is something they invented in the big cities. There it can obviously become a gigantic problem for a couple to decide who is going to clean an apartment floor which consists of a few pitiful square metres. Our house is ten by twelve metres, and there's never a question about who's going to clean the floors. I do that.

But doesn't it still happen far too often that the woman works more than the man? That she does double duty?

You probably know that a lot is written on that subject here. The husbands are usually called the 'Knights of the Sofa'. As I said, I consider this a problem city people have invented. It's a problem for those who have no warm water in the kitchen, and floors that are two by three metres. If the woman cleans the floor and her husband sits around and watches, it demeans her. But if one has a house and garden besides, the question of who's going to do this or that doesn't even come up.

What do you consider typical women's problems here?

In this country? Women's problems? I can't see any special women's problems. Is that supposed to be the new fashion?

Do you know anything about the so-called women's movement in the West?

Which one? There are so many of them. For emancipation? (*She laughs.*) We don't need that here. We've already passed that stage. Emancipation is part of our style of life. I assure you that question isn't a problem here. We don't separate the women's movement from our usual activities, from society in general. Here, women have finally got the emancipation they're entitled to. Do you realize what that means?

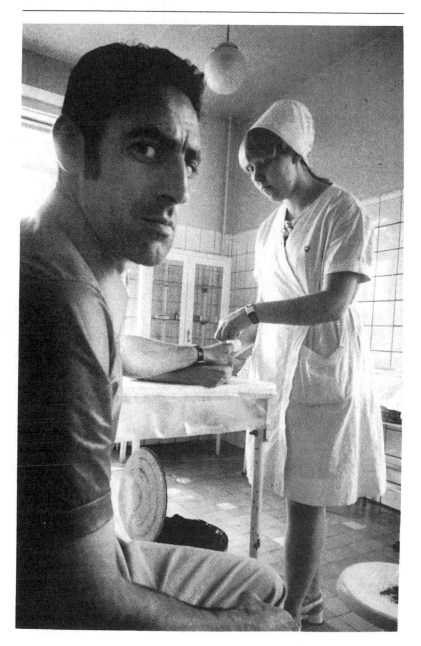

Photographs by Jean Mohr

CAROLYN FORCHÉ
EL SALVADOR: AN
AIDE-MÉMOIRE

The year Franco died, I spent several months on Mallorca translating the poetry of Claribel Alegría, a Salvadoran in voluntary exile. During those months the almond trees bloomed and lost flower, the olives and lemons ripened, and we hauled baskets of apricots from Claribel's small *finca*. There was bathing in the *calla*, fresh squid under the palm thatch, drunk Australian sailors to dance with at night. It was my first time in Europe and there was no better place at that time than Spain. I was there when Franco's anniversary passed for the first time in forty years without notice—and the lack of public celebration was a collective hush of relief. I travelled with Claribel's daughter, Maya Flakoll, for ten days through Andalusia by train, visiting poetry shrines. The *gitanos* had finally pounded a cross into the earth to mark the grave of Federico García Lorca, not where it had been presumed to be all this time, not beneath an olive tree, but in a bowl of land rimmed by pines. We hiked the eleven kilometres through the Sierra Nevada foothills to La Fuente Grande and held a book of poems open over the silenced poet.

On Mallorca I lost interest in the *calla* sunbathing, the parties that carried on into the morning, the staggering home wine-drunk up the goat paths. I did not hike to the peak of the Teix with baskets of *entremesas* nor, despite well-intentioned urgings, could I surrender myself to the island's diversionary summer mystique.

I was busy with Claribel's poems, and with the horrific accounts of the survivors of repressive Latin American régimes. Claribel's home was frequented by these wounded: writers who had been tortured and imprisoned, who had lost husbands, wives, and closest friends. In the afternoon, more than once I joined Claribel in her silent vigil near the window until the mail came, her 'difficult time of day', alone in a chair in the perfect light of thick-walled Mallorquín windows. These were her afternoons of despair, and they haunted me. In those hours I first learned of El Salvador, not from the springs of her nostalgia for 'the fraternity of dipping a tortilla into a common pot of beans and meat', but from the source of its pervasive brutality. My understanding of Latin American realities was confined then to the romantic devotion to Vietnam-era revolutionary pieties, the sainthood of Ernesto Che rather than the debilitating effects of the cult of personality that arose in the collective memory of Guevara. I worked into the late hours on my poems and on translations, drinking '101' brandy and chain-smoking Un-X-Dos. When Cuban writer Mario Benedetti visited, I questioned him about what 'an American' could do in the struggle against repression.

'As a *North* American, you might try working to influence a profound change in your country's foreign policy.'

Over coffee in the mornings I studied reports from Amnesty International, London, and learned of a plague on Latin exiles who had sought refuge in Spain following Franco's death: a right-wing death squad known as the 'AAA'—Anti-Communista Apostólica, founded in Argentina and exported to assassinate influential exiles from the southern cone.

I returned to the United States and in the autumn of 1977 was invited to El Salvador by people who knew Claribel. 'How much do you know about Latin America?' I was asked. Then: 'Good. At least you know that you know nothing.' A young writer, politically unaffiliated, ideologically vague, I was to be blessed with the rarity of a moral and political education—what, at times, would seem an unbearable immersion; what eventually would become a focused obsession. It would change my life and work, propel me towards engagement, test my endurance and find it wanting, and prevent me from ever viewing myself or my country again through precisely the same fog of unwitting connivance.

I was sent for a briefing to Dr Thomas P. Anderson, author of *Matanza,* the definitive scholarly history of Salvador's revolution of 1932, and to Ignacio Lozano, a Californian newspaper editor and former ambassador (under Gerald Ford) to El Salvador. It was suggested that I visit Salvador as a journalist, a role that would of necessity become real.

In January 1978 I landed at Ilopango, the dingy centre-city airport which is now Salvador's largest military base. Arriving before me were the members of a human rights investigation team, headed by then Congressman John Drinan, S.J. (Democrat of Massachusetts). I had been told that a black North American, Ronald James Richardson, had been killed while in the custody of the Salvadoran government and that a North American organization known as the American Institute for Free Labour Development (AIFLD, an organ of the AFL-CIO and an intelligence front) was manipulating the Salvadoran agricultural workers. Investigation of the 'Richardson Case' exposed me to the *sub rosa* activities of the Salvadoran military, whose highest-ranking officers and government officials were engaged in cocaine smuggling, kidnapping, extortion, and terrorism; through studying AIFLD's work, I would learn of the spurious intentions of an organization destined to become the architect of the present agrarian reform. I was delivered the promised exposure to the stratified life of Salvador, and was welcomed to 'Vietnam, circa 1959'. The 'Golden Triangle' had moved to the isthmus of the Americas, 'rural pacification' was in embryo, the seeds of rebellion had taken root in destitution and hunger.

Later my companion and guide, 'Ricardo', changed his description from 'Vietnam' to 'a Nazi forced labour camp'.

'It is not hyperbole,' he said quietly. 'You will come to see that.'

In those first twenty days I was taken to clinics and hospitals, to villages, farms, prisons, coffee mansions and processing plants, to cane mills and the elegant homes of American foreign service bureaucrats, nudged into the hillsides overlooking the capital, where I was offered cocktails and platters of ocean shrimps; it was not yet known what I would write of my impressions or where I would print them. Fortuitously, I had published nationally in my own country, and in Salvador 'only poetry' did not carry the pejorative connotation I might have ascribed to it then. I knew nothing of political journalism but was willing to learn—it seemed, at the time, an acceptable way for a poet to make a living.

I lay on my belly in the *campo* and was handed a pair of field glasses. The lenses sharpened on a plastic tarpaulin tacked to four maize stalks several hundred yards away, beneath which a woman sat on the ground. She was gazing through the plastic roof of her 'house' and hugging three naked, emaciated children. There was an aqua plastic dog-food bowl at her feet.

'She's watching for the plane,' my friend said. 'We have to get out of here now or we're going to get it, too.'

I trained the lenses on the woman's eyes, gelled with disease and open to a swarm of gnats. We climbed back in the truck and rolled the windows up just as the duster plane swept back across the field, dumping a yellow cloud of pesticide over the woman and her children, to protect the cotton crop around them.

At the time I was unaware of the pedagogical theories of Paulo Freire (*Pedagogy of the Oppressed*), but found myself learning *in situ* the politics of cultural immersion. It was by Ricardo's later admission 'risky business', but it was thought important that a few North Americans, particularly writers, be sensitized to Salvador prior to any military conflict. The lessons were simple and critical, the methods somewhat more difficult to detect.

I was given a white lab jacket and, posing as a North American physician, was asked to work in a rural hospital at the side of a Salvadoran doctor who was paid two hundred dollars a month by her government to care for 100,000 *campesinos*. She had no lab, no X-ray, no whole blood plasma, or antibiotics, no anaesthetics or medicines, no autoclave for sterilizing surgical equipment. Her forceps were rusted, the walls of her operating room were studded with flies; beside her hospital, a coffee-processing plant's refuse heaps incubated the maggots, and she paid a *campesina* to swish the flies away with a newspaper while she delivered the newborn. She was forced to do Caesarean sections at times without enough local anaesthetic. Without supplies, she worked with only her hands and a cheap ophthalmoscope. In her clinic I held children in my arms who died hours later for want of a manual suction device to remove the fluid from their lungs. Their peculiar skin rashes spread to my hands, arms, and belly. I dug maggots from a child's open wound with a teaspoon. I contracted four strains of dysentery and was treated by stomach antiseptics, effective yet damaging enough to be banned by our own Food and Drug Administration. This doctor had worked in the *campo* for years, a lifetime of delivering the offspring of thirteen-year-old mothers who thought the navel marked the birth-canal opening. She had worked long enough to feel that it was acceptable to ignore her own cervical cancer, and hard enough, in Salvador, to view her inevitable death as the least of her concerns.

I was taken to the homes of landowners, with their pools set like aquamarines in the clipped grass, to the afternoon games of canasta over quaint local *pupusas* and tea, where parrots hung by their feet among the bougainvillea and nearly everything was imported, if only from Miami or New Orleans. One evening I dined with a military officer who toasted America, private enterprise, Las Vegas, and the 'fatherland', until his wife excused herself, and in a drape of cigar smoke the events of 'The Colonel' were told, almost a *poème trouvé*. I had only to pare down the memory and render it whole, unlined, and as precise as recollection would have it. I did not wish to endanger myself by the act of poeticizing such a necessary reportage. It became, when I wrote it, the second insistence of El Salvador to infiltrate what I so ridiculously preserved as my work's allegiance to Art. No more than in any earlier poems did I choose my subject.

The following day I was let into Ahuachapán prison (now an army *cuartel*). We had been driving back from a meeting with Salvadoran feminists when Ricardo swung the truck into a climb through a tube of dust towards the run-down fortification. I was thirsty, infested with intestinal parasites, fatigued from twenty days of ricocheting between extremes of poverty and wealth. I was horrified, impatient, suspicious of almost everyone, paralyzed by sympathy and revulsion. I kept thinking of the kindly, silver-haired American political officer who informed me that in Salvador, 'there were always five versions of the truth.' From this, I was presumably to conclude that the truth could not therefore be known. Ricardo seemed by turns the Braggioni of Porter's 'Flowering Judas' and a pedagogical genius of considerable vision and patience. As we walked towards the gate, he palmed the air to slow our pace.

'This is a criminal penitentiary. You will have thirty minutes inside. Realize, please, at all times where you are, and whatever you see here, understand that for political prisoners it is always much worse. OK?'

We shook hands with the chief guard and a few subordinates, clean-shaven youths armed with G-3s. There was first the stench: rotting blood, excrement, buckets of urine, and corn slop. A man in his thirties came towards us, dragging a swollen green leg, his pants ripped to the thigh to accommodate the swelling. He was introduced as 'Miguel' and I as a 'friend'. The two men shook hands a long time, standing together in the filth, a firm knot of warmth between them. Miguel was asked to give me a 'tour', and he agreed, first taking a coin from his pocket and slipping it into the guard station soda machine. He handed me an orange Nehi, urging me somewhat insistently to take it, and we began a slow walk into the first hall. The prison was four-square with an open court in the centre. There were bunk rooms where the cots were stacked three deep and some were hung with newsprint 'for privacy'. The men squatted on the ground or along the walls, some stirring small coal fires, others ducking under urine-soaked tents of newspaper. It was suppertime, and they were cooking their dry tortillas. I used the soda as a relief from the stench, like a hose of oxygen. There were maybe four hundred men packed into Ahuachapán, and it was an odd sight, an American woman, but there was no heckling.

'Did you hear the shots when we first pulled up?' Ricardo asked. 'Those were warnings. A visitor—behave.'

Miguel showed me through the workrooms and latrines, finishing his sentences with his eyes: a necessary skill under repressive régimes, highly developed in Salvador. With the guards' attention diverted, he gestured towards a black open doorway and suggested that I might wander through it, stay a few moments, and come back out 'as if I had seen nothing.'

I did as he asked, my eyes adjusting to the darkness of that shit-smeared room with its single chink of light in the concrete. There were wooden boxes stacked against one wall, each a metre by a metre, with barred openings the size of a book, and within them there was breathing, raspy and half-conscious. It was a few moments before I realized that men were kept in those cages, their movement so cramped that they could neither sit, stand, nor lie down. I recall only magnified fragments of my few minutes in that room. I was rooted to the clay floor, unable to move either towards or away from the cages. I turned from the room towards Miguel, who pivoted on his crutch and with his eyes on the ground said in a low voice, '*La oscura*', the dark place. 'Sometimes a man is kept in there a year, and cannot move when he comes out.'

We caught up with Ricardo, who leaned towards me and whispered, 'Tie your sweater sleeves around your neck. You are covered with hives.'

In the cab of the truck I braced my feet against the dashboard and through the half-cracked window shook hands with the young soldiers, smiling and nodding. A hundred metres from the prison I lifted Ricardo's spare shirt in my hands and vomited. We were late for yet another meeting, the sun had dropped behind the volcanoes, my eyes ached. When I was empty the dry heaves began, and, after the sobbing, a convulsive shudder. Miguel was serving his third consecutive sentence, this time for organizing a hunger strike against prison conditions. In that moment I saw him turn back to his supper, his crutch stamping circles of piss and mud beside him as he walked. I heard the screams of a woman giving birth by Caesarean without anaesthetic in Ana's hospital. I saw the flies fastened to the walls in the operating room, the gnats on the eyes of the starving woman, the reflection of flies on Ana's eyes in the hospital kitchen window. The shit, I imagined, was inside my nostrils and I would smell it the rest of my life, as it is for a man who in battle tastes a piece of flesh or gets the blood under his fingernails. The smell never comes out; it was something Ricardo explained once as he was falling asleep.

'Feel this,' he said, manoeuvring the truck down the hill road. 'This is what oppression feels like. Now you have begun to learn something. When you get back to the States, what you do with this is up to you.'

Between 1978 and 1981 I travelled between the United States and Salvador, writing reports on the war waiting to happen, drawing blueprints of prisons from memory, naming the dead. I filled soup bowls with cigarette butts, grocery boxes with files on American involvement in the rural labour movement, and each week I took a stool sample to the parasite clinic. A priest I knew was gang-raped by soldiers; another was hauled off and beaten nearly to death. On one trip a woman friend and I were chased by the death squad for five minutes on the narrow back roads that circle the city; her evasive driving and considerable luck saved us. One night a year ago I was interviewing a defecting member of the Christian Democratic Party. As we started out of the drive to go back to my hotel, we encountered three plainclothesmen hunched over the roof of a taxicab, their machine guns pointed at our windshield. We escaped through a grove of avocado trees. The bodies of friends have turned up disembowelled and decapitated, their teeth punched into broken points, their faces sliced off with machetes. On the final trip to the airport we swerved to avoid a corpse, a man spread-eagled, his stomach hacked open, his entrails stretched from one side of the road to the other. We drove over them like a garden hose. My friend looked at me. *Just another dead man,* he said. And by then it had become true for me as well: the unthinkable, the sense of death within life before death.

II

'I see an injustice,' wrote Czeslaw Milosz in *Native Realm.* 'A Parisian does not have to bring his city out of nothingness every time he wants to describe it.' So it was with Wilno, that Lithuanian/Polish/Byelorussian city of the poet's childhood, and so it has been with the task of writing about Salvador in the United States. The country called by Gabriela Mistral 'the Tom Thumb of the Americas' would necessarily be described to North Americans as 'about the size of Massachusetts'. As writers we could begin with its location on the Pacific south of Guatemala and west of Honduras and with Ariadne's thread of statistics: 4.5 million people, 400 per square kilometre (a country without silence or privacy), a population growth rate of 3.5 percent (such a population would double in two decades). But what does 'ninety percent malnutrition' mean? Or that 'eighty percent of the population has no running water, electricity, or sanitary services?' I watched women push faeces aside with a stick, lower their pails to the water, and carry it home to wash their clothes, their spoons and plates, themselves, their infant children. The chief cause of death has been amoebic dysentery. One out of four children dies before the age of five; the average human life span is forty-six years. What does it mean when a man says, 'It is better to die quickly fighting than slowly of starvation?' And that such a man suffers towards that decision in what is now being called 'North America's backyard'? How is the language used to draw battle lines, to identify the enemy? What are the current euphemisms for empire, public defence of private wealth, extermination of human beings? If the lethal weapon is the soldier, what is meant by 'nonlethal military aid'? And what determined the shift to helicopter gunships, M-16s, M-79 grenade launchers? The State Department's white paper entitled, *Communist Interference in El Salvador,* argues that it is a 'case of indirect armed aggression against a small Third World country by Communist powers acting through Cuba'. James Petras in *The Nation* (March 28 1981) has argued that the report's evidence 'is flimsy, circumstantial or nonexistent; the reasoning and logic is slipshod and internally inconsistent; it assumes what needs to be proven; and finally, what facts are presented refute the very case the State Department is attempting to demonstrate.' On the basis of this

229

Carolyn Forché

report, the popular press sounded an alarm over the 'flow of arms'. But from where have arms 'flowed', and to whom and for what? In terms of language, we could begin by asking why North American arms are weighed in dollar value and those reaching the opposition measured in tonnage. Or we could point out the nature of the international arms market, a complex global network in which it is possible to buy almost anything for the right price, no matter the country of origin or destination. The State Department conveniently ignores its own intelligence on arms flow to the civilian right, its own escalation of military assistance to the right-wing military, and even the discrepancies in its final analysis. But what does all this tell us about who is fighting whom for what? Americans have been told that there is a 'fundamental difference' between 'advisers' and military 'trainers'. Could it simply be that the euphemism for American military personnel must be changed so as not to serve as a mnemonic device for the longest war in our failing public memory? A year ago I asked the American military attaché in Salvador what would happen if one of these already proposed advisers returned to the US in a flag-draped coffin. He did not argue semantics.

'That,' he said, smiling, 'would be up to the American press, wouldn't it?'

Most of that press had held with striking fidelity to the State Department text: a vulnerable and worthy 'centrist' government besieged by left- and right-wing extremists, the former characterized by their unacceptable political ideology, the latter rendered non-ideologically unacceptable, that is, only in their extremity. The familiar ring of this portrayal has not escaped US apologists, who must explain why El Salvador is not 'another Vietnam'. Their argument hinges, it seems, on the rapidity with which the US could assist the Salvadoran military in the task of 'defeating the enemy'. Tactically, this means sealing the country off, warning all other nations to 'cease and desist' supplying arms, using violations of that warning as a pretext for blockades and interventions, but excepting ourselves in our continual armament of what we are calling the 'government' of El Salvador. Ignoring the institutional self-interest of the Salvadoran army, we blame the presumably 'civilian' right for the murder of thousands of *campesinos,* students, doctors, teachers, journalists, nuns, priests, and children. This requires that we ignore

230

the deposed and retired military men who command the activities of the death squads with impunity, and that the security forces responsible for the killings are under the command of the army, which is under the command of the so-called centrist government and is in fact the government itself.

There are other differences between the conflicts of El Salvador and Vietnam. There is no People's Republic of China to the north to arm and ally itself with a people engaged in a protracted war. The guerrillas are not second-generation Vietminh, but young people who armed themselves after exhaustive and failed attempts at non-violent resistance and peaceful change. The popular organizations they defend were formed in the early seventies by *campesinos* who became socially conscious through the efforts of grass-roots clergymen teaching the Medellín doctrines of social justice; the precursors of these organizations were prayer and Bible study groups, rural labour organizations and urban trade unions. As the military government grew increasingly repressive, the opposition widened to include all other political parties, the Catholic majority, the university and professional communities, and the small-business sector.

Critics of US policy accurately recognize parallels between the two conflicts in terms of involvement, escalation, and justification. The latter demands a vigilant 'euphemology' undertaken to protect language from distortions of military expedience and political convenience. Noam Chomsky has argued that 'among the many symbols used to frighten and manipulate the populace of the democratic states, few have been more important than terror and terrorism. These terms have generally been confined to the use of violence by individual and marginal groups. Official violence, which is far more extensive in both scale and destructiveness, is placed in a different category altogether. This usage has nothing to do with justice, causal sequence, or numbers abused.' He goes on to say that 'the question of proper usage is settled not merely by the official or unofficial status of the perpetrators of violence but also by their political affiliations.' State violence is excused as 'reactive', and the 'turmoil' or 'conflict' is viewed ahistorically.

It is true that there have been voices of peaceful change and social reform in El Salvador—the so-called centrists—but the US has never supported them. The US backed one fraudulently-elected military régime after another, giving them what they wanted and still want: a steady infusion of massive economic aid with which high-ranking officers can insure their personal futures and the loyalty of their subordinates. In return we expect them to guarantee stability, which means holding power by whatever means necessary for the promotion of a favourable investment climate, even if it requires us to exterminate the population, as it has come to mean in Salvador.

The military, who always admired 'Generalissimo Franco', and are encouraged in their anti-Communist crusade, grow paranoid and genocidal. Near the Sampul River last summer, soldiers tossed babies into the air for target practice, during the cattle-prod roundup and massacre of six hundred peasants. Whole families have been gunned down or hacked to pieces with machetes, including the elderly and the newborn. Now that the massacre and the struggle against it have become the occasion to 'test American resolve', the Salvadoran military is all too aware of the security of its position and the impunity with which it may operate. Why would a peasant, aware of the odds, of the significance of American backing, continue to take up arms on the side of the opposition? How is it that such opposition endures, when daily men and women are doused with gasoline and burned alive in the streets as a lesson to others; when even death is not enough, and the corpses are mutilated beyond recognition? The answer to that question in El Salvador answers the same for Vietnam.

III

We were waved past the military guard station and started down the highway, swinging into the oncoming lane to pass slow sugar-cane trucks and army transports. Every few kilometres, patrols trekked the gravel roadside. It was a warm night, dry but close to the rainy season. Juan palmed the column shift, chain-smoked, and motioned with his hot-boxed cigarette in the direction of San Marcos. Bonfires lit by the opposition were chewing away at the dark hillside. As we neared San Salvador, passing through the slums of Candelaria, I saw that the roads were barricaded. More than once Juan attempted a short cut, but upon spotting military checkpoints, changed his mind. To relieve the tension, he dug a handful of change from his pocket and showed me his collection of deutsche marks, Belgian francs, Swedish öre and kronor, holding each to the dashboard light and naming the journalist who had given it to him, the country, the paper. His prize was a coin from the Danish reporter whose cameras had been shot away as he crouched on a roof top to photograph an army attack on protest marchers. That was a month before, on January 22 1980, when some hundreds lost their lives; it was the beginning of a savage year of extermination. Juan rose from his seat and slipped the worthless coins back into his pocket.

Later that spring, Rene Tamsen of WHUR radio, Washington, DC, would be forced by a death squad into an unmarked car in downtown San Salvador. A Salvadoran photographer, Cesar Najarro, and his *Crónica del Pueblo* editor would be seized during a coffee break. When their mutilated bodies were discovered, it would be evident that they had been disembowelled before death. A Mexican photo-journalist, Ignacio Rodriguez, would fall in August to a military bullet. After Christmas an American freelancer, John Sullivan, would vanish from his downtown hotel room. Censorship of the press. In January 1981, Ian Mates, South African TV cameraman, would hit a land mine and would bleed to death. In a year, no one would want the Salvador assignment. In a year, journalists would appear before cameras trembling and incredulous, unable to reconcile their perceptions with those of Washington, and even established media would begin to reflect this dichotomy. Carter policy had been to play down El Salvador in the press while providing 'quiet' aid to the repressive forces.

Between 1978 and 1980, investigative articles sent to national magazines mysteriously disappeared from publication mail rooms, were oddly delayed in reaching editors, or were rejected after lengthy deliberations, most often because of El Salvador's 'low news value'. The American interreligious network and human rights community began to receive evidence of a conscious and concerted censorship effort in the United States. During interviews in 1978 with members of the Salvadoran right-wing business community, I was twice offered large sums of money to portray their government favourably in the American press. By early 1981, desk editors knew where El Salvador was and the play-down policy had been replaced by the Reagan administration's propaganda effort. The right-wing military co-operated in El Salvador by serving death threats on prominent journalists, while torturing and murdering others. American writers critical of US policy were described by the Department of State as 'the witting and unwitting dupes' of Communist propagandists. Those who have continued coverage of Salvador have found that the military monitors the wire services and all telecommunications, that pseudonyms often provide no security, that no one active in the documentation of the war of extermination can afford to be traceable in the country; effectiveness becomes self-limiting. It became apparent that my education in El Salvador had prepared me to work only until March 16 1980, when, after several close calls, I was urged to leave the country. Monsignor Romero met with me, asking that I return to the US and 'tell the American people what is happening.'

'Do you have any messages for certain exiled friends?'

'Yes. Tell them to come back.'

'But wouldn't they be killed?'

'We are all going to be killed—you and me, all of us,' he said quietly. A week later he was shot while saying mass in the chapel of a hospital for the incurable.

In those days I kept my work as a poet and journalist separate, of two distinct *mentalidades*, but I could not keep El Salvador from my poems because it had become so much a part of my life. I was cautioned to avoid mixing art and politics, that one damages the other, and it was some time before I realized that 'political poetry' often means the poetry of protest, accused of polemical didacticism, and not the poetry which implicitly celebrates politically acceptable values. I suspect that underlying this discomfort is a naive assumption: that to locate a poem in an area associated with political trouble automatically renders it political.

All poetry is both pure and engaged, in the sense that it is made of language, but it is also art. Any theory that takes one half of the social-aesthetic dynamic and accentuates it too much results in a breakdown. Stress of purity generates a feeble aestheticism which fails, in its beauty, to communicate. On the other hand, propagandistic hack work has no independent life as poetry. What matters is not whether a poem is political, but the quality of its engagement.

In *The Consciousness Industry,* Hans Magnus Enzensberger has argued the futility of locating the political aspect of poetry outside poetry itself, and that:

Such obtuseness plays into the hands of the bourgeois aesthetic which would like to deny poetry any social aspect. Too often the champions of inwardness and sensibility are reactionaries. They consider politics a special subject best left to professionals, and wish to detach it completely from all other human activity. They advise poetry to stick to such models as they have devised for it, in other words, to high aspirations and eternal values. The promised reward for this continence is timeless validity. Behind these high-sounding proclamations lurks a contempt for poetry no less profound than that of vulgar Marxism. For a political quarantine placed on poetry in the name of eternal values itself serves political ends.

All language, then, is political; vision is always ideologically charged; perceptions are shaped *a priori* by our assumptions, and sensibility is formed by a consciousness at once social, historical, and aesthetic. There is no such thing as non-political poetry. The time, however, to determine what those politics will be is not the moment of taking pen to paper, but during the whole of one's life. We are responsible for the quality of our vision; we have the say in the shaping of our sensibility. In the many thousand daily choices we make, we create ourselves and the voice with which we speak and work.

From our tradition we inherit a poetic, a sense of appropriate subjects, styles, forms, and levels of diction; that poetic might insist that we be attuned to the individual in isolation, to particular sensitivity in the face of 'nature', to special ingenuity in inventing metaphor. It might encourage a self-regarding, inward-looking poetry. Since Romanticism, didactic poetry has been presumed dead, and narrative poetry has had at best a half-life. Demonstration is inimical to a poetry of lyric confession and self-examination, therefore didactic poetry is seen as crude and unpoetic. To suggest a return to the formal didactic mode of Virgil's *Georgics* or Lucretius's *De Rerum Natura* would be to deny history, but what has survived of that poetic is the belief that a poet's voice must be inwardly authentic and compelling of our attention; the poet's voice must have authority.

I have been told that a poet should be of his or her time. It is my feeling that the twentieth-century human condition demands a poetry of witness. This is not accomplished without certain difficulties; the inherited poetic limits the range of our work and determines the boundaries of what might be said. There is the problem of metaphor, which moved Neruda to write: 'The blood of the children/flowed out onto the streets/like...like the blood of the children.' There is the problem of poeticizing horror, which resembles the problem of the photographic image that might render starvation visually appealing. There are problems of reduction and over-simplification; of our need to see the world as complex beyond our comprehension, difficult beyond our capacities for solution. If I did not wish to make poetry of what I had seen, what is it I thought poetry was?

At some point the two *mentalidades* converged, and the impulse to witness confronted the prevailing poetic; at the same time it seemed clear that eulogy and censure were no longer possible and that Enzensberger is correct in stating: 'The poem expresses in exemplary fashion that it is not at the disposal of politics. That is its political content.' I decided to follow my impulse to write narratives of witness and confrontation, to disallow obscurity and conventions, which might prettify that which I wished to document. As for that wish, the poems will speak for themselves, obstinate as always. I wish also to thank my friends and *compañeros* in El Salvador for persuading me during a period of doubt that poetry could be enough.

THE COLONEL

What you have heard is true. I was in his house. His wife carried a tray of coffee and sugar. His daughter filed her nails, his son went out for the night. There were daily papers, pet dogs, a pistol on the cushion beside him. The moon swung bare on its black cord over the house. On the television was a cop show. It was in English. Broken bottles were embedded in the walls around the house to scoop the kneecaps from a man's legs or cut his hands to lace. On the windows there were gratings like those in liquor stores. We had dinner, rack of lamb, good wine, a gold bell was on the table for calling the maid. The maid brought green mangoes, salt, a type of bread. I was asked how I enjoyed the country. There was a brief commercial in Spanish. His wife took everything away. There was some talk then of how difficult it had become to govern. The parrot said hello on the terrace. The colonel told it to shut up, and pushed himself from the table. My friend said to me with his eyes: say nothing. The colonel returned with a sack used to bring groceries home. He spilled many human ears on the table. They were like dried peach halves. There is no other way to say this. He took one of them in his hands, shook it in our faces, dropped it into a water glass. It came alive there. I am tired of fooling around he said. As for the rights of anyone, tell your people they can go fuck themselves. He swept the ears to the floor with his arm and held the last of his wine in the air. Something for your poetry, no? he said. Some of the ears on the floor caught this scrap of his voice. Some of the ears on the floor were pressed to the ground.

TODD MCEWEN
EVENSONG

L eave my wife alone I said. No he said I will not leave your wife alone, I love her. And so saying he went from the doorstep and taking a small green tent he set it up in the garden and every morning thereafter I was irritated awake by the smell of his infernal little cookstove and a bit later tortured by that of his squalid fried breakfast. He hired a small boy to bring love letters to the front door 16 times a day, hourly. My wife gave the boy 5p every time; this angered me but as she said it is not the boy's fault. Besides he is from a poor family. But at 5p x 16 hrs = 80p *per diem* might I not end up in the poorhouse myself? But it was not the money. It was the situation. And the smell every morning. My wife's one pronouncement was It is just a phase. But a phase for who? I said And how long? She, lovely, went to the other side of the garden and planted leeks in silence. While she planted the leeks I was left to answer the door and pay the boy the 5p every hour. Can't you see she's just over there by the hedge? I said after he had handed me the third letter. He smiled at me mutely. So he was retarded as well as poor! Darling, I love you, I can't live without you, be mine. Your worshipper. I stopped reading the letters, they were all the same. And the envelopes were all the same, addressed merely to She. In the morning the letters were often stained with cooking fat or some kind of jam. The letters that came at midday were relatively clean (I think he ate only salads for lunch, made from herbs and flowers growing on the cat's grave by the tent). The evening letters often smelled of whisky or canned beer and potato crisps. I left the letters in a neat pile on my wife's table. She would come in from planting leeks and glance at the letters, occasionally sifting through them to see if the message varied which as I have said it did not. Characteristically my wife refused to be drawn into the situation while I became obsessed with it. Even the coalmen stepped around the tent without disturbing him while they made their delivery. It's probably just a phase! one of them whispered to me. One evening as I sat and watched the smoke from his wretched stove drift past the window I said to my wife Don't you realize we are tenants of a noble? A man with a title? He'll take care of this. My wife sewed placidly. She refused to be drawn into the situation but I had become obsessed with it. I dialled the castle. What! groaned a voice. I I I want to talk to his lordship I said This is me at the west farm. What's the matter with you? said the voice Do you know what time it is? I do I said What's the matter with you? His lordship is asleep said the voice and is always asleep at this hour. Dog's life, being a life peer I snarled. What is the nature of your business? said the voice. There is a man in a tent in my garden I said. Squatter eh? said the voice. Most indubitably I said feeling I was getting somewhere. Why don't you tell him to clear off? said the voice. I have I said. Why don't you call the police? said the voice. There's no point I said As you well know only his lordship can evict someone from *feudal* land. With the *f* I filled the mouthpiece with foam. Is he causing trouble? said the voice. He writes love letters to my wife I said. Oh? said the voice lighting a cigarette. He was interested now. Hourly I said They are delivered by a little backward boy who lives down the road. Yes I know the place said the voice His father was gamekeeper to his lordship for many years. Isn't that marvellous? I said. The estate cannot mix in affairs of the heart said the voice It's not good business. It's not an affair of the heart I said My wife wants nothing to do with him or the letters. Well perhaps she's pursuing the best course then eh? said the voice I must ring off now but it has been most interesting. He hung up. I hung up and looked at my wife who was trying to tune in her radio. I put on my hat and stamped out of the house and out the gate slamming it for effect of which there was none and glaring at the tent I stalked down the road toward Muckhart's house. Muckhart was cleaning his nose, absorbed in its reflection in the window over his kitchen sink. Because of complicated lighting conditions the window acted as a mirror in the interior of the house but approaching from the road I could see Muckhart cleaning his nose. I banged on the door and Muckhart opened it. His dog barked at me immediately and without cessation. Muckhart! I shouted over the dog din Muckhart! Realizing the dog would not stop barking Muckhart came out on to the step and closed the door behind him. Immediately the barking stopped. He gave me a merry look and turned toward the door again but as soon as his touch had disturbed the mechanism of the doorknob the furious barking began again. We'd best stay out here! I shouted and he nodded and turned back to me. Muckhart I said There is a man in my garden in a tent. Aye I've seen that he said Friend o yours? Not at all I said He is a squatter. Och! A squatter? said Muckhart. Yes I said feeling I was getting somewhere. Weel hae ye askit him tae leave? said Muckhart. It's more complicated than that I said He's writing love letters to my

wife, once an hour, delivered by a retarded boy. Muckhart scratched
his head. Aye that would be the wee boy fae the cottage by the water. I
suppose so I said impatiently. Weel dinnae fash yerseel said
Muckhart I'll awa and hae a blether wi his mam in the mornin. No! I
said No No No! Not the boy. Oh so ye dinna mind aboot the letters?
said Muckhart queerly. I do mind! I said turning red But it's the man
in the tent! I want you to get rid of the man in the tent. But I cannae do
onythin aboot that spluttered Muckhart suddenly resentful Ye kens
it's ony the laird as can evict a squatter. He made to enter the kitchen
but I stayed him. Listen I said Can't you arrange to (here I moved my
clawlike hands in a foolish imitation of quotation marks)
'accidentally' run over the tent with your tractor? Muckhart eyed my
gesture without comprehension but took his hand away from the
doorknob. He looked out at the evening and taking a pipe out of his
pocket he sat down on the step. I sat down beside him and watched
him fill the pipe. He tamped the tobacco firmly with his alarming
brown thumb which had been in India during the war. He lit the pipe
and smoked, silent, staring at the byre. No he said eventually I cannae
do that. Why not? I whined. Ye ask me if I couldnae arrange tae
accidentally run ooer the tent wi ma tractor and the onser tae that is
no. Ye see said Muckhart If I *arranged* tae dae it it wouldnae be an
accident noo would it? And I micht truly accidentally run ooer the
tent but I couldnae predict it and indeed the possibility is verrry
verrry slim considering (here he got up) yer gairden is separatit fae the
road by a ditch and yer wife's flooers and the grave of yer puir auld
puss. He knocked his pipe against the step. Evenin to ye he said and
went inside. I was left alone with my thoughts and the road home. It
was twilight. Approaching my house and the tent with its accursed tin
chimney I suddenly hied into the ditch which rendered me invisible
from the garden. I prised up a large stone from the moocky bottom
and hurled it at the tent. To my delight it struck the tin chimney,
knocking off its little Chinese hat. Hey! came a cry from the tent.
Woo! I said Woo! Who's there? he said still inside. I rustled the weeds
on the garden side of the ditch in a supernatural manner. Woo! I said
I am the Spirit of this Place. There is great danger here. Woo! He put
his head out of the tent, frightened. Woo! I said Leave this place leave
this place leave this place. Woo! For God's sake! he cried Who's
there? Woo! I said It's me, an awful raw-head bloody-bones! Fly for

your life! Woo! The head disappeared into the tent and I heard nothing. Rummaging in the ditch I felt another stone which to my disgust turned out to be a dead toad. Yet I flung it and managed to knock down the tent pole. With a tremendous clatter the whole of him emerged from the collapsed tent. He was wearing an overcoat and had a rope tied around him from which hung his damned pots and pans. He stood and looked with uncertainty at the lifeless toad on the tent, the whole of which was catching fire owing to the stove being upset. *Woo!* I howled like the wind. *Wah!* With a shriek he leaped over the fence and began to hurry down the road. Every few yards he tripped over the pans, some of which were very large. I continued to wail until he had disappeared down the road to the south. Bloody Sassenach. I had difficulty in extracting my legs from the mud in the ditch but eventually got up to the garden hauling myself by thistles and brambles. I stood and watched his tent burn and made up incantations which I recited. When I entered the house my wife was still trying to tune her radio. She had refused to be drawn into the situation while I on the other hand had become obsessed with it. The next morning the retarded boy knocked at the door but he had no letter. I was almost happy to see him. I gave him 50p and told him to go home but he came back in an hour, again with no letter and the next hour and the next and the next and the next and the next.

LETTERS

Literature or Politics?

To the Editor:

The last two issues of *Granta*, which arrived in quick succession, provoked very different reactions in this subscriber/admirer/supporter. The *Best of Young British Novelists* (issue seven) seemed to me a brilliant feat of publishing—full of interest and entertainment, useful to readers, and a marvellous shop window for the writers concerned. *A Literature for Politics* (issue 6), on the other hand, caused me some disappointment and even dismay, not so much because of the contents themselves (though I wonder whether a magazine dedicated to the encouragement of new imaginative writing is really the place for political essays that are bound to date quickly, or for cultural analysis for which there are plenty of other periodical outlets) as because of the tone and drift of the editorial, and the slogan under which the whole collection was published.

A Literature for Politics. If the phrase is not just empty rhetoric, it must imply some kind of subordination of literature *to* politics, that is, of literary discourse to political dis-course. Because 'politics', like 'literature', is a discourse, or complex of discourses, not a non-verbal reality which literature must strive to represent or articulate. As discourses, literature and politics are distinct and different ways of organizing and making sense of human experience. They overlap and interact, but they also inevitably compete, because their priorities are different; and history suggests that for literature to subordinate its priorities to those of politics is likely to be disastrous for both.

One of the priorities of literature (*i.e.* of verbal *art*) is play, and that is surely what Milan Kundera is affirming when he describes himself as 'a hedonist trapped in a world politicised in the extreme.' I must say that the editor seems to me perversely to misinterpret Kundera's contribution in his editorial. When Kundera celebrates writing in which '*everything* is in question, *everything* is doubtful; *everything* is the object of the game; *everything* is entertaining (without shame in being entertaining)—with all the consequences this implies for the form of the novel,' it doesn't sound to me like the manifesto of 'a literature for politics'. It sounds more like what I thought *Granta* was about before I read its editorial. I hope the latter was only a temporary aberration. Issue seven encourages me.

David Lodge

All letters are welcome and should be addressed to *Granta,* 44a Hobson Street, Cambridge CB1 1NL.

Department of English Language and Literature, The University of Birmingham

Letters

To the Editor:

I am full of admiration for your splendid issue *A Literature for Politics,* but am slightly mystified by the way it was received by the press, most notably by Conor Cruise O'Brien in the *Observer.* Surely the point of the editorial was that the very familiar division of *pure* literature and *pure* politics is distorting. We have arrived at such a strange stage in the way we talk about literature. On the one hand, we accept that all writing is, in its workings, non-representational—a discourse, a construct in language, an assembly of signs. But we do not accept that that is only one part—and arguably the least important part—of the argument. Writing is also *representational.* It has to be: it's what establishes our relationship with what is 'out there'. And, for me at least, the only meaningful literature is one that, in some way, addresses what is 'out there', that it be prepared to confront the issues that matter, that it be, in short, willing to locate itself among political concerns. What I enjoyed so much about *A Literature for Politics* was that the writers in it were in fact brave enough to confront those concerns but were sophisticated enough not to succumb to the pressure to make a didactic statement about them. Their work was, as it were, both detached and engaged at the same time. Conor Cruise O'Brien, while quite rightly admiring your editorial selections, insisted on seeing them merely as examples of literature and not politics. Is it not possible to see them as they are—as examples of

both? Can't people see that to insist that literature be kept sanitized—washed of all political concerns—is a reactionary stance, can only be a reactionary stance, and is in itself, and in the most insidious of ways, political.

I should add, in passing, that I thought your *Best of Young British Novelists* was a load of rubbish.

Robert Sullivan

Edinburgh, Scotland

To the Editor:

Your issue *A Literature for Politics* is extraordinary, piece by piece and as a whole. It offers startling portraits of victim and oppressor, and without editorial intrusion they remind the reader how short the distance is between either of those and himself.

Tobias Wolff

Syracuse, New York

To the Editor:

A Literature for Politics nearly pressed me to abandon *Granta.* I believe that literature has no effect on politics whatsoever, and I have waited in vain for someone to give me even one example of a work of literature—a novel, say—that has wrought any improvement on the human condition via politics or politicians. Unlike previous issues, *A Literature for Politics* had nothing of interest for me, with the possible exception of its editorial, which was, I admit, a very good polemic. But does it not come down to this in the end: whatever a writer has to 'say', be it political or precious, depends on how well he or she can write? Even your apparent *bete noire*, John Barth, *can* write a good story: *Chimera*, for instance.

Surely the value of *Granta*, as demonstrated in the *Best of Young British Novelists* and the earlier issues, is in its being a showcase for contemporary fiction: in giving me the chance to read stories or extracts from novels that lead me either to buy an author's work or to save my money in not buying the books that inflated reviews might have pointed me to. I enjoyed the *Best of Young British Novelists*, which has confirmed my indifference to Martin Amis, demonstrated the utter dreariness of the highly touted Lisa St Aubin de Teran, and given me a good find in Pat Barker.

Jeremy Cartland

Brighton, Sussex

Israel and the Holocaust

To the Editor:

While I respect Boaz Evron as an Israeli journalist ('The Holocaust Reinterpreted: An Indictment of Israel' in issue six), I was dismayed by his glib use of etymology to distort the magnitude of Hitler's destruction of seventy-five percent

of the Jews living in the areas he conquered. I'm sure that no other European Jew is likely to be misled. Of course, Jews were not the only victims, and, if we are going to argue along these lines, Germans were not the only murderers. But the killings, however gruesome and horrible, do not represent the entire point. For aside from isolated and miraculous acts of bravery, and with the exception of Denmark and Norway, the resistance to Nazi labelling, segregating and removing of Jewish victims was lamentable throughout Europe. The point is antisemitism and, if gentile knowledge of some of these facts has inhibited antisemitism for a generation or so, European Jews may be grateful. The effects of this knowledge may well be dissipating.

But even while this was so, I can hardly accept Evron's point that European governments have insistently put their national interests aside in the defence of Israel. Britain was surely not denying its national interests when it turned back the refugee ships that were making their way to Palestine or when it withdrew from the Middle East fully aware of the military superiority of the Arabs. National interests were not being denied when Nasser regretfully announced his intention to maintain his blockade in 1967. And national interests were hardly being denied when the oil weapon was being used in earnest. It is ironic that Evron singles out France as being the only nation that relates to Israel in a rational manner—that is, that it is the only nation that does not deny its national interests—when, throughout the fifties, France was Israel's only real ally.

One final point: British Jews are far from regarding themselves as bound to support whatever any Israeli government does. They are in fact usually among the first to criticize Israeli policies. I myself signed a letter of protest to *Maariv*. If I would not willingly write to the English press in the same way, it is only because, contrary to what Evron asserts, there is more than enough space devoted to hostile criticism of Israel there already.

Elaine Feinstein

Cambridge

To the Editor:

'The Holocaust Reinterpreted' (issue six) dealt with, among other considerations, Israel's relationship to Europe and the United States. I was not able to discuss in detail the implications of that relationship within Israel itself. One incident—concerning the press—is worth noting.

A short while ago, I, along with a number of other journalists, was invited to the occupied territories by three individuals living there. The three individuals—Bashir Barguit, Mamum el Sayad, and Akram Hanya—are the editors of the Arab papers in Israel, and they asked that we travel to see them because they were unable to come to see us: they are not allowed to cross the Green Line, the 'border' between Israel and

the occupied territories, and have been restricted, by a town detention order, from ever leaving the cities where they live.

Three years ago, these editors received an injunction forbidding them to leave the boundaries of their towns. They asked for an explanation; they were offered none. They were not accused of having committed an offence, and the security authorities refused to show the lawyers representing the editors any of the charges that were presumably being made against them. They are, therefore, unable to defend themselves; they cannot appeal. When they approached the Supreme Court, the Court decided that it was unable to interfere in what it regarded as a consideration of security.

The editors now find themselves in a rather curious way. The papers they edit are published in Jerusalem, where they are forbidden to go: they edit, it seems, by remote control. More curious, their papers are forbidden in the occupied territories: in principle, they are not allowed to see the papers they edit. What is the possible intention of the Israel authorities? I assume it is to keep the editors, obviously influential in the shaping of public opinion, closely under supervision. They are not to be brutalized; they are not to be pressured; but they are to know that they can be closed down at any moment: they are always threatened by 'the blow'. For surely the Israeli authorities know that these editors are, by whatever means, disobeying their injunction. And disobedience is, of course, a very proper reason for arrest. How quickly we are learning the colonists' tricks.

No less interesting was the editor Bashiv Barguit's observations of the Palestinians in the occupied territories. Throughout the West Bank, a social revolution is taking place. The old feudal society—with its exchange markets, its money-lenders, its archaic loyalties—has disappeared, and a new society is taking its place, shaped entirely by its dealings with the well-developed Israeli capitalism. The occupation has introduced, among the Arabs, an entirely new awareness of politics and class and nationalism. The occupation is, in effect, forming the Palestinian people. Sixty years ago, many of these Arabs still regarded themselves as part of greater Syria; today, after sixty years of Zionism and Israeli domination, they know very well how to regard themselves: they are Palestinians. And Israel has created them and continues to create them. All attempts to diminish this new awareness only strengthens it—as the war in Lebanon has shown. I suspect that the Palestinians have the greatest national awareness within the Arab world, with the possible exception of Egypt. In the past, these people were among the most underdeveloped in the Ottoman Empire. Today, the people I meet are clever and sophisticated: and they crave education. I have read recently that the number of Palestinian university graduates, here and in the Palestinian diaspora, equals the number of Israel university graduates. They call themselves, sometimes, 'The Jews of the Middle East'. It is as if we have printed ourselves on a population that is now turning into our mirror image: a stubborn people, cunning, courageous and imaginative.

Boaz Evron

Tel Aviv
Israel

Complaints

To the Editor:

I subscribed to your magazine to see what was happening in modern literature, but the idea was not a success. T. Coraghessan Boyle (issue five) was discovered by my sister-in-law, who insisted on wrapping it up well before putting it in the dustbin, in case the garbage men, on seeing it, were corrupted.

The adjectives which come to mind are 'adolescent', 'grubby', and 'obscene'. I might have admired the stuff forty years ago (when we were excited by the same old naughty words), but, since then, I've grown up. Now it merely makes me sad. I shall not be renewing my subscription.

J. Smalley
London

Back issues of *Granta*—including *A Literature for Politics* and *Best of Young British Novelists*—are available from *Granta*, as either part of a £10.00 subscription or at £3.50 each.

The Hudson Review

35th Anniversary Issue

EMBRACING OMNICIDE Louis Rene Beres
THE PREVIOUS TENANT Louis Simpson
THE RIDGE FARM A. R. Ammons
BUSINESS AND POETRY Dana Gioia
FIFTY-SEVEN VIEWS OF FUJIYAMA Guy Davenport

Theodore Ziolkowski
Charles Tomlinson
Gail Mazur
Sonya Rudikoff
Marvin Mudrick
T. R. Hummer
Robert Asahina
Vernon Young
Roger Rosenblatt
Richmond Lattimore
Joseph Epstein
Paula Deitz

The Hudson Review, 684 Park Avenue, New York 10021

SLEEPWALKING
Meg Wolitzer

Already published to great acclaim in the United States, this moving story of a young student's emotional crisis is one of the major first novels of 1983. 'She writes with remarkable poise and understanding. She makes us see the painful, confusing world of young women in love with literature and death.'
MARY GORDON
£7.95

IN THE MOOD
Keith Waterhouse

Auberon Waugh insists that Keith Waterhouse 'is one of the few great writers of our time... he is not only among the funniest, he is also among the wittiest and most observant' – and this new novel, set in the nineteen-fifties, is his most hilarious to date.
Publication: May 9th
£7.95

NEW FICTION FROM MICHAEL JOSEPH

LISTENERS
Sally Emerson

The Editor of **Books and Bookmen** made her fictional debut to great acclaim in 1980 with **Second Sight**: 'Strong, individual and full of promise' **Financial Times**. 'I cannot but admire such an ambitious first novel' **Daily Telegraph**. Her second novel, which continues the story of Jennifer Hamilton, fulfils all the promise of that remarkable beginning.
Publication: April 25th
£7.95

DIARY OF A GOOD NEIGHBOUR
Jane Somers

'The Diary treats an almost untouchable subject with great courage and sensitivity... but even more impressive, it does so with fire and passion. Utterly authentic and disturbing. I greatly admired and enjoyed it... a pleasure to read.'
MARGARET FORSTER
£7.95

Contributors

Duncan Bush's third collection of poetry is to be published this year by the Poetry Wales Press, and he is currently preparing his first collection of short stories. He lives in Wales. **Michael Herr** is the author of *Dispatches* and is completing a book on the history of rock and roll. He lives in London. **Russell Hoban**'s most recent novel, *Pilgermann*, was published in February. His previous contributions to *Granta* were in issues three and five. **Marek Nowakowski** lives in Poland and, until recently, was in prison there. 'War Reports' is to be included in a collection of short pieces about Poland entitled *The Canary and other Tales of Marshal Law* to be published by the Harvill Press later this year. **Angela Carter** is the author of seven novels, two collections of short stories, a non-fiction monograph, *The Sadeian Woman*, and a collection of journalism published last year, *Nothing Sacred*. Her essay is the first of three pieces by women on their fathers that will appear in *Granta* and that will be published in *Reflections on Fathers* by the Virago Press in November. **Carola Hansson** works as a writer and editor for Swedish radio and television. **Karin Liden** is the author of a number of books on the Soviet Union, and works in the Education Department of Swedish Broadcasting. Their interviews of Moscow women are being collected and will be published by Pantheon Books in the United States. **Jean Mohr** has worked with John Berger on a number of books, including *Ways of Seeing* and *Another Way of Telling*. He has also worked as a photographer over the last twenty years for UNESCO, the World Health Organization, and the International Red Cross. He lives in Geneva, Switzerland. **Carolyn Forché** has published two books of poetry, *Fathering the Tribes*, and *The Country Between Us*. Between 1978 and 1980 she made a number of trips to El Salvador, where she worked as a journalist and a human rights advocate. **Todd McEwen**'s first novel, *Fisher's Hornpipe*, has just been published. Until recently he lived with his wife on an estate in Scotland, and claims to know feudalism first hand. 'Evensong' is his first published short story.

THOMAS PALMER
The Transfer

'Thomas Palmer is very, very good.' Mario Puzo
'... deserves to be placed next to the works of Hammett and Chandler. And you can't say better than that.' *Time Out*
'The Florida Everglades are so miasmally evoked that susceptible readers might be advised to rub themselves with mosquito repellent.' *Guardian*
0 00 222721 5 £8.95

GILLIAN AVERY
Onlookers

'Two comedies of errors, one set in modern academe and the other in the mid-19th century ... together make a splended whole.' *Spectator*
'The modern section is lively, with velvet over the claws; the second half is a quite haunting definition of place and period.' *Guardian*
0 00 222673 1 £6.95

PETER STRAUB
Floating Dragon

'Peter Straub's fictions are the fastest chillers in the west.' *Observer*
Peter Straub is the 'young master of the tradition of Hawthorne, Poe and James.' Carlos Fuentes
0 00 222714 2 £9.95

MAGGIE ROSS
Milena

The second novel by the author of *The Gasteropod*, winner of the James Tait Black Prize and widely recognised as one of the outstanding debuts of its decade.
0 00 222602 2 £8.95

Collins

New Fiction from
The Bodley Head

WILLIAM TREVOR
Fools of Fortune   £7.50

DAVID WHELDON
The Viaduct   £5.95

Winner of the Triple First Award

PETER DICKINSON
Hindsight   £7.95

STEPHEN BENATAR
When I Was Otherwise   £7.95

CRAIG NOVA
The Good Son   £7.95

BETTE PESETSKY
Author from a Savage People   £7.95

KING PENGUIN

TWO YEARS ON

THE BOOK OF LAUGHTER AND FORGETTING

MILAN KUNDERA

'No question about it. The most important novel published in Britain this year ... a whirling dance of a book ... mingles a hedonist's love of eroticism, fantasy and fun with a knife-sharp political satire ... a masterpiece'
— Salman Rushdie in the *Sunday Times*

'Sinuously intelligent ... one is torn between profound pleasure in the novel's execution and wonder at the pain that inspired it'
— Ian McEwan in the *Observer*

£2.50